AUG 0 5 2014

Praise for

Real Wifeys: Hustle Hard

"A well laid out plot spiced with wild sex moves Mink's story right along. Readers will keep turning pages to see if Suga succeeds as she moves toward redemption. Mink's books are the real deal."

—*Library Journal*

"Mink's energy and grit make it a fun read."

—*Juicy Magazine*

Praise for

Real Wifeys: Get Money

"Mink's brisk combination of insult, profanity, and pop culture is what street lit is all about . . . Another powerful story of women orbiting the hip-hop world . . . Luscious is both a villain and a heroine whom readers will embrace. Order in anticipation of high demand."

—*Library Journal*

"Unexpected story lines . . . Very realistic . . . A quick read with an engaging main character."

—Huffington Post

Praise for

Real Wifeys: On the Grind

"Marking her solo debut with this new series launch, Mink (coauthor, *The Hood Life*; *Shameless Hoodwives*; *Desperate Hoodwives*) gives Kaeyla a snappy and profane voice laced with sarcasm. She's a charismatic woman, both vulnerable and tough. Female readers will love her, but men may want to check their own woman's purse for Taser wires. Load your shelves with multiple copies."

—*Library Journal*

"A gritty new urban series with a down-and-dirty intensity that's heartbreaking."

—*Publishers Weekly*

"The *Real Wifeys* series tells the tales of strong female characters who overcome obstacles while standing by or getting over the men that they love."

—AllHipHop.com

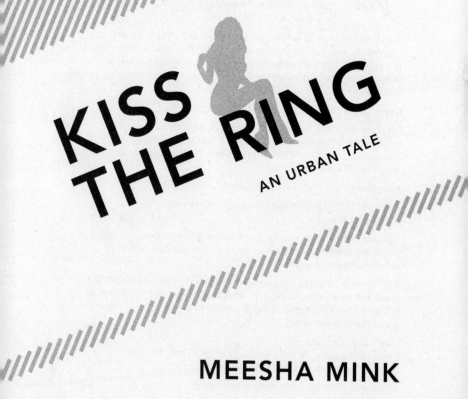

KISS THE RING

AN URBAN TALE

MEESHA MINK

A Touchstone Book
Published by Simon & Schuster
New York London Toronto Sydney New Delhi

Touchstone
A Division of Simon & Schuster, Inc.
1230 Avenue of the Americas
New York, NY 10020

First Touchstone trade paperback edition August 2014

TOUCHSTONE and colophon are registered trademarks
of Simon & Schuster, Inc.

For information about special discounts for bulk purchases,
please contact Simon & Schuster Special Sales at 1-866-506-1949
or business@simonandschuster.com.

The Simon & Schuster Speakers Bureau can bring authors to your live
event. For more information or to book an event contact the Simon &
Schuster Speakers Bureau at 1-866-248-3049 or visit our website at
www.simonspeakers.com.

Interior design by Akasha Archer
Cover photographs: Woman © Eric Hood/E+/Getty Images,
Diamond letters © dgbomb/Shutterstock

Manufactured in the United States of America

10 9 8 7 6 5 4 3 2 1

Library of Congress Cataloging-in-Publication Data

Mink, Meesha.
  Kiss the ring : an urban tale / Meesha Mink.—First Touchstone
trade paperback edition.
      pages cm
  "A Touchstone book."
    1. African American women—Fiction. 2. Revenge—Fiction.
3. Gangs—Fiction 4. Inner cities—Fiction. 5. Newark (N.J.)—Fiction.
I. Title.
  PS3552.R8945K57 2014
  813'.54—dc23

                                    2014005439

ISBN 978-1-4767-5530-4
ISBN 978-1-4767-5534-2 (ebook)

*For those with big dreams
and the inner hustle to make them come true*

Prologue

My son is dead. Just fourteen short years he lived on this earth and now it's been snatched away from him. Chased and run down in the street like a stray dog. Left to die like his life ain't meant shit.

Naeema Cole pushed the folder away from where she sat at her kitchen table. She picked up her glass pipe, dick-shaped, the balls hollowed out and filled with Lime Haze, her favorite strain of medicinal marijuana. She had a connect named Mook and not a doctor in sight trying to cure an illness. Pressing her lips to the tip, she took a deep toke, letting the smoke fill her mouth and then her lungs as a tear filled with her pain and regrets raced down her cheek. Exhaling the thick smoke through her nose, she shifted her slanted ebony eyes to the copy of the Newark Police Department's official record of the investigation into the murder of Brandon Mack.

Just one day after being released from the hospital with her newborn son she had placed him in the arms of Ms. JuJu, an older woman who lived down the street from the group home Naeema hated so much. She wanted Ms. JuJu to bless her son with all the kindness she'd shown every last one of the misguided group home girls where she volunteered.

I never was a mother to him but I loved him because he was mine. He came from me.

A tear of guilt followed the other as she shifted in the

cheap black chair, causing it to loudly scrape against the dull laminate tile covering the floor. Pain hit her deeply in a place she never knew existed until the moment she got the call from Ms. JuJu telling her of her son's death. His murder. Naeema closed her eyes and opened her mouth slightly to exhale in short puffs as the words she read in the police report formed a mental image while she envisioned the night of his death . . .

The sound of feet pounding against pavement echoed heavily through the long stretch of alley flanked by two towering brick buildings. His heart pounded furiously in his chest and his throat was dry and pained from inhaling deep gulps of air as he ran for his life. Death was on his heels and fear was his adrenaline.

He didn't want to die at fourteen.

"Shit!" he swore, his eyes squinting when a pair of bright headlights suddenly flashed on him from the other end of the alley.

The light illuminated the panic in his eyes.

His harsh and labored breathing echoed more loudly as he stopped running and looked left and right for an escape route. There was none. "Shit!" he swore again, looking back into the bright lights as the vehicle suddenly accelerated toward him.

He turned and ran back down the alley, wishing his presence was as large and looming as his shadow cast against the brick by the towering streetlights. Then he wouldn't feel so afraid . . . so alone . . . so near death.

He burst from between the buildings and paused just

long enough to decide if he should jet left or right. In that moment that shit felt more like choosing life or death.

The rumble of the engine steadily became louder behind him.

He took off to the right, his hands balled into fists and arching upward like he could make himself run faster. The muscles in his thin thighs burned and his chest ached from the exertion.

He didn't know, when he finally headed home after midnight and took a shortcut through West Side Park, that he would have to outrun death. That the same route would lead to much too much isolation for anyone to even hear his scream for help at that time of the night.

"Fuck this shit," he swore under his breath, turning the corner and fighting the urge to spin around and beg them to leave him alone.

Va-room!

He looked over his thin shoulder just seconds before the car jumped the curb and rammed his body back against a chain-link fence. Pain pierced his legs and ribs as the bones broke from the unrelenting pressure. He felt his bladder empty and the smell of his piss filled the air. As he closed his eyes, his upper body fell forward with a heavy thump against the hot hood over the rumbling motor.

The car jolted when it was switched into reverse.

He cried out in a high pitch as the car pulled his body forward, causing his broken legs to drag against the concrete of the curb and then the black asphalt of the street for a few feet before he finally slumped off the hood. Tears flooded his cheeks while he lay writhing in pain.

This ain't no way to die, man.

Even though his eyes were squeezed shut, the headlights lessened the darkness behind his lids.

Va-room.

"God help me," he whispered, feeling an odd blend of pain, fatigue, and fear.

The weight of the car rolled across his body with the first set of tires and then the second. This time he shitted on himself and the sounds of his bones crushing echoed around him. His body felt warm all at once and then cold chills caused his limp and battered body to shiver.

The pain was unbearable. The smell of blood was cloying.

"Take me, God," he begged, already feeling his ability to breathe fail.

He opened his eyes at the sound of footsteps, the last of his fourteen years of life seeping from him. A pair of boots came to stand in his blood that stained the street.

"Fuck you, motherfucker," a voice floated down to him, filled with rage.

He didn't understand. He knew the man standing above him. The man was someone he thought was a friend.

He'd thought wrong.

In the final seconds, as life left his body and his eyes became vacant, he felt his head being lifted from the concrete just before the acrid burn of a knife dragged across his throat.

His lips moved but the words wouldn't form. God forgive me, he thought just before his eyes filled with death.

Almost every night since Ms. JuJu called her, that was her dream. Her nightmare. Her vision of the night her son died.

The invasion of peaceful sleep. It had her fucked up for real. She had no idea if the last moments of his life were better or worse than her imaginings. Only thing she knew for sure was her son was dead and the police had his friends listed as "persons of interest," but that was as far as their sorry-ass investigation had gotten in the last few weeks. As far as she could tell they never even questioned any of them. It was clear they could care less about another dead black boy in the streets of Newark.

Did I care any more than them when I never made sure my son even knew who I am?

Naeema lowered her head into her hands and cried so hard that her shoulders shook and her chest heaved. She screamed from the pit of her stomach until the veins in her neck strained. She stood up so forcefully that her chair slid back across the floor and slammed into the front of the refrigerator.

Somebody has to pay.

She sniffed and angrily swiped the rest of her tears from her eyes as she picked up the 9mm sitting on the kitchen table next to the file. It fit nicely in her hand and her finger itched to fire off a round as she flipped through the pages of the folder with her free hand. She spread the photos. Four of them.

Four guilty motherfuckers as far as she was concerned.

Smiling bitterly, tears of anger raced down her cheek as she tapped each face in the photo with the barrel of the gun. Hatred burned her gut like an inferno was lit inside her. One of her son's friends had become a lethal foe. She just knew it. She always trusted her gut.

Biting her bottom lip, she flinched as she fired off the gun, blasting a hole through each of the faces.

POW!

POW!

POW!

POW!

The wood of the table shattered and flew up in the air around her like confetti with each blast. She didn't give a fuck that she'd demolished it and filled her kitchen floor with bullets. She didn't give a fuck if the cops came knocking. She didn't give a fuck about anything but flushing out her son's murderer and making him beg her for forgiveness just before she blew his brains out.

Dropping the gun, she let her body sink down to the floor. "I'm so sorry," Naeema whispered, closing her eyes, letting the pain consume her and fuel her need for revenge.

1

Four months later

"Don't die today, motherfucker."

Steely brown eyes were all that showed through the ski mask as the barrel of the gun was pressed against the fleshy cheek of the bank's lone security guard. His eyes were filled with fear, shifting to the left to try to view the holder of the gun.

"Look forward."

He immediately did, and raised both of his pudgy hands up into the air without being requested.

"Good boy," the assailant mocked in a throaty male voice, pressing the gun deeper into the guard's cheek until the soft tissue dimpled.

Don't die today.

Three others dressed all in black with the same ski masks took their positions around the small bank. Number One, Bastian "Bas" Jones, stood by the glass door poised with a gloved hand on the 9mm still resting in the leather holster. Number Two, Nelson Hunter, quickly walked across the small foyer of the bank and raised the handgun to point in the air between the shoulders of the two tellers on duty. And Number Three, Jamal "Red" Manning, stood beneath the surveillance camera with an AK-15 sniper rifle pointed in the vicinity of the few bank customers unlucky enough to be in line.

And I'm Number Four.

It was most definitely a holdup and everyone in the bank was clear about that. Surprisingly, no one screamed.

Nobody move. Nobody get hurt.

"Countdown! Let's go," Bas shouted loudly, a stopwatch in his gloved hand.

"Get your asses on the floor," Red demanded in a hard, take-no-shit voice and eyed each one with a glare.

The elderly man who looked like he was ready to head right back to a life of leisure in his recliner before the television set.

The middle-aged woman dressed like a teacher running errands on a brief break.

And the young black girl still in her Dunkin' Donuts uniform probably wishing she had waited to cash her check.

Their morning run to the small South Orange bank with the stone exterior and warm decor just got fucked all the way up. All. The. Way.

"May God forgive you," the woman suddenly cried out in a high-pitched voice.

Red moved forward and used one strong grasp to lift the barrel of the assault rifle high enough to ease it between her thin crimson-painted lips. "Bitch, you want to ask him about it face-to-face?" he asked, his voice mocking but his eyes all too serious.

Uh-oh. Shit just got real as hell.

In the midst of the silence of the bank, the sound of her swallowing over a lump in her throat echoed like a bomb blasting off. Her pale blue eyes widened as tears pooled in them before they raced down her wobbling cheeks and her entire body shook in fear. Her moment of foolish bravado was gone.

Red bent his head to the side and then cocked the gun. The boldness, defiance, and daring in his eyes could not be hidden.

She whimpered and then passed out, falling to the floor as if she lacked any bones in her frame. Red roughly snatched his boot from beneath her body before backing away as the others looked up at him from their spots stretched out on the white tiled floor. He obviously gave zero fucks about her and whether she was passed out or dead. Zero fucks.

Red is not the motherfucker to test.

"Countdown. Number Two . . . let's go," Bas shouted loudly. "Number Four . . . handle that!"

The orders were clear.

"Get low, Rent-A-Cop." The gun was shifted from the guard's fleshy cheek to the back of his unkempt head as brown eyes quickly shifted to take in Nelson tossing the leather duffel bag over the counter to the tellers.

"Empty all the cash drawers. Make it happen," Nelson snapped, shifting the gun to point in a direct line on one teller's heart and then the other's as they quickly scrambled to grab and then shove all the cash from the drawers into the duffel bag.

The security guard was still frozen on his knees.

"Down, motherfucker."

"Please don't shoot," he begged, in a voice filled with his worries.

Hardheaded motherfucker.

"Down."

He finally pressed his rotund belly against the cool tiles as he lay flat.

Damn!

There was no denying the highly charged energy pulsating in the air. Nervous gestures. Tears. Whimpers. Prayers.

"Thirty seconds," Bas called out, his slanted eyes seeming even brighter against the blackness of the mask.

The energy shifted again and crackled in the air like white noise.

"Hurry the fuck up," Nelson snapped at the tellers, turning his hand sideways to twist the gun in the air.

It was one of those moments when anything could happen at any moment. Any fucking thing.

"Twenty seconds." Bas stepped his tall figure back and roughly pushed the glass door of the bank wide open.

The pale redheaded male teller pushed the bag over to the black female teller with short dreads that needed more growth if she didn't want to look like she was being electrocuted. She bit her bottom lip as she hoisted the bag up to pass over the counter. It suddenly tumbled over the edge and fell to the floor with a THUD.

Everybody froze and the air seemed to be sucked from the room.

Nelson looked down at the bag and then up at the teller as his wrist snapped and the barrel of the gun jerked up. He cocked it.

Click.

No!

She cried out and took a step back. "Please," she begged, her eyes pooling with tears as she raised her hands and covered her face with splayed fingers.

Everything about the stance of his body said he was fighting not to put a bullet in her.

"Get the fucking bag and let's go, Number Two," Bas said in a hard voice.

And just like that the tension left his rotund body as he did just that and turned to run through the open door.

"Number Three . . . OUT!"

Red held the AK-15 steady as he quickly backed his large, muscular frame out the door.

"Number Four . . . OUT! Let's go."

Thank God.

With one last glance at the scared faces peering up from the floor and then down at the guard, there was nothing to do but walk backward out the door before turning to round the corner of the bank building. A white, battered Lincoln Continental awaited them.

It looked like a shitty getaway car but the motor underneath the jagged hood purred like a kitten. Kenney "Hammer" Charles, the final masked man behind the wheel, made sure of that.

Let's get the fuck outta here!

"Come on, Bas," Hammer said, his gloved hands tightly gripping the steering wheel as he leaned forward to peer through the windshield.

His voice was filled with the nerves, urgency, and adrenaline they all felt as the last of their crew—the leader of their crew, Bas—finally came running around the corner of the bank to slide into the front passenger seat of the car. He barely slammed the heavy door shut before the Continental accelerated forward with a peel of the tires against the street.

Hammer sped the vehicle through the normally serene suburban streets of South Orange township at high and furious speed. They had just sharply turned the corner leading into a short tunnel as the whir of police sirens sounded in the distance.

Everyone glanced over their shoulder or checked side-view mirrors.

"Shit," someone swore.

A lone police car was closing the three-block gap between them. It was clear—and expected—that one of the tellers had sounded the silent alarm to alert the police to the holdup.

Fuck this shit.

"I ain't in the fucking mood," Bas said, the husky tone of his voice more evident when he spoke normally and wasn't yelling out commands. With his mask still in place he checked his 9mm before lowering the window to point it back behind them.

No the fuck he ain't . . .

"Yo . . . chill, Bas," Hammer insisted, reaching over to grip his wrist. "Not yet. I got this, son."

The gun stayed pointed out the window, aimed and ready to fire, Bas's finger still on the trigger even as he gazed down at Hammer's hand with hard eyes. Eyes that shifted up to lock on his friend's profile in the mask.

Everyone in the car froze.

What the fuck?

Hammer instantly slid his hand off Bas and back onto the steering wheel.

POW!

THIS motherfucker just blasted off without even looking to see where the bullets might land. Hurt. Destroy. Injure. Kill.

POW! POW!

Yes the fuck he did.

Again everyone checked over their shoulders or in the mirrors as hearts pounded and the sweat of fear filled the small confined space. The police car was still on their asses even with the front windshield shattered by Bas's bullets.

Hammer turned a corner sharply and the wheels burned black streaks on the brick paved roads. He swerved suddenly to miss a woman pushing a stroller across the street. They could still hear her high-pitched scream as he left the outskirts of South Orange and entered the city limits of Newark through its Ivy Hill section.

The flash and blare of sirens were still close behind them, almost overpowering the sounds of early summer.

"Let's go, Hammer," Red shouted, pounding his gloved fist against the back of the front seat.

He screamed the words they all felt as their hearts pounded and their pulses raced even faster than the car. Nearly all.

Bas calmly kept his slanted eyes on the rearview mirror, his body relaxed in the seat as he tapped his gun against his knee. "Go up two lights and make a right," he said, his voice just as steady and sure as the hand ready to fire off another round. "Get off these main avenues."

Hammer deftly followed Bas's commands until they

finally reached a one-way street devoid of homes or traffic. He was able to open up the car and zoom ahead, steadily increasing the distance between them and the police. They knew the streets of the Brick City and used that knowledge to their full advantage, taking small side streets and short-cuts from one street to the next via openings where homes once sat. Soon the police were left behind to wonder where their prey disappeared.

Thank God.

Hammer slowed the car as the sounds of sirens completely faded. His shoulders and his stance in the seat relaxed a little. Shit was less tense. Less on the edge.

They did the crime but no one gave a fuck about doing the time.

Even without the presence of the police on their necks, no one said shit and the silence inside the vehicle was deafening. Everyone was lost in their thoughts. How to spend the money they just stole? How long before they were caught? What would the news say about them? When was the next bank robbery?

Would they make it out alive the next time?

Crime? Fine.

Time? Fuck that.

We just robbed a bank. I just helped rob a bank.

Hammer drove the streets at a much less noticeable speed but he still was taking no shorts in getting them to the spot. He slowed down as he neared an old garage attached to a two-story abandoned brick church with its stained glass windows covered with sheets of wood. One push of the remote clipped to the sun visor and the door lifted for him to drive inside.

It wasn't until he put the car in park and closed the garage door that they finally removed their black masks and climbed from the vehicle. Seconds later the almost indiscernible "click" of the generator sounded before the overhead light illuminated the windowless garage. The machine hummed loudly as it provided the electricity they wouldn't dare request from PSEG.

The garage smelled damp and musty and was just big enough to house the Lincoln and a large metal cabinet. In silence they quickly removed their gear, knowing they were leaving it all behind to be used again.

Nelson's bright eyes gleamed from his deep chocolate complexion as he moved his short, thick figure forward to toss the leather duffel bag at Bas. "I'm guessing ain't shit but 'bout ten grand," he said, wiping the sweat beading around the edge of his short 'fro, and not looking anything more than his nineteen years of age.

Bas caught it easily with one hand before tossing it onto the hood of the Lincoln. "We made better time and better money in Uniondale a couple of months ago," he said, unzipping the black all-in-one jumpsuit they all wore. He stepped out of it and tossed it onto the floor by the rear tire of the car to stand in his Ralph Lauren orange V-neck T-shirt and khaki shorts. He had a deep brown complexion that was smoother than melted chocolate, tall and thin in build but short as fuck in temper. Bas was just in his mid-twenties but his willingness to get physical was legendary. When something sparked off his anger it was crucial as hell. He appeared to be laid back and cool-headed, but to anyone who knew him—or knew of him—it was clear that could all change in a heartbeat.

Red's mask, gloves, and uniform fell onto the pile next. He stretched every firm muscle in his brick-house frame and then flexed his thick neck. "I did my part to keep shit straight," he said, his voice like rocks being crushed, and wiped his large hands over his bald head. His imposing build, jagged scar across his forehead, and the words KILLA tatted across the back of his shiny head left little doubt that he stayed ready to fuck shit up. Just one word or the right look from Bas and someone was completely dealt with. No questions asked.

"Congrats for not knocking that old lady the fuck out," Bas said.

"That woulda most definitely kept shit . . . less than straight, son," Hammer said, walking up to drop his things onto the growing pile on the concrete floor as well. He turned to check out his reflection in one of the car's windows. Hammer was caramel fine and knew it. He slung his dick like he was scared to lose it. He had enough women— and kids—to prove he put all of his fine-ass looks to use.

Red didn't laugh and the side-eye he gave Hammer made clear he wasn't in the mood to.

"And Nelson, you gotta check your fucking temper," Bas said, turning to unlock the metal cabinet and remove one of the three money-counting machines on the lowest shelf.

"I got you, Bas," Nelson said, gathering up all the guns to carefully place on the empty shelves of the cabinet.

"You better," he said in a cold voice, cutting his serious eyes up from loading the machine to lock on the youngest member of their crew.

Nelson nodded, shifting his eyes away from Bas while he gathered up the pile and jammed everything into a huge garbage bag. It was clear as day that Bas's approval meant a lot to him.

"And you did a'ight for your one and only ride," Bas said, his cool eyes warming as he came over to stand before the last person in the garage.

"One and only is right," said a male voice, as the black jumpsuit was unzipped to reveal a shapely body that was pure curves in a black form-fitting catsuit. Solid. Thick. Undeniably female. With a smile, she pulled off the ski mask and the hands-free voice changer she wore, and reached up to stroke the side of his square and handsome face. "A dare is a dare. I told you I could handle that shit," she said.

Bas smiled and eased one strong arm around her waist to pull her body close before bending his head a bit to taste her mouth. His hand dipped down to slap and then squeeze one of her plush ass cheeks as his tongue flickered against the tip of hers. "Don't start something you *know* you not ready to finish, Queen."

The other men all groaned in annoyance.

"I wish y'all would just fuck already," one of them said.

Bas chuckled before giving her another slap on the ass, then moved back across the small space to place rubber bands around the money. "Twelve lousy grand," he said, tossing the money back into the bag.

He never split up the take from the bank. He used money from his own stash that had already been laundered to make sure the chances of the stolen cash being traced back to them were lessened. He was most definitely the leader and the brains of the Make Money Crew, and everyone in the group respected that and played their own positions well.

Bas held the duffel in one hand and locked the cabinet

with the other as everyone filed out of the garage by the side door leading directly into the church's basement, where the kitchen had been housed. Queen slowed her steps and glanced back over her shoulder just as Bas snorted a bump of coke from the side of his hand. His sniffs echoed loudly in the quiet just before he cleared his throat.

She turned and rushed from the kitchen and then down the hall to where dimly lit steps led up to the vestibule of the sanctuary. No part of her enjoyed being in his presence when he was high. Over the last couple of months she'd watched him go from cool, calm, and collected to a short-tempered, not-to-be-slept-on ninja after just a line of that shit. Protect your neck and keep your back knife-free if he dared to do two. Thank God he was just on the recreational level.

She looked around at the abandoned space, which retained hints of its former beauty in the aged woodwork. Twenty years ago the church had been vibrant and beautiful. Now it was just a shell of its former self surrounded by waist-high weeds and bushes, the stained glass windows covered by boards and the gleam of the cherry wood dulled by dust and neglect.

The hangout of a band of thieves and bank robbers.

She still couldn't believe she had convinced Bas to let her go along with them on the robbery. She had been scared shitless the entire time but it had been important to gain their trust. Plus she felt like she needed to see it all go down. She needed to learn more about the people she'd moved among for the last two months. Details about them were vital. Important. Necessary as hell.

She looked through the diamond-shaped window panes on the wooden doors leading into the sanctuary. Her cat-shaped eyes rested on each person. Nelson stretched out on the front pew. Hammer lounging in the pulpit on his cell phone. Red was doing sit-ups on the floor in front of the leaning collection table.

Her gaze shifted as the door behind the pulpit, leading directly back down a set of stairs to the office in the basement, opened. Bas walked through it carrying stacks of money in his hand, each held together with a rubber band. He had swapped the cash for the money he kept in the office in a huge locked safe for which only he had both the key and the combination.

She looked on with squinted eyes as he tossed each wad to the men. She looked from one to the other over and over again, feeling the heat of hatred burn her stomach until she could retch. Bas, Hammer, Nelson, and Red. Bas. Hammer. Nelson. Red.

She made a fist so tight that her nails pinched the flesh of her palm. Her hatred for them nearly choked her. One of them had killed her teenage son and left him for dead in the streets. She was going to find out which one and then she was going to take pleasure in killing him. *Eye for an eye.*

"Queen, you a better bitch than me."

Naeema forced her body to remain relaxed even as she turned to smile at Vivica, Red's girlfriend and her bridge into the crew. There were many times she had to remind herself that these motherfuckers knew her as Queen. For them, Naeema—the mother of Brandon Mack—didn't exist. "It was a'ight," she said, shrugging her shoulder as she took in the slender light-skinned beauty with wide-set eyes and full lips.

Vivica played with her hot-pink cornrows that reached

the top of her ass in the shorts she wore. "I'll spend the money but fuck putting myself in the line of fire to get it," she said, walking past Naeema to open one of the double doors.

Bitch, if you had anything to do with killing my son, you're already in the line of fire.

"Queen, you coming?" Vivica asked, looking back over her shoulder.

Naeema followed the other woman into the sanctuary, very aware that she was living among a den of thieves and a murderer that she was hell-bent on fleshing out.

2

*N*aeema gathered her bag as the driver of the green cab made the right on Eastern Parkway in Newark. She climbed from the back of the taxi and closed the door. She barely had time to take a step forward before the African cabbie pulled off up the street. She scratched at the synthetic bob wig on her head as she looked up and down the length of the street that sloped downward like a slide. The street was made up of one-family homes that had once belonged to Jewish business owners before the great exodus of white folks out of Newark back in the late 1950s and 1960s.

Whether the house was still living up to its former glory or took a turn for the worse all depended on whether the owner—or the tenants—gave a fuck about curb appeal.

Naeema eyed one of the two brick houses flanking her home. Freshly painted shutters, shiny brass house numbers, and cute mailbox adorned the front brick façade. The metal railings had a shiny black coat without a single peel. The landscaping behind the wrought iron fence was on point.

She shifted her eyes to the other brick home. It was the exact opposite, like an image in a weird mirror that flipped shit. Thing was, Naeema was in no position to play pot to the black kettle.

Biting her full bottom lip, she squinted against the afternoon sun as she stepped up on the curb and eyed her happy home. The windows of the second floor and attic were still boarded and one of the ones on the first floor was cracked and held together with tape. Some bricks were missing in spots with large red letters on it for whatever gang had decided to tag the once-abandoned building. The falling fence served no real purpose and the stack of old newspapers on the porch was an eyesore and a fire hazard. She never had signed up for a subscription to the *Star Ledger* but the papers came like clockwork and she wasn't turning down shit that was free.

"I am dead-ass wrong for this shit," she mumbled before she hitched her tote up higher on her shoulder and bent over to pick up the fence gate that was damn near hanging to the ground.

Twice she tried to prop it against the rusted fence. Twice she failed. Twice she swore.

"Fuck it," she said almost wearily, letting it fall back to hang near the ground before she stepped over it in her black wedge sneakers to jog up the stairs and unlock the front door.

Rolling her eyes, she lifted the door up by the knob and shoved hard against it with her shoulder to dislodge it from the frame. She'd hired a bootleg carpenter—with more brag on his skill than actual skills—and the door had been his one and only project when he couldn't even put *that* motherfucker on straight.

Doing the same trick to close and lock it, Naeema kicked off her sneakers and dropped her tote onto the floor before she snatched off the short black wig to rub her slender fin-

gers and long stiletto-shaped nails over her closely shaven
head. For a second, she stood there in the large living room
with its faded wallpaper, scratched hardwood floors, and
decrepit fireplace. She could close her eyes and almost picture the days she'd spent growing up there.

The house once belonged to her grandfather and now it
was hers.

She was the owner of a home that had seen better days,
and although she cared that it still looked like the abandoned and battered shithole it became after her grandfather's death, she didn't have the money to fix it up the way it
deserved. The way he would want.

*But it's mine . . . what's left of this raggedy motherfucker
anyway.*

The brick colonial had been her home since the day her
grandfather had had to choose whether to let her go into
the foster care system or raise her. A drunk driver took her
mother away and her father was never there. That left her
grandfather to grieve the death of his daughter and raise his
eleven-year-old grandchild, who was filled with grief and
anger and lack of understanding.

As soon as she hit her teens she took his age for granted.
She had a love for hanging out in the streets—she'd inherited
it from her father—and she'd let it lead her to sneaking out
of the house at night or running away for days to discover
parties, weed, and dicks—and not in that order. The years
between thirteen and fifteen were a messy-ass blur.

Just fucking wild and reckless.

There were plenty of women who came in and out of his
life to help, but Willie Cole had done the work of raising a
little girl. He cooked. He cleaned. He shopped. He talked.

He listened. He did his best to do her hair. He made sure she went to school. He took care of her. He loved her. He was *there*. He didn't deserve the nights he stayed up looking for her or waited for her to come home safe. Naeema paused in her steps as an ache radiated across her body from missing the only stable person in her life.

The pain was a mix of longing and grief and guilt. Lots of guilt.

Pushing away her thoughts with the release of a heavy breath, she reached behind her back to unzip her catsuit before pulling it from her curvaceous body to eventually kick it onto the pile of dirty clothes stacking up in front of the brick fireplace. She was using the living room as her bedroom until she could afford to replace the glass broken out of the bedroom windows by the rocks of bored children. The 1920s colonial had three floors, five bedrooms, three full baths, a semifinished basement, and even an old garage, but her entire existence was limited to the first floor. There were two clear paths from the living room to the bathroom on the left and then the living room to the kitchen at the rear of the house.

Back and fucking forth like she was trapped in a cage or fish bowl.

Still, she was blessed to have a roof over her head, a pot to piss in, and the window to throw it out of. There was a time when she hadn't. Her grandfather's death left her with her own life choice at fifteen: be pushed into the foster care system or run.

She ran like hell and lived pillar to post. She didn't want to remember some of the shit she did—the things she compromised—to have a place to sleep for a night. Lying. Stealing. Conning. Overlooking some dude's uglies—face, body, or attitude—so he'd buy a motel room long enough for him to bust a nut and for her to enjoy its comfort until the front desk staff called at checkout.

She had been like Malcolm X. By *any* motherfucking means necessary.

Over the last year since she'd moved in, she was able to sweep and scrub the floor of every room clean and empty it of whatever sad remnants of drug abuse or homelessness had been left behind by transients or junkies after her grandfather's death. But it was obvious the house was in serious need of some tender loving care. She felt lucky it was still standing and not burned to a crisp by the fire used to heat crack or cold bodies.

It was home.

Walking past the metal full-size bed in the center of the room, her eyes locked on her reflection in the mirror. Nothing about her spoke to being a mother to a teenage child and far less to being of an age to outlive him. She was tall like her grandfather and curvy like her mother. Since she was thirteen her profile had been a letter *S*—all ass and breasts. It drew the eye of many a young horny boy and far too many grown men.

"They'll run right through a pretty girl like you," her grandfather said one night as he sat in her bedroom, surprising her as she climbed back through the window she'd snuck out of hours before. "And it's always you pretty ones looking for some man to tell you what you should be able to see for yourself in the mirror. And by the time you really take a good hard look at yourself life and a string of lyin'-ass men done fucked you over and left nothin' but hard times on your face. Keep fallin' for the okey-doke, Naeema, and you gon' regret that bullshit for sure."

A hard head and hot behind kept her from listening to him. Thinking she knew it all and then some. Just dumb and young and filled with cum.

She needed that guidance and love from him and she fought it so hard. Then when she became a parent she never once mustered up the ability to offer the same to her child.

My son is dead and I hadn't laid eyes on him since he was less than a week old.

Turning from her image in pain she opened the top drawer of her dresser and removed the Payless shoe box snuggled with her socks and panties. She removed her dick pipe and loosely filled the balls with weed. She used to keep the pipe on the top of her dresser like an award or some shit, but coming home to find a mouse perched on the top where she placed her lips led her to throwing that one in the trash and buying another that she kept protected in a box.

She smiled at the first toke, enjoying how the first hit had a real subtle taste of lime. Dropping down onto the center of her bed, she picked up the remote and turned on the nineteen-inch flat screen sitting on top of many containers stacked along the wall. Most of them held her shoes or her beloved spandex or Lycra clothing that showed off her curves and never required ironing. That was a helluva two-fer as far as she was concerned.

Knock.

She looked over her shoulder at the sound of the solitary rap of strong knuckles against the door in the kitchen that led down into the basement. With the hint of a smile, she took another toke and held it in her lungs as she rose to pull on an oversize football jersey that dwarfed her curvy frame like crazy. The man who once owned the jersey had made her feel just as small by his size. The name TANK printed on the back had suited him well.

Exhaling the smoke of the weed that guaranteed her a delicious high for a straight four or five hours, Naeema walked across the length of the living room and into the kitchen that fancy white folks would call retro and she just called outdated. It was clear not a damn thing about it had changed since the late seventies, including the orange walls, dull walnut cabinet, and yellow appliances. The absence of her table and the bullets lodged in the floor where it once sat didn't upgrade things worth a damn.

"Hey, Sarge," she said as she pulled the door open.

She eyed the gray-haired man in his mid-sixties as he entered the kitchen. The army vet was just as gruff in looks and manner as Fred Sanford. He rarely smiled and even less rarely ventured up the stairs from where he lived in her basement. If he heard her moving about the kitchen he would knock on the door leading from the basement and wait for her permission to enter. She guessed it was his way of still giving her some privacy.

She held her breath at the first sight of him but then remembered he now regularly used the shower in the small basement at her urging. She'd tried for way too many weeks to deal with the stench of an unwashed body until she had to straight handle that problem.

When she took possession of the house, Sarge was squatting in it, and after getting over the urge to press a Taser to the neck of the wild-looking man in the dirty army uniform she hadn't had the heart to put him out . . . yet. In the depths of his eyes she had seen surprise at her sudden appearance but also a fear that the shelter he had come to cherish would be gone. Although his stink was high enough to rise to the heavens above and she had no idea if he would murder her in her sleep, Naeema's gut had guided her to let him stay. Unlike the bullshit decisions she'd made in her teens, Naeema had learned to trust her instincts in her twenties. Now they rarely led her wrong.

In truth, knowing he was downstairs was a comfort to her. It was a disjointed version of her former life living with her grandfather for all those years. Sarge had become a constant as she struggled to readjust to the recent changes in her life.

"That shit ain't good for you, Naeema."

She shrugged one shoulder as she released a thick stream of smoke. Her nerves were still shot to hell from the bank robbery earlier that morning. That had been a big risk, but if it meant getting closer to the people she thought were responsible for her son's death, then it was well worth it. "You hungry, Sarge?" she asked, opening the fridge.

"The South Orange police department is currently investigating a bank robbery at the Township Bank this morning."

"My belly full," he answered gruffly.

Naeema barely heard him. Her body stiffened and her head cocked at the sound of the local news on the television.

"Four masked gunmen entered the bank just a few minutes after its opening and demanded the bank employees empty its registers."

"Just wanted to lay eyes on you," he said.

Naeema nodded as she swung the door to the fridge

closed and walked back into the living room. Her eyes were locked on the screen as she picked up the remote.

"The unidentified men fled the bank with an undisclosed amount of cash. The robbers were pursued in a late-model white Lincoln Continental without plates but lost the police once the chase entered neighboring Newark, New Jersey . . ."

She raised the remote as her heart seemed to lurch forward in her chest.

Click.

"I helped to rob a motherfucking bank," she mouthed, biting her full bottom lip as her eyes filled with the trouble she felt.

She took a few moments and then a few more trying to get her shit together before she turned. Sarge was standing in the doorway, the tips of the old and scuffed Timberland boots he always wore were firmly pressed to the metal saddle separating the two rooms. He never came beyond the kitchen, never crossed that metal line, like he thought he was a fly that would get zapped if he even dared to fuck with it.

He squinted his eyes as he shifted them from the television to her face.

Naeema forced herself to relax her face as she walked over to him. Before she could open her mouth he grunted and turned to walk away. She heard the door leading down to the basement slam.

WHAM!

She moved no farther.

The sudden silence was loud as a no-good motherfucker. The quiet had never been a friend of hers. "Fuck this shit," she said, taking another deep puff from the cool ceramic tip, then made her way to her front door, set the pipe on the floor, and stepped out onto the porch.

Futilely fanning herself to beat back the summer heat, Naeema closed her eyes and absorbed the sounds of the city. They were always present. Always vibrant. Large trucks grinding and rattling down the streets. Car horns. Music blaring through opened car windows. Raised voices. Children laughing. Police or fire sirens wailing in the distance. All kinds of noise.

She needed that shit bad as hell.

The sudden screech of tires seemed to override everything. Naeema stiffened in surprise.

THUMP.

The sound of a woman slamming her hand down against the hood of a rusted red vehicle echoed in the street. Naeema's body filled with relief. At least the car hadn't run her over.

"Get your high ass out the street!" the driver shouted out the window, his accent unrecognizable.

"Fuck you!" the woman shouted back, punctuating the exchange with a thorough-ass flip of her middle finger.

He maneuvered his car past her on the narrow one-way street lined with parked cars.

Naeema looked on in growing surprise as the woman scratched her ample ass in the brightly colored leggings she wore, stepped up onto the sidewalk, and pushed her tangled and matted weave from her face.

Naeema's eyes widened when she recognized one of her neighbors. Coko stepped up onto the sidewalk and stumbled, falling forward. "Well, damn," Naeema gasped as she rushed down the stairs in her bare feet. She struggled briefly with the wayward gate of the fence before running down the street to kneel beside the woman.

"Who da fuck are you?" Coko asked as she struggled to rise.

Naeema gagged at the stench of her breath, offended as hell. It smelled like a mix of shit and everything else fucked up in the world. The fuck?

"Get the fuck off me. Shit!"

Oh, to hell with this stank-breath bitch . . .

Naeema rose and stepped back while Coko fought like a bitch to rise to her feet in the scuffed and tattered heels she wore. Her movements made the funk of her unwashed ass rise up in the summer heat. Naeema didn't know what was worse: her breath or her twat smelling like cat piss and old sex juices.

Long after Coko moved up the steps and into her brick house just two doors down from her own, Naeema stood there thinking of the demons that had chased yet another woman into the arms of drug abuse. It was clear the death of her man, Keno, had pushed her with far too much ease toward getting high. Word was thick on the streets that Keno pissed off one of the factions of the Mafia when he took over an underground gambling and loan-sharking business after his best friend, Dane, got busted by the police. The only thing everyone knew for sure was somebody blew his ass up in a warehouse explosion.

In the year since Keno's death, Coko had slid from being a sexy thick chocolate chick to an ashy shadow of her former self. Even the little Asian "thot"—that ho over there—that used to trail behind her had stopped coming around. Still, though Naeema knew she was busy on the trail of her son's killer, she'd had no clue Coko had fallen off so much. She was strung the fuck out and Naeema would bet her light bill money that some of her stench was from tricking to support her habit.

She gave the little brick house one last look over her shoulder as she made her way back to her own home. Naeema wasn't one to judge. She had come close as fuck to crossing the line into addiction herself. These days she relied on her medicinal weed to elevate her but she could just as easily have become Coko years ago when she was young and trying anything a young boy with a hard dick and a slick tongue offered her.

Drugs wasn't shit to play with because there was no way to win in that game.

She jogged up the stairs of her house and entered, pausing long enough to pick up her weed pipe before she lifted the door and then firmly shut it by pressing her body against it. Feeling the effects of the weed, she set the dick on the dresser and opened her Louis Vuitton handbag—the only authentic bag she owned. She pushed aside the wad of fifty-dollar bills—her share of the take from the bank—Bas had surprised her with to grab one of her two cell phones. One was a touch screen that she'd had for over a year. The other was a twenty-dollar throwaway or burner phone she used just to chitchat with the Make Money Crew. The cheap flip phone was lit up. She had three missed calls from Vivica.

"Fuck her," Naeema muttered, dropping down to sit on the stool in front of her full-length mirror.

Honestly, she knew she shouldn't be so hard on Vivica. When she saw her name listed as Red's girlfriend in the police report, Naeema had gone to their address and followed the woman until she found a reason for them to meet so she could get in with Bas and the crew through her. It was clear real quick that Vivica loved Red, shopping, and clubbing. One stop by On Your Back, her favorite clothing store downtown, and Naeema had chatted her up about clothes and clubbing. Soon "Queen" and Vivica became the best of friends. Just a few weeks later Vivica introduced "Queen" to Bas at Club 973.

Truly she knew she owed Vivica big time.

Anytime in the last couple of months that Naeema went deep undercover, it was Viv and Red's apartment where she slept. She lied and said she lived with her mother and hated going home. They bought it. She was in. She became like Vivica's shadow and soon she was hanging out at the church with the crew. She had been accepted. Step one was complete.

She needed a break from them motherfuckers. On and off for the last two months she had gotten lost in their world but she needed to shut the door on them. Everything about her dealings with them mofos was fake as a five-dollar pack of weave hair. For just one night she wanted to forget.

Forget the revenge.

Forget the crime she helped commit that day.

Forget the murder she planned to commit.

Forget that she was an "ain't shit" mother with a dead son she never knew.

Tears, guilt, and pain welled up.

"Shit," she swore, reaching in the bag to pull out the wad of cash.

She held it tight as hell in her fist and wished she wasn't so broke that she could burn the money and feel all righteous about not making a dime off her son's death. Coulda, shoulda, fucking woulda.

Standing up, she flung the wad against the opposite wall, knowing the whole time she would be on her knees looking for that loot first thing in the morning.

Naeema picked up her cell phone and hit 69 on her speed dial. It rang twice.

"Whaddup, Na?"

"Come thru," she said in a whisper filled with her need.

The line stayed quiet for a few seconds.

"Who dat, Tank?"

Naeema tensed at the female voice questioning him from the background. She instantly felt hot with anger and jealousy.

"Yo," she stressed, pressing her eyes closed. "Fuck her. Come *thru*."

"Naee—"

Click.

She hung up on his protests and checked the time on her phone, then dropped it onto her bed and crossed the room to the small bathroom just behind the stairs leading to the second floor. By the time she'd finished a long hot shower and douched she heard the roar of a motorcycle come up the drive. With nothing wrapped around her curves but her damp lime-green towel, Naeema made her way to the front door and opened it just as the lights of the Harley blacked out and a tall figure climbed off it to cut through the opening in the side gate. She bit her bottom lip and leaned back against the door, her eyes heavy from the weed and from straight wanting him to make her forget like only he could.

She turned and walked back inside. She spotted the wad

of money just peeking out from under the radiator and she dashed across the room to push it out of sight with her toe.

"You need to do something about this raggedy-ass door. Hell . . . and this raggedy motherfucka too," he said, his tall, broad body looking as fine and fit as it was in the black tee he wore with jeans. Broad shoulders and narrow hips. Muscles. A body built to please.

"Shut up, Tank," she said, letting the towel drop to the floor.

He removed his helmet and she smiled at his fine Laz Alonzo–looking ass and his square face, slanted eyes, and soft lips.

"Yo, Naeema, you be trippin'," he said.

She lay back on the bed and spread her thick thighs wide. Even as he stood there like he was frozen in one spot, his sexy eyes dipped down to her pussy as she spread her lips and worked her inner muscles.

"This what you call me to come thru for?" he asked.

"Legally . . . that's my dick . . . and this your pussy," Naeema said, her eyes locked on his. "Come thru."

"You left me. You said we was done. You said you was sick of arguing—"

She flipped over onto her knees on the bed and twerked her ass muscles. "Last chance, hubby," she said, looking over her shoulder at him.

Tank was every bit of six foot five and strong as a dozen oxen but she knew her pussy was his weakness. Always had been. Always would be.

Moments later she bit her bottom lip at the hot feel of his fingers massaging her buttocks before he slapped first one ass cheek and then the other.

WHAP. WHAP.

"Say please," he ordered her as he pressed his thumb against her clit.

She moaned in pleasure, already imagining him sliding all of his eleven thick inches deep inside her. She knew without looking that his pants were down around his ankles and his dick was hard, heavy, and in his hand. Just waiting.

Naeema was just as anxious. The truth was his dick was her weakness too.

"Please," she cried out as he slapped her buttocks with his dick.

Always was. Always would be.

3

Naeema glanced up at the clock on the pristine white walls of the kitchen before she finished cutting the ham sandwich in half and then pouring a glass of milk to sit beside it. She wiped her hands on the dish towel that hung neatly from the apron around her waist and protected the polka dot dress she wore with black kitten heels and pearls. Leaving the kitchen, she walked across the well-furnished living room to stand at the foot of the stairs.

"Brandon," she called in a perfect singsong as she patted her bob.

"Yes, Mother."

Smiling, she looked up at her teenage son standing at the top of the stairs in his pink polo shirt, khaki shorts, and leather Sperrys. Her heart swelled with love. "Lunch is ready, honey. Come on down," she said.

"I'm reading, Mom," he said with perfect diction.

"Bring your book down with you," she said.

"Yes, ma'am."

Naeema turned and spared a few moments to smooth wrinkles from the sofa and fluff up the throw pillows before heading back into the kitchen. She was setting a bag of chips next to the saucer holding the sandwich when Brandon strolled into the kitchen with his book in hand. He took his seat and she bent a bit to press a kiss to his temple. "You know you're the best thing God could have ever blessed me with?" she asked.

Brandon nodded and glanced up at her with a smile before taking a big bite of his sandwich.

She turned to open the cabinet over the sink that she kept filled with snacks.

"Too bad this bullshit is phony as fuck, Ma."

Naeema's body went stiff as hell as she looked over her shoulder at her son in surprise. She gasped to find him standing behind her silently. She screamed out and pressed her back to the sink at the sight of the blood seeping from a crack in his skull. His thin neck was ripped open by a jagged slash. Tire tracks covered his clothing. His eyes were bloodshot. His bones were broken and protruding through his skin. His body jerked roughly and he coughed up blood that spurted from his mouth and neck, spraying against her face and shirt.

"No!" she cried, squeezing her eyes shut as she turned to run toward the door leading into the small backyard.

The stench of his blood got stronger in the air and she knew he was behind her. Closer.

"No, Brandon. No!" she screamed at the top of her lungs as she fought to open the door.

"You never loved me," he said, his voice gurgling from the blood filling his throat. "You never wanted me."

Her tears and fears caused her shoulders to shake as she felt her legs give out from beneath her as she slid down to the floor. "I'm sorry," she whimpered.

"It's all your fault."

"I fucked up. Forgive me. Please," she begged, her voice barely above a harsh whisper.

"You ain't shit . . . Na-ee-ma," he said with snide emphasis.

She covered her face with her hands as his blood began to drip down onto the top of her head and he leveled his mangled body over her . . .

"Hey, Na, wake up. What's wrong?"

Naeema shook her head and struggled between the world of her nightmare and a sleep-fueled reality as she was awakened.

"Na . . . why you cryin'?"

She opened her eyes and sat up with a gasp. Her face was wet with her tears and her heart still pounded hard as fuck in her chest. She wiped her face and pulled her knees to her chest, pressing her exposed breasts against her thighs as she wrapped her arms around her legs. The darkness of the house only did a little bit to cut the summer heat and she could feel the dampness of both her and Tank's skin when he sat up in bed beside her.

"What's goin' on with you, yo?" he asked.

Licking her lips she turned her head atop her knees and reached for the remote to turn the television on. The light from it gleamed against their bodies while the sound of the local news filled the air. "I'm good," she lied, knowing she couldn't tell her husband that a dream that started out with her faking the funk like she was Michelle Obama or some shit spiraled into a nightmare about her son—a child she never told him or anyone else in her life about.

"You ain't shit, Na-ee-ma."

He was right.

Tank took the remote and put the television on mute before he wrapped a strong arm around her shoulders and pulled her body on his as he lay back down. She pressed her face into his neck and took a deep inhale of the scent of his cologne. She could so easily get lost in him and the madness that was their love. So fucking easy. It wouldn't be the first time.

When Naeema got dressed to hit the clubs that night back in 2006, the last thing she had been looking for was love. Drinks? Weed and Ecstasy pills? Good music? Cute dudes? Dancing? Some fun with her girls? Hell *yes* to all of that. Still, the first sight of the sexy man at the door of Club Infinity with SECURITY written across his shirt had her gone . . . especially when she saw that the fly motherfucker was feeling her too.

He flirted. She flirted back.

She didn't even go inside the club at all that night. She chilled with him, giving zero fucks about the other dudes eyeing how good she looked in the off-shoulder latex dress she wore like a second skin against her curves. Even when her friends had left the club early to make a diner run, Naeema had stayed behind with the sexy bouncer and part-time celebrity security guard until the club shut down.

Naeema went home with him too. No sex, just good conversation . . . but all that talking went out the window on the second night. And they both went in. Nothing left undone. Their conversations were cool—sometimes deep and thoughtful, other times playful and fun—but it was the sex that fucked them both up.

She moved into his three-bedroom house a month later and two years after that they flew to the Bahamas and got married. It lasted close to six years before she packed her shit and left. The fire in their marriage was just as heated in the bedroom as it was when they argued about dumb shit.

It had been about a year since she left, and besides occasional fuck fests, they were living separate lives. They only thing ever drama-free between them was sex.

Rolling away from his body she quickly moved to straddle his hips.

Tank brought his hands up to cup her hips, his eyes taking in her full breasts, flat stomach, and bald pussy. He shifted his hand to stroke his thumb against his name tattooed against the smooth skin of her mound.

Naeema shook her head in shame. "You had my head all fucked up back then when I got this," she said, sucking in what little gut she had to look down at it.

"This good *dick* had you fucked up," he bragged, his voice deep.

"True," she agreed, bringing her legs up to press her ankles against the sides of his head.

Tank quickly grabbed her calves when her ankles tightened. "You wouldn't know how to do it even if you wanted to," he taunted her, giving her a slow wink as he opened his hands to free her and then spread his arms wide as if daring her to try.

He was right. Even if she had the skill to straight snap his neck with her ankles, she could never do anything to hurt Tank. First, because he had a black belt in martial arts and what few maneuvers she knew he'd taught her, and second, because she loved him. She reached down to stroke the tip of his dick that was pressed between her thighs. She instantly felt his heat and then his hardness. Tank moaned and closed his eyes in pleasure, rolling his hips to stroke his dick upward.

Quickly she raised one leg and brought it down sharply toward his nose. Just millimeters before the blow landed he captured her heel in one of his large hands. "It's levels to this young girl . . ." he rapped, imitating Meek Mill.

He turned his head on the pillow and sucked her smooth heel as he kept his eyes locked on her.

Naeema arched her back and cried out a little. Achilles' heel was his weakness and it was hers too. It was a weird-ass hot spot and Tank was the only man to ever find it and exploit it. "Shit," she swore as her nipples tightened and goose bumps raced across her caramel skin like crazy.

As soon as his grip weakened, she freed her foot and quickly rolled her body off his to the floor and tumbled away before jumping up to her feet with a solid THUD.

Tank had the nerve to laugh at her as he clapped his hands.

Bam-bam-bam.

Naeema motioned with her finger for him to be quiet as Sarge rang his ghetto bell from below to let them know they were fucking with his peace. Tank made a face as he rose from the bed and raised his leg like he was about to stomp on the floor.

"Don't you fuck with it, Tank," she said, coming across the room to push against him and knock him back against the bed.

Being playful, he lightly plucked one of her taut nipples before he flipped her like a pancake onto her stomach and then slipped his arms and legs around her. She felt his smooth chest hairs against her back and the hair around his dick tickling her ass as he pressed her into the bed beneath his weight. "He lucky his crazy ass even up in here," Tank said, his cool breath fanning against the side of her face.

Tank didn't mean that shit.

One of the reasons she let Sarge stay was because she'd asked Tank to use his connects at the Newark Police Department to run a background check on the vet to make sure he was straight.

"Now tell me why you're havin' nightmares about that murdered kid," he demanded, his voice now low and husky and sexy as shit.

Naeema stiffened before she could catch herself. "What?" she asked, turning her head to avoid him licking circles against her cheek.

"You asked me to pull strings to get his file and now you're having nightmares and screamin' out his name in your sleep and shit," Tank said, his body dwarfing hers by close to a foot in height and thirty pounds in weight.

As much as they argued because they both were hot-headed and jealous as hell, her son was the one thing Naeema never revealed about herself to Tank. They never lied to each other. She closed her eyes and licked her lips. "I guess just looking at all those photos from the crime scene been fucking with me. You know I ain't used to that shit," she said, skimming the truth.

"Who is he?" he asked, shifting their bodies so they now lay on their sides with his body still like a claw around hers.

She was trapped and immobile but the pressure of his body against hers was sexy and comfortable all at once. She let herself have that moment when she didn't have shit to do but let Tank hold her. *Tell him.*

He brought one hand over to lightly stroke her nipple. She moaned.

Tell him.

He sucked her neck just below her ear. She shivered.

Tell him.

As much as she wanted someone to lift some of the burden of her grief and anger from her shoulders, she couldn't fuck with him looking at her different because she was one of them chicks that didn't choose to raise her child. In those four years between handing her baby over to Ms. JuJu and meeting Tank, her life hadn't amounted to shit. Partying and bullshit mostly.

She let being a mother come second to that?

"You ain't shit, Na-ee-ma."

Her body went weak with grief. Just straight limp. "Let me go, Tank," she pleaded softly.

He did in an instant. "What's up with you, Na?" he asked as she rolled away from him, curled her body into a tight ball, and pressed her face into one of the pillows on the bed.

She heard him but she was too busy trying to get her shit together. Trying to keep from becoming a crying mess. Trying and fucking failing like crazy.

Naeema opened her eyes as he gripped her upper arms and lifted her up to face him as he now stood on the side of the bed. "Just go home, Tank. I'll holler at you later," she said, looking over his shoulder to avoid his eyes as she tried to shrug out of his grasp.

He shook her a little in frustration. "Who is this little boy?"

Her anger came with a quickness and she broke out of his grasp and mushed his hard chest with both of her hands to step down off the bed and move past him. Again she knew he let her get away with that. "Just leave it the fuck alone, Tank—"

"Hold up one sec, yo."

She looked on as Tank flipped the covers to find the remote before he turned up the volume on the television.

"The weekend shooting of ten-year-old Olivia Hawkins brings the city's murder rate for the year to fifteen . . ."

As Tank turned the volume back down on the television, Naeema turned away from the picture of the slain little girl still on the screen. Her son was one of the dead counted in that number.

"Another unsolved murder," she muttered.

"Just like Brandon?" he asked pointedly.

She avoided answering him as she picked up his football jersey that she wore earlier and slid it on. "Listening to the news makes it seem like a war zone out there."

Tank sat down on the bed. "That's true as hell."

"It's too many young-ass cock-strong motherfuckers roaming the street that don't give a fuck about life. Theirs or anybody else's," she said, thinking of Bas and the way he moved through life like he owned the world.

She flinched at the memory of him shooting that gun without even looking back to see where his bullets landed. Somebody like that could have easily run a young boy over to kill him. *Or order his goon to do it.*

In the time since she'd been around them she hadn't found a reason for any of them to want Brandon dead. Not yet. She just had to push a little harder. Helping on that bank robbery would give her a closer in with Bas and hopefully she'd be more than Vivica's cute friend that he flirted with.

"The mayor supposed to hire more police," Tank said.

Naeema twisted her mouth as she climbed on the bed behind him and pressed her titties against his back and settled her chin atop his head. "Them motherfuckers ain't to be trusted."

"Good thing because then you wouldn't have that file you wanted, right?" he reminded her, leaning forward to look back at her.

"So there ain't no dirty-ass cops, Tank?" Naeema asked with attitude.

"Fuck yeah it is," he assured her. "Come on now. I ain't no lame, Na. There's good and bad in everything and the streets ain't safe, because not every police give a fuck. These kids gotta make better decisions about how they movin' through these streets."

"Like Olivia?" she shot back, mentioning the little girl just discussed in the news story.

"You know that ain't what the fuck I mean. Olivia and Brandon are two different scenarios."

Naeema sat back on her haunches and eyed him hard. "So Brandon deserved to die?" she asked him in a cold voice even as the heat of her anger burned her belly.

"Fuck no and if you tell me what this is all about I'll help you find out what happened."

Naeema forced herself to chill as she climbed off the bed. She knew everything Tank said was the realest shit ever. She knew firsthand that her son was in thick with a band of thieves. He wasn't completely an innocent like Olivia and so many others. Still, he didn't deserve to die.

"If you just let me know anything I can do, yo, to help you out you know I will," he said, pointedly looking around at her crazy living situation. "*An-y-thing.*"

Naeema shrugged. "I'm good."

Tank opened his arms wide as he stared at her. "It's hot as a *motherfucka* in here. I think a mouse just ran across my foot being a rude little bastard. And who knows what the fuck *he* got goin' on downstairs."

Naeema bit her bottom lip to keep from laughing.

"Yo, I'm serious as a heart attack. Let me at least put air in this bitch and call a fuckin' exterminator," he said.

Another point of contention in their marriage was Tank being the neat freak and Naeema caring far less whether everything was in its proper place. "What's the purpose of me jettin' if you still taking care of me?"

Tank shook his head. "But I can come thru and fuck you when you ask for that, right?"

"I didn't ask," she countered, pointing one of her long stiletto-shaped nails at him.

"No, you ordered—"

"And you obeyed," she teased.

At Tank's continued silence Naeema looked over her shoulder at him. His dark eyes rested on her. She rolled her eyes and moved past him to pull her pipe out of the box in the drawer. She turned on the lamp sitting on the corner of the dresser, giving the room more light before she packed it with new loud. "Want some?" she asked before she lit it.

"From that?" he balked.

"Yours is bigger, daddy," she assured him in a soft voice before she licked the tip and took a toke.

"Nah, I'm good," Tank said.

"But I'll make it better," she said, pushing him back down on the bed with her free hand before she sat on his lap.

Tank's hands came up to rest on her buttocks beneath the jersey. Naeema took a long toke as she swiveled her hips in tight little circles and looked him directly in those sexy fucking eyes she loved. He lightly slapped her ass as she felt his dick get harder and brush against her thigh as it grew.

Cupping the back of his head with one hand she pursed her lips and exhaled a stream of thick weed smoke. He eased his hands around to massage her soft inner thighs as he opened his mouth and inhaled. "This that good," she promised him in a whisper.

"The weed or the pussy?" he asked, freeing the smoke to swirl densely in the air between their mouths.

"Both."

Naeema took another toke as Tank raised the jersey. "Hmmmmmm," she moaned, stroking his hard dick with her hand as she held the smoke in her lungs.

His tongue felt feather light and hot against her hard nipples before he sucked one deeply into his mouth.

"Shit," Naeema swore as her clit swelled and throbbed with its own pulse.

"Give me some," he moaned against the deep hot valley between her breasts as he wrapped his arms around her.

"The weed or the pussy?" she asked, letting her head fall back as she released the last of the smoke up into the air in one long stream that floated up to the ceiling.

"Both."

She took one last strong toke before reaching down to set the pipe on the floor. She rose up on her knees and held his thick curving dick straight up to lower her pussy down onto it slowly. She paused with just the smooth tip inside her and worked her walls to clasp and release it a few times before sliding down the full length of him with a tiny circle of her hips.

"You a bad bitch," Tank told her, his eyes hot as he stared at her.

Naeema held his fine face in her hands and tilted it back before she blew a slow and steady stream of smoke into his nose as she worked her hips to ride his dick.

"The baddest bitch," he swore.

Pushing his upper body down on the bed, she sat straight up and pulled the jersey over her head to fling across the room before she pressed her hands into his hard chest and leaned forward just enough to lift her hips and slide her pussy back up to his hot tip before she slammed it back down again.

"Damn," Tank swore, pressing his hips up off the bed as he formed his lips into an O.

The weed was kicking in and she smiled with a little laugh as she enjoyed the base of his dick stroking against her clit and rode him with a slow up-and-down motion, finishing with a tight spin of her hips. The thickness of him pressed against her. The curve of his dick caused the tip to stroke her walls. The feel of his hands massaging her nipples pushed her over the edge.

"I'm staying the night and in the morning I want some more of this pussy." He pulled her upper body down to suck at her nipples again before reaching behind her buttocks to massage the small space between her pussy and ass with his thumb.

Naeema cried out as her walls tightened against the rock-hard length of him. "You big-dick motherfucker," she moaned, biting her lip, and she picked up the pace to ride him harder and faster as she felt a strong nut building.

"Make me cum," he breathed hotly against her damp nipples. "Make this dick cum."

And she did, crying out hoarsely, feeling a million different explosions go off inside her as she came with him. She rode the dick through it all even while it felt like the room was spinning around them.

Tank's body went stiff from head to toe as she felt each jolt of his dick when he filled her with his nut. She slowed the ride, squeezing her walls to draw every bit of his seed from him, and peered down at him as he made crazy sexy faces.

He puckered his lips and she instantly bent down to kiss him.

It had been months since they last made love and nothing about it had cooled off. She felt her love for him rise up in her and she forced herself to slide off his now limp dick, lying on her side with her back to him, shivering from the aftereffects and forcing herself not to say those three words.

4

*N*aeema awoke with a start, lifting her head from the pillow as she looked around. The living room was empty. She looked to her right, surprised to find the other side of the bed empty too. Turning over, she sat up and the sheet fell to her waist, exposing her breasts.

She knew Tank was gone and not just in the bathroom or downstairs fucking with Sarge. Sometime during the night he had hauled ass and not even woken her. *Guess he changed his mind on some early-morning pussy . . . or he's getting it somewhere else.*

Refusing to let herself get riled the hell up with jealousy, she kicked off her sheets and again grabbed the jersey from the floor to pull on before she headed to the kitchen. She washed her hands in the sink and opened the fridge. That motherfucker looked like hunger, desperation, and a complete lack of food stamps. A carton of milk she knew was sour as Coko's breath and an old takeout container of fried chicken and fries she had last week were lonely as hell on them empty shelves.

She had been spending so much time with MMC—the Make Money Crew—and Vivica that she hadn't been around to cook. "Or carry my ass to work," she mumbled, turning to look out the window over the kitchen sink.

"The fuck is this?" she asked aloud coming closer to the sink to peek through the curtain at Sarge sitting next to a lit-up grill in the backyard.

Naeema rushed into the living room to pull on a pair of her old Jordans before heading back through the kitchen and out the back door. She almost forgot half the bricks from one of the bottom steps were gone and had to catch herself before she tripped.

"Careful," Sarge called over, the summer sun making his silver hair shiny as hell. Or she figured it could be sweat soaking his scalp from being dressed in his army fatigues. Long-sleeved shirt and all. Like his ass was still on duty and ready to salute a general or some shit.

Just crazy.

"Sarge, what you doin'?" she asked, coming to stand beside him.

She looked down at the pot of beans bubbling away on the mini charcoal grill and pinched the bridge of her nose in irritation.

"I'm cooking," he said, leaning forward to use the small spoon he held to stir the pot.

Naeema released a heavy breath. "You can cook in the house, Sarge," she said, looking over into the backyard of her neighbors to see if they were witness to the fuck shit as well.

"It was too hot in that basement for the grill today."

"*Today*? Huh? What?" she asked, making an incredulous face. "No . . . no . . . no. You can cook on the stove in the kitchen."

"No," he said simply, reaching in the pocket of his shirt for a small metal container that he shook over the pot.

The whole scene reminded her of a photo she'd seen on

hotghettomess.com where some fool had an air conditioner duct-taped inside the back window of an old car with a generator rigged to the trunk giving that bitch power.

Just dumb shit that made no sense.

When she discovered he was still using a bucket for a toilet even though there was a working bathroom in the basement, that had taken a lot of patience and her putting her foot down for him to stop *that* shit.

Fighting not to vomit at the memory, she shook her head and swallowed hard. "Sarge, I let you stay here because I want you here. So please stop trying not to be a burden, because the things you *choose* to do is more of a burden than if you just . . . like relaxed and enjoyed the little bit of amenities we do have around here like lights and running water. You know?" she asked as she watched him take the pot off the grill and stand up with it in his hand.

"Have some," he said, with a twinkle in his eyes because he knew damn well she would not.

"Nah, I'm good. Thanks."

Sarge walked back across the small paved yard and into the house as he whistled some tune. Naeema walked over to grab the hose and turn on the outside faucet it was attached to and doused the charcoal. In the end she was laughing when she walked back into the house as her stomach growled from the scent of the beans lingering in the air.

With one last look through the fridge and equally empty cupboards, Naeema walked back into the living room and stooped down to pick up the money from beneath the cold radiator. Her brow furrowed as she rose to her full height. She used her thumb to stroke the rubber band holding the money together in a roll.

Spending it didn't seem right.

Dropping the wad back into her handbag, she headed to the bathroom to shower. As she stood under the steaming hot spray of the separate shower stall, she wished the master bath upstairs worked. But the water didn't work in that bath and so she dealt with the half bath on the ground floor. She was a bath girl and would much prefer sitting her punani in hot water scented with bath oils and overrunning with bubbles.

Drying off with one of the towels folded neatly on the built-in shelves flanking the green commode, she wrapped it around her body before she brushed her teeth and gave herself a facial. Rushing, she fast-walked into the living room. She checked the time on her cell phone. "Shit," she swore, jumping up and over the bed to grab a bra and thong from her top dresser drawer before turning to reach in a bin for black spandex leggings and a half-shirt.

She barely spared a second to swipe on deodorant and spray on her favorite body mist—a mix of lavender, vanilla, and lemon that she'd blended herself. She was late but she had to take time to get her makeup straight. Most men had more hair on their head than she did and a beat face was a must—lashes and all.

Dressed and done with strapping on a pair of wedge high-top black and gold sneakers that matched the black half-shirt with BOSS BITCH splayed across her ample bosom in gold letters, she dropped all the shit from her real Louis into a fake Gucci book bag that she pulled on.

Her steps thudded against the floor as she rushed into the kitchen. "Sarge, I'm gone," she called, standing by the open door leading into the basement.

He grunted.

Naeema left the house and crossed the yard to the weathered and battered one-car garage that had only remnants of its dark green paint left. She unlocked it and lifted the door, smiling as more and more of her motorcycle was revealed. She loved it. It was a third-year anniversary gift from Tank. She stroked her fingers over the words *Tank & Naeema 4Ever* painted on the gas tank.

They both believed that shit back then.

Once she had on her hot-pink helmet and was riding the motorcycle down the drive, she felt like herself for the first time in a minute. No weaves. No extra crazy outfits. No faking the funk like she was a naive hood chick. Just Naeema headed to work like she had done every other day for the last nine years. Before she went undercover with the MMC, she had never missed a day of work unless she was traveling with Tank during one of his security jobs. Even if she got white-girl wasted or faded as hell the night before or headed straight to work from the club, Naeema had always clocked in and made her money.

As she dipped and moved through the heavy Newark traffic the hot summer air brushed against her skin but it felt good to her. A day without looking in them motherfuckers' faces was always an Ice Cube level good day. She pulled to a red light on Springfield Avenue next to a bright rust-colored mini-Hummer. From the corner of her eye she spotted the tinted windows lower. The sounds of Jay-Z's "Open Letter" filled the air. Glancing over at them from behind the pink tint of her helmet's visor, she quickly counted four dudes all looking at her ass spread on the seat of the motorcycle as she leaned forward ready to zoom off.

She was used to that shit and didn't let it gas her head.

Dudes loved a fat ass, and a fat ass on a bike made their eyes big and their dicks *real* hard.

She was just revving her motorcycle when she suddenly felt a slap against her ass. Her head whipped around quick as shit. The dude in the passenger seat was hanging half his body out the open window with a big grin on his face as his boys laughed and cheered them on. The driver in the car behind her blew his horn like he was co-signing the bullshit move.

Disrespectful motherfuckers.

Naeema flipped up the shield. "You like that?" she called over to him, sitting up straight on the seat of her motorcycle as it continued to vibrate with life between her legs and against the ass he'd assaulted.

"Hell yeah," he answered, a round-faced cutie with deep dimples.

Naeema reached up quick as shit and grabbed the collar of his plaid shirt in her left fist tight as hell as she pressed the clutch with her right and started to drive ahead, steering with one hand.

"Hey," he hollered in a high-pitched squeal like a straight bitch as his body jerked out of the window some more.

Naeema kept rolling forward slowly even as he gripped her wrist and tried to free her hold on his disrespectful ass. The driver of the Hummer accelerated to keep up with her and to keep his boy from falling out of the window as he kept hollering like a fucking pig being dragged to slaughter. "You punk bitch," she hollered to him.

She glanced forward real quick and spotted a police car in the distance headed toward them. Letting his shirt go and then slapping the shit out of him, she accelerated ahead with a laugh and rested low in her seat as she left them clowns behind easily before turning down Clinton Avenue.

Her heart was pounding and her pulse racing as she jetted the rest of the way to Hawthorne Avenue. Slowing down the motorcycle, she turned off the busy street and pulled to a stop in one of the parking spots lining the front of the minimall. She parked and removed her helmet.

"Whaddup, Naeema."

She smiled and waved to whichever of the dudes already lounging in the lot had spoken. It was just a little past eleven but the spot was already crunk with those who didn't have shit to do all day but chill or hustle. She knew as she crossed the lot and walked into the building that every eye of every dude posted up on the cars outside was on her. She didn't even need to look back to confirm that shit. It wasn't ego, just knowledge about horny-ass dudes in a pack acting like they were about to pounce.

The scent of the aftershave hit her as soon as she stepped inside the barber shop. It smelled good as hell to her. Familiar. Just like all the faces of the dudes she worked with. "Whaddup, y'all," she said with a smile as she looked up and down the two rows of ten chairs each, then she removed her book bag and set it on her station at the front of the shop.

Naeema steeled herself for the bullshit she *knew* was about to go down.

"Look who turned the fuck back up."

"Well, damn, where the hell you been?"

"Whaddup, Naeema."

"I thought you quit, shit."

"We was 'bout to do a APB on this bitch!"

Naeema sat down in the chair, swiveling back and forth as she removed her clippers from the book bag. "Come on, that's all y'all got? Y'all had a whole week to get y'all shit together. For real," she teased, crossing her legs as she waved her fingers to beckon more of the teasing.

"Don't let these negroes fool you. They missed you."

She twirled in the chair and looked up at the owner, Derek Majors, standing on the second level outside his glass office. He motioned with two fingers for Naeema to come upstairs, then turned before he could even see if she agreed and walked back in his office.

The men turned their conversation off Naeema's sudden reappearance while she stood up and made her way to the back of the shop to jog up the stairs.

"Look, I wouldn't give a damn how long it takes or how effed up the website was at first. I wanted in on Obamacare and my black, uninsured, sick of running up high-ass emergency room bills and fucking up my credit 'cause I don't pay those ER bills self, was patient as a motherfucker. Ya heard me?" one of the barbers said from behind her.

Naeema glanced back over her shoulder as the men, barbers and customers alike, all threw their opinions in the mix.

"Obama should have made sure there was a smooth rollout—he gave the Republicans all the bullshit they needed to complain," someone said.

"Oh man, your ass. Y'all know damn well them Republicans paid somebody to mess that website up. Don't be a dumb-ass your whole life."

The voices rose up again.

Naeema laughed at the ruckus and knocked on the black door, which was already cracked open. She left it that way when she walked in. Derek was an ex-dope dealer turned legit businessman in his mid-thirties. He was married but he kept enough random women streaming in and out of the barber shop, liquor store, and hair care store he operated in the mini-mall that Naeema didn't trust his ass at *all*.

Especially since they'd fucked before.

It was years ago. He wasn't married yet or completely out of the dope game. She was just an eighteen-year-old self-taught barber cutting hair for the fellas in the neighborhood in between living life to the fullest. Her boyfriend at the time, a dude named Romeo, had talked her into getting her barber's license so she could eventually work in a shop and make more money than she got doing bootleg cuts. Derek had come to the school to recruit new barbers and she'd caught his wandering eye. When she peeped his whip and his fly gear, she forgot how ugly he was or that she had a boyfriend when he offered her a job as an apprentice . . . if she let him smash.

That was over ten years ago and she hated that she had a memory of how rough he fucked. Dick too big and thrusts too hard for that shit to be any good. Maybe he had finessed his sex game since then? Naeema didn't give a fuck either way.

"Hey, Derek."

He gave her a once-over before he dropped the pen he held onto his desk that was straight out of the 1990s. "Welcome back, Na," he said, leaning back in his chair.

His looks were hard to define. He straddled the line between ugly and cute. It all depended on where you stood when you looked at him and if your eyes were squinted. Like the old folks used to say: he was so ugly he was cute.

What earned him all the pussy was his money, his popularity in the hood, and his style. He stayed dressed nice, haircut, jewelry in place, swagger in a thousand, and smelling good. The women—especially the young ones—loved it.

"Thanks . . . but you know only my husband calls me Na," she said.

He smiled. "Word on the street y'all not together," he said. "My bad."

She smiled too. "It's still his. Matter of fact he just got it last night," she said.

Derek's eyes dipped down to her pussy print in the leggings. "Damn," he swore under his breath in obvious envy.

They had an odd vibe. She knew he wanted to fuck. He knew she wasn't having it. In all the years since she worked at A Cut Above he never brought up that night she let him hit it from behind right in his office on the floor, before he even had a desk. Still, she knew he never forgot and wouldn't turn it down if she offered it to him funky. She also knew he kept her around because she was eye candy for the customers and she had a steady clientele of dudes wanting her to cut their hair. *And probably give 'em some cut.*

Again, not ego, just knowledge of the allure of a big ass for a black man.

"If you need *that* much time off again just let me know something first," he said, picking up his pen and giving his attention to the papers on his desk.

"You're right, Derek, I shoulda handled that better. I apologize," she said, then turned and left his office.

She gave him that respect because he gave her the respect of not telling any of the fellas in the shop that she had fucked to get put on. Even if it was so long ago, the knuckleheads wouldn't let it ride. Once a woman was classified as a ho there wasn't a damn thing she could do to change it.

She made her way back to her station, her eyes instantly glancing out the window to make sure her motorcycle was okay. Not that anybody would dare mess with it. There were too many fellas hanging outside the shop for one, and second, there wasn't too many fools looking to set Tank on their heels. He was well respected and well feared.

Tell him.

She stood behind the leather barber chair and rested her head in her hand as she peered out the window but didn't even notice the heavy traffic flowing back and forth up Hawthorne Avenue. She had no doubt in her mind that Tank could straight find out more info on Brandon's death than she could. But she also knew he didn't respect liars and she couldn't reveal to him that she kept such a huge part of her past a secret. Plus, she wanted to be the one to put in the work. It was her homage to her son.

No, I gotta do this on my own.

"Yo, Naeema. Check this out, right."

She released a heavy breath and turned to find Mone, one of the original barbers in the shop, handing her his iPhone 5s. Mone was tall, skinny, and high yellow. When he irked her nerves she was the first to tell him to get his banana-looking ass out of her face. "What's this?' she asked, taking the phone and reaching for a cloth to wipe away some of the sweat marks and crusty residue from the touch screen.

"Me and this little honey dip was tryna to do a little somethin' at her spot, right, and handlin' my BI. I look down and see *this* foul shit," he said, tapping his long slender fingers against the screen. "Was I wrong to bust one and jet?"

Naeema frowned and leaned back a little at the sight of her woman's ass covered with spots like she just sat there all day and busted blackheads on it.

"Ex-*act*-ly," Mone said at the sight of her face. "Fuck her. I got me and got the hell on."

The voices rose up. Another debate raged on. Barbershop politicking.

Naeema handed him the phone back. "She wrong . . . but you dead wrong for posing mid-stroke to take a picture of her ass. That's so disrespectful, Mone," she chastised him.

"Nah, those spots on her ass is mad disrespectful," he said, handing the phone to one of the customers sitting in the black leather chairs lining the front wall.

The dude nodded. "Yo, this is some disrespectful shit right here," he said.

"Ex-*act*-ly," Mone emphasized again.

"'Til Mone saw that shit he was in that nanni like 'Ooh . . . ooh kill 'em. Ooh,'" joked Fatz, a heavyset brown-skinned dude who'd just started cutting hair at the shop last year.

Naeema tossed the towel she still held at Fatz as he raised his arm and did the Cousin Terio dance. The entire shop broke out laughing.

"Please leave that shit in 2013," she said.

Damn near all the fellas jumped to their feet.

"Oooh, kill 'em," they said in unison as they did the dance.

Naeema started to get on them about it, but on the television she spotted the image of the bank the Make Money Crew robbed yesterday. "Turn that up," she said, her palms starting to sweat.

One of the customers stood up and turned up the volume.

"Police are still investigating the robbery of a South Orange bank early yesterday morning, but there are currently no leads. If you have any information leading to the identification of the four masked men pictured here, please contact Crimewatchers . . ."

Naeema's heart was racing like crazy and she felt like she might pee her damn self. There were moments in the last twenty-four hours that she got so comfortable, she forgot she'd helped robbed a bank. She ain't never been a snitch bitch, but the MMC would get no loyalty. The very first time the police rang her bell it was on.

"Yo, the cops always catch bank robbers. That's Fed time. You can't fuck with the Feds, everybody know that."

Naeema focused on the convo going down about the robbery as her stomach started to bubble with nerves.

"You only hear about the ones they catch. You think they bragging about the ones that got away?" one of the customers said.

"True," someone agreed.

Bas told them to lay low until he reached out to them but Naeema reached in her purse for her burner cell and called Vivica's phone number as she walked outside.

It went straight to voice mail.

"This Viv. Do what you do."

Naeema turned her back on the crowd of fellas lounging in front of the liquor store, some with paper bag–covered bottles of Hennessey and blunts already blazing in their hands.

"Hey, Vivica, this Queen," she said, changing her voice like she was chewing a piece of gum. "I see you called me yesterday but I . . . didn't know my phone was on silent. Hit me up when you get dis."

Ending the call and making sure her phone was closed, Naeema headed to the liquor store for a bag of pork rinds and a grape soda to feed her hunger before walking back to the shop. She motioned for one of the walk-ins to sit in her chair as she set the phone and her snack on the counter of her station.

Before she could dig into her rinds or even get the drape around her client's shoulders, the cell phone sounded off. She dug it out of her bag and rushed back outside. "Hell-o," she said.

"Whaddup, *bitch*," Vivica said.

"Nothin'. Whaddup with you?"

"Bored as hell. Red just left and I'm just sitting around here chillin'," she said with both a loud television and bass-driven music booming in the background. "Ride over here."

Naeema bit her lip and looked up as she pulled a lie from her ass. "I can't right now. I'm gettin' my hair done . . . in Bridgewater," she added in case Vivica tried to invite herself. She didn't have a car and the hour-long drive was not an option for her.

"Bridgewater?" she said. "Damn, black people really spreadin' out, huh?"

"Yup." Naeema turned and spotted her customer about to get up from the chair. "I gotta go but let's go out tonight."

"A'ight, call me when you leave there."

"A'ight." She hung up the phone before she rushed inside.

"I'm sorry, I had an emergency, but I'm ready now," she said, walking over to lightly press her hands against his shoulders and guide him back into the chair.

She forced herself to focus on the dude's fade and not on her schemes to flesh out her son's killer *and* to make sure no one was acting sheisty like they was about to rat out on the bank robbery. There wasn't a damn thing she could do to Brandon's killer from behind bars.

5

"Queen, I think Red is cheating on me."

Naeema took a sip of her Crown Royal and Red Bull as she looked at Vivica over the rim of her glass at the bar of Club 973 in Newark. Not knowing what to say, she took another deep sip before she set her glass down. "What makes you think that?" she leaned in to ask as Kirko Bangz's "Drank in My Cup" played loudly around them in the dark club.

"He don't wanna fuck like he used to no more," Vivica said without any hesitation in telling all of her personal business.

Naeema wasn't a selfish and coldhearted chick but her goal in befriending Vivica was not to be the bearer of all her troubles . . . *especially* whether Red's crime-ridden ass was dipping out on her or not. She seriously could not give less of a fuck. Fighting not to roll her eyes and say as much, Naeema took another sip. "Girl, you trippin', Red loves your ass," she said, standing up. "Let's go dance and forget about all that crazy shit you dreamin' up."

But Vivica didn't rise. Instead she reached into her rhinestone-covered purse and pulled out her cell phone. She flipped her waist-length pink braids back over her shoulder before she pressed the phone to her ear.

Going forward with the eye roll, Naeema smoothed her hands over the skintight jeans she was wearing with sky-high bright pink heels and a white tank with FUN written in neon colors. Her Pocahontas wig was synthetic and making her scalp sweat and itch. She was more irritated than a motherfucker.

Reaching into her the small heart-shaped neon green chain bag, she pulled out her cell phone and checked the time with a swipe of the thumb across the screen. 12:30 a.m.

Shit, it's still early and she ain't talking 'bout shit I want to hear.

"You wanna leave now and go home to Red?" she asked, motioning for the bartender. *If I'm gonna sit and listen to her ass whine all night, I have got to be fucked up.*

"He somewhere with Bas." Vivica twirled the ends of one of her braids around her finger.

"I thought he say to lay low for a while?" Naeema asked, pretending to still be nonchalant.

"Not them two. They thick as thieves," Vivica said.

As Beyoncé's "Drunk in Love" filled the air and women began singing along with the music, Naeema ordered two more Crown Royals and Red Bulls, sliding one in front of Vivica as she sipped from hers. She thought about her next words, trying not to trip up and say the wrong thing. "Bas wouldn't pull him away from you if it wasn't mad important," she said, meaning to sound gullible.

Vivica just shrugged. "Me, Bas, and Red go way back. He wouldn't do shit to hurt me," she said, then started to sway to the music as she raised one hand in the air.

Vivica was another loyal soldier in the Bas army.

"We woke up in the kitchen saying, 'How the hell did this shit happen' oh baby," she sang, motioning with her hands and dancing in her seat.

"You always been the only girl 'round them?" Naeema asked, trying to get her attention back.

Vivica nodded and took a sip of her drink. "Bas ain't fucking shit but that powder and his thug dreams . . . Hammer got way too many girlfriends, side-chicks, babymamas, and tricks to even think about picking one to chill. Nelson can't pull shit, let alone a bitch cute enough to bring around and not get clowned on. Brandon died before they even knew 'bout Brianna."

Naeema's heart pounded in her chest almost as loudly as the bass of the music around them. *Brianna?* She didn't remember that name anywhere in the file.

"How come you knew her and nobody else did?" she asked, raising her hand to tap her fingernail against her teeth as her mind worked a dozen different possibilities.

Since she was in high school and first got a set of acrylic tips, she had picked up that habit and hadn't kicked it since. It helped her to think and right then her mind was racing at the new info dropped into her lap.

"She work in a diner over by where we live and I used to see Brandon there with her."

Naeema decided to back off that, not wanting to scare her by seeming too nosy. Vivica sometimes talked about Brandon and she was always sure never to pry too much. She learned early on in their friendship that Vivica revealed more when she was uninterrupted. And Naeema needed to hear—to know—more.

What role did Brianna play in this?

"Bas don't know what to do with you, Queen," Vivica said, picking up her phone again and tapping a text with her thumb.

"Huh?" Naeema asked, obviously distracted by her thoughts.

"Oh, he wants to fuck you . . . we all know that, but letting you ride on the job yesterday was all about him seeing if he could trust you," Vivica said.

And to have something to hold over my head in case he didn't.

Vivica picked up her phone when it lit up. Her whole face changed. Dick-sprung.

Naeema knew it was Red. "Your ass ready to go now," she teased.

Vivica smiled and stood up. "We'll chill another time," she said, looking sorry. "You wasn't stayin' wit me tonight, was you?"

"No, I'm carrying my black ass home. You go 'head, I'm'a stay. It's early," she lied. She just wanted Vivica to leave before she offered her a ride home. Naeema never did and had no plans to let them know where she really lived.

"A'ight. Call me tomorrow."

Naeema reached out and grabbed her wrist. "Viv."

She turned.

"Suck his balls and jack him off when he's about to nut," she said in her ear.

Vivica made a face and laughed. "Queen, girl, you crazy . . . but I'll let you know how it go."

Moments later her thin figure disappeared in the crowd . . .

Naeema squinted her eyes as she sat in a taxi outside the L&B Diner on Fourteenth Avenue and replayed the scene with Vivica from the club the last night. She had wanted to remember as much of it as she could to make sure she didn't miss shit. The little tip she gave her was in exchange for the one Vivica didn't even know she gave to her.

"You getting out?"

Naeema looked away from the diner to find the cabdriver turned around in his seat eyeing her. "The meter still running, right?" she snapped. "Then chill."

He mumbled something under his breath as he roughly shifted around in his seat.

She looked back out the window. She didn't even know if Brianna was at work.

And you never will if you don't get your ass out the car.

"Will you wait for me?" she asked as she slid her tote on her arm.

"You pay first," he said, turning around in his seat again.

Naeema reached into her purse. Her hand brushed the rolled-up money but she pushed that aside and reached for her bright red wallet instead to pull out a twenty-dollar bill. "Please wait. I won't be but a hot second," she said, pushing the bill into the metal slot of the bulletproof partition dividing them.

"Meter on," he said.

"Man, fuck you," Naeema mouthed as she climbed from the cab. She hadn't driven her motorcycle because, like her short hair, it was too big a fact for somebody to remember and she didn't want anything connecting back to her real life. So she was stuck with crabby cabbie and his whackness.

She looked up and down the nearly deserted street for oncoming traffic before she crossed.

From the looks of L&B's you would think it was closed

and deserted. On both sides of the entire block there was nothing but empty lots where houses and apartment buildings once stood. The diner sat in the middle of the block and nothing but a few cars was parked outside of it. It was in bad need of a good pressure wash and a paint job. The windows were covered by bars, and old weathered graffiti, probably dating back to the eighties or nineties, covered the broken stucco.

It looked like the perfect spot to get got. No witnesses. Nowhere to run and hide. A straight-up jack spot.

She paused on the street to see if she could spot the three-bedroom apartment building where Red and Vivica stayed. She doubted that she could, since it was a block over, but she checked anyway. She wanted to get in and get out before Vivica's noncooking ass showed up. Naeema called her phone to see where she was and got no answer.

As she stepped closer to the diner she could smell the grease frying everything from eggs to chicken wings. She couldn't front that her stomach liked it and grumbled away in hunger.

The front door opened and a tiny dude with a short 'fro held the door open for her. "Thank you," she said, smelling the scent of weed and the diner's scent of greasy food heavy around him.

"No problem, ma."

The inside was not a mismatch with the exterior. It was small with a long counter and just four booths near the front door. There was barely room for two people to walk down the length of the diner at the same time. The walls were filled with cards showing the different meals offered and they looked like they hadn't been updated since the eighties or nineties either. She did appreciate that the air was blowing like crazy and the cool restaurant was a welcome from the heat outside.

The truth was, Naeema had seen and eaten at a lot worse. Sometimes it was these little dives that had the best food. As she took a seat at the counter she brushed back her black Chinese bob wig and eyed the older woman flipping burgers on the grill with one hand, the other on her hip. "What can I get you?" she asked, looking briefly over at Naeema.

"A cheeseburger combo to go, and I was looking for Brianna," she said, turning when she felt something brush against her ass.

It was just the bag of a woman making her way out the diner.

"I'm Dianna," the cook said. "Who you?"

"Monifa," she lied, as she took in the woman who had to be thick into her forties or even fifties.

I know damn well Brandon was not choppin' down this old lady.

"A friend of mine, Ms. JuJu, raised this boy named Brandon that got killed—"

The woman's face changed. "Oh, I thought you said *Di*-anna," she said with emphasis. "Brianna is my granddaughter."

Thank God.

Naeema felt her body relax. She was glad she didn't have to whup this old lady's ass for molesting her son. And she meant straight fuck her up for all eternity.

"What you want with her?" Dianna asked, sounding suspicious as she slid burgers onto buns sitting on plates, like she'd been doing it for years.

"Ms. JuJu found a girl's ring in his stuff and wanted to

get it back to Brianna if it was hers," Naeema said smooth as hell, using the lie she had benched and ready. To top it off, she pulled out a fake gold ring she'd bought at the dollar store.

"Brianna went downtown. You can leave it with me," she said, turning away to set the plates in front of two elderly men sitting at the end of the counter.

"Okay," Naeema said, even as her mind worked double time for a backup plan she didn't have. *Shit.* "Thank you."

Dianna came over to lean her short and square figure against the counter as she held her hand out. "Damn shame how he died," she said.

Naeema handed her the ring. "I'm just in town for the week and Ms. JuJu don't really talk about it. What happened?" she asked, sounding curious.

The bell over the door rang.

"It's hot out there."

Dianna looked past Naeema and smiled. "I told you to wait 'til that sun went down to go out in that heat."

Naeema's pulse raced. She swirled on the stool and looked at a tall, slender teenage girl with a curly weave walking toward them carrying a Payless plastic shopping bag. She had that pretty and perfect dark complexion and wide bright eyes with deep dimples.

Naeema saw a brief image of her son and Brianna sitting at one of the booths across from each other, smiling and flirting and not noticing anything around them as they got caught up in each other the way teenagers did when they were crushing on someone hard.

"Here, give it to her yourself."

Naeema turned and looked down as the ring was pushed

back into her hand. "Thanks," she said softly, not sure why she felt all discombobulated and shit.

"We was just talking about Brandon," Dianna said before she turned to go handle her grill.

Naeema was watching the teenager and she saw the pain flash across her face. The dimples flattened and her eyes got sad. His death was still messing with her.

"You knew Brandon?" she asked, her eyes stopping at different points on Naeema's body.

Her face.

Her body in the strapless peach sundress she wore.

Her nails.

Even the sandals showcasing the French pedicure on her feet.

Naeema knew she looked much younger than her twenty-nine years. She'd heard every age from twenty to twenty-four but never a number close to thirty, and she definitely looked young enough for Brianna to get jealous that *she* was one of Brandon's chicks.

If only you knew, little girl . . .

Knowing the ring would piss her off, Naeema slid it back into her bag and stood up to step closer to her. "I'm a friend of Ms. JuJu and I was at her house and she wondered how you was dealing with everything."

"Ms. JuJu? Who dat?" Brianna asked, her thin face showing every bit of her confusion.

Shit. Naeema was confused as shit herself. Maybe her and Brandon wasn't that close?

"That's the lady that raised Brandon," she explained. "He must've been so caught up in you because he told her all about you."

Lies was slipping from her lips like breaths of air. Just easy. Too easy.

But very necessary.

Brianna's face softened as her dimples reappeared with a smile. "I really liked him," she said, sitting her bag on a table before she slid into one of the booth seats.

Prayers up that her grandmother too busy on that grill to stroll her ass over here and sit down . . .

"I didn't get to meet him but Ms. JuJu talks about him a lot," Naeema lied. She hadn't seen or spoken to the woman since she'd learned of Brandon's death. Naeema couldn't face the one person who knew she turned her back on her own son.

"He was real cool. Real laid back . . . but not no punk," she said, twisting one of her tight curls around her slender index finger. "I was a junior and he was just a freshman but he was cocky enough to holler at me in front of all my friends one day in the caf. Plus he was *too* cute."

Was.

"I was talking to this other kid named Rico and he felt like Brandon dissed him and all of that drama." Brianna reached across the table and lightly touched Naeema's hand like they were hangout partners. "Brandon whupped that ass. In front of the whole school too."

Naeema's heart skipped a beat. Maybe two.

Rico? Another damn lead the police missed?

"Rico Lopez? I think I know his mother," she lied.

Brianna shook her head. "Oh no, this Rico is black. Rico Anderson."

"Oh. Okay."

"And *then* somebody put that shit online. YouTube.

WorldStar. Facebook. Twitter. Instagram. Umph-umph-umph. Whoo, that ish was wild." Brianna shook her head. "For a hot second I felt bad for Rico but yo, if you start sum'n there gon' be sum'n so be ready or don't even start it, you know?"

"Shit, I woulda dropped out after that," Naeema said.

"Me too. But he didn't. Matter fact . . . Brandon the one that dropped out," she said.

Naeema's heart pounded hard as another new fact was dropped in her lap. Something else for her to feel guilty about. She knew more about her son in death than she had when he was alive. "Maybe Rico scared him or something."

Brianna shook her head. "Nah, that was because of his guidance counselor."

Naeema stayed quiet.

Brianna played with one of her curls again. "He didn't like how Mr. Warren stepped to him one day after school in detention. He really liked Mr. Warren too. He trusted him. That's why it fucked with him. I told him to report his perverted ass but . . ."

Naeema couldn't hide her frown. Another blow. Another missed opportunity to protect her son.

Brianna just shrugged her shoulders as her face filled with sadness again. "I'm glad you told me he talked about me to the lady because we had just really started talking," she said, her voice soft as her big eyes filled with tears. "It's fucked up. He was so cool and funny and smart. It's just fucked up. Right?"

"It's real fucked up," Naeema said, blinking to keep from joining her in showing her sorrow. "You think Rico had something to do with it?"

"Nah. He got locked up for a stolen car in March. I don't even know if he out yet."

Another dead end?

Brianna stood up and grabbed her bag, using her free hand to swipe away her tears. "Tell that lady I'm sorry I missed the funeral. I just couldn't see him like that. You know?"

Naeema knew all too well. She hadn't been at the service either. "I'll tell her."

"Poor thing stayed in bed crying, her eyes puffy and red for a week after," her grandmother said, walking up to hand Naeema a bag with grease already seeping through at the corner.

Standing up, Naeema pressed a ten-dollar bill into her hand. "I better get going," she said, feeling far too many emotions swirling around her like a hurricane.

She needed a fucking moment. Or two.

"What's your name?" Brianna called behind her.

Naeema had just opened the door and sounded the bell. She turned.

I'm Naeema, Brandon's mother.

She opened her mouth wanting to speak the truth but instead she said, "Monifa. I'm Monifa."

She was just about to leave the restaurant when she turned and came back in. Brianna looked up in surprise. "I'm glad Brandon had you in his life. Even if for a little while, Brianna," Naeema said truthfully before she turned and hauled ass again, hurrying to climb into the back of the cab.

"Where to now?" Crabby Cabbie asked.

"Just drive off," she said, closing her eyes as she let her head fall back against the headrest.

"I need somewhere to drive off to."

She was ready to straight cuss him out until he sat down and had a long talk with himself to reevaluate every bit of his life. "Broad and Market," she snapped.

Just in case a trail led back to her coming to that diner, Naeema didn't want them to be able to call the cab company and trace the cab back to her and where she lived. These days her life was all about "just in case" and trying to think three steps ahead of every fucking decision. On guard. Making moves. Telling lies. Playing fucking I Spy With My Little Eye and shit.

I don't have a choice.

Naeema refused to turn her back on her son again.

The next night Naeema sat in the glass shelter of a bus stop across from O'Malleys Bar in Hoboken. Her eyes were trained on the large wooden front door with its black metal latches. The number 40 bus came and went. The door opened and two white men with medium-length brown hair exited. She squinted her eyes as she peered at their faces and then swiped her thumb across her touch screen to double-check the photo she saved to her phone.

Not him.

The door opened three more times and each time she did her check.

Squint. Swipe.

She would go inside if she didn't think she would stick out like she wore a sign that stated the obvious: Lone Negro in the Building. Hoboken was miles away from Newark, and in terms of differences between the two, the distance might as well have been a million miles.

The door opened again.

Squint. Swipe.

She sat up straighter.

Bingo, motherfucker. B-I-N-G-O.

Naeema kept her eyes locked on the man as he walked down the street and turned the corner. She was already up on her sneaker-covered feet and crossing the street on his heels. She was nervous. She was unsure. She even thought she was going slightly crazy. But more than that, she was pissed the fuck off. Pissed always trumped every other emotion.

He removed keys from his pocket and unlocked the doors to a bright blue smart car.

Fucking figures. The perfect car for this clown-ass fool.

"Mr. Warren," she called out.

He turned and his face became puzzled.

The wide-leg stride that brought her so close to him paused at a vision of him standing over Brandon in a small office with his hand reaching down between her son's thighs.

"Can I help you?" he asked, his keys readied in his hand.

"No, but you can stop helping yourself to little boys at the school where you work," she said.

Blue eyes shifted to the left and right real quick. "Excuse me," he said, sounding offended.

Like I give a fuck.

Naeema came to stand before him. They were the same height and she was able to look him directly in the eye beneath the glow of the streetlamp. "You wanna play with dicks and balls, bitch, find you a grown-ass man. West Side High ain't your motherfuckin' playground."

"Get the fuck out of my face," he snapped, pushing her shoulder.

Naeema stumbled back. She couldn't front. He surprised her. *What if he flips on me? Can I beat his ass?*

He was at least twenty pounds heavier.

But fuck that. This white dude just put hands on me. Fuck, this look like the 1860s in this bitch?

Naeema slapped him across the face twice.

WHAP! WHAP!

"Hey," he cried out, his blue eyes wide as he pressed a hand to his reddening cheeks.

"Hey hell. Keep your fucking hands to yourself," she said, curving her fingers into tight fists in case he tried it. "And that comes to getting physical with a female *and* fondling little boys."

His blue eyes shifted again. "I didn't—"

"You *did*," she emphasized, feeling her anger at him rise. "Your bullshit caused one little boy to drop out of school."

"I—"

"Shut up," Naeema snapped, looking back over her shoulder at the sound of voices. "You don't get to molest boys. You don't get to use them for your perverted bullshit. You don't get to front to your wife, *Olive*, like your ass don't love dick. And you don't get to work in a fucking school around kids."

She saw his surprise as she flung his wife's name at him. Naeema had a picture of the pretty redhead in her phone too.

"I got proof," she lied. "And if I see your ass back at West Side or any other school, I'm going to your wife and then the police. Just try me."

Naeema turned and walked back out of the lot, brushing past the people who were headed to their cars. She crossed the street, passed the bus stop, and headed down two blocks to where she hid her motorcycle behind a pizzeria. Unlocking the helmet and the bike, she was soon racing down the street, leaving behind the man whose actions made her son drop out of school.

"Motherfuck him," she muttered.

Facebook was a tattle-telling bitch.

It had taken her less than ten minutes to search his name and pull up his public Facebook profile and a lot of his business along with it—including his plans for the night. He led her right to him.

She didn't think Mr. Warren had anything to do with Brandon's death—although she wasn't striking him off her list of suspects. Rico was another thing. Brandon stole his girl and whipped his ass in front of the school. Still, Brianna said he was locked up and couldn't do it.

Naeema didn't think it could hurt to double-check that and it didn't mean he couldn't have gotten somebody else to handle his dirty work.

//

     $\mathscr{I}$t had been a week since the bank robbery, and Naeema only felt some of her nerves about it fade since she knew the Feds were the "sit it out and wait until the evidence was real good" type of law enforcement. They would wait it out for years just to make sure their case was airtight. Still no word from Bas but she knew everything was straight through Vivica. She kept her focus on her own investigation. In the time since visiting Brianna at the diner, Naeema had discovered that Rico, the boy Brandon fought at school, had been in jail but got out a month ago. She hadn't been able to find him—especially with school out for the summer—but his Facebook posts were all about his new boo so she had a feeling he was laid up somewhere with her. Mr. Warren's Facebook page was now private. So was his wife's. Didn't matter. As soon as school was back in a couple of weeks she was going to make damn sure his ass wasn't strolling through the halls of West Side High.

     As much as she didn't trust the police, if she had any real proof she would turn his ass.

     Sitting on the middle of her bed in nothing but a sports bra and shorts, she read through the police file for the hundredth time and studied the crime scene photos wishing her CSI game was tight enough where something out of the ordinary would be clearer to her. *That shit always seemed so easy on television.*

Closing the file, she laid back on the bed and wished her new ceiling fan produced cool air and didn't just cut through the heat. She'd made good money at the barber shop over the last few days and she was steadily putting it into her building fund. The house needed major repairs and that would take major coinage. The robbery cash was still in her purse. She hadn't added it to her own stash in the shoe box and she never could bring herself to spend any of it.

She wasn't ready to do something noble like donate it to charity or something like that either.

Picking up her phone, she opened up her pictures and flipped through to the photos of Brandon she swiped off his Facebook page in the days after Ms. JuJu told her about his death. She smiled sadly at him sitting on a stoop with a bunch of other teenage boys, with his hands posed up in the air. Her boy was handsome. Tall and thin with a square chin, high cheekbones, and long lashes, smooth caramel skin. She could see plenty of herself and his father in him.

What kind of future could he have when she gave him away and his father ran away before he even came into the world . . .

"So whatchu gon' do, Naeema?"

Naeema pressed her hands against her belly swollen with nearly six months of pregnancy and felt the baby inside it move as she looked up at her boyfriend Chance's mother standing over her with a fat blunt blazed. Ms. Mack—or just Mack, like she said to call her—was a stud. Long hair

*in cornrows. Titties taped down. Oversize white tee and
sagging jeans in place. Lover of pussy.*

*Naeema knew that for sure when she woke up one night
while Chance was out slinging dope and Mack was in their
bedroom pulling down her drawers and asking to eat her
out. She made it clear to Mack that she didn't roll that way.
Thankfully she let it be and strolled her dyking ass out the
room.*

*From then on Naeema slept in jogging pants and wedged
a shoe under the thin fake wood door whenever Chance
wasn't there. She never told him about it. She wanted to but
she didn't want Mack to throw her out on the street.*

*"I don't have nowhere to go, Mack," she said, feeling her
fear rising.*

*Mack shrugged one broad shoulder and flicked the ashes
from the tip of her blunt onto the grungy floor. "Not my
fucking problem, bitch," she said. "Chance said that ain't his
fucking baby, so you and your burden need to get the fuck
up outta my place."*

*Naeema's eyes got wide as she looked around the room,
stalling for time, trying to think of some way to make things
different. In the year since she'd moved in with Chance
and his mother, the dingy little bedroom had felt more like
home and stability than anything since her grandfather's
death.*

*Four months ago Chance was rubbing her belly and
coming up with baby names. Then the touches came less.
No more names were mentioned. His attention toward her
faded.*

And now this?

"Chance wouldn't say that," she said, looking at a pic-

ture taped to the wall that they took months ago in New York on New Year's Eve.

"You calling me a liar, yo?" Mack asked, coming over to stand where Naeema sat on the edge of the thin mattress.

Naeema, pushing the memories of happier times away, looked over at Mack.

"Get what little shit your homeless ass got in here and get the fuck out," Mack said, kicking a pair of Naeema's shoes with her Timberlands.

Naeema didn't know what the fuck to do. Chance had left the apartment that morning and ever since he hadn't come back and he didn't answer the phone whenever she called. She didn't trust Mack not to fight her or call the police. She started pulling what little clothes she had from the two large garbage bags in the corner.

"I ain't got all night, Naeema," Mack said, coming over to roughly brush her out of the way before she picked up both garbage bags and emptied them onto the middle of the bed. "You got ten minutes. Whateva shit ain't packed by then . . . then oh the fuck well."

As soon as Mack left the room, Naeema reached for her prepaid phone. She called Chance's cell number twice. No answer. She texted him: "Your moms throwing me out. Come help me."

After a few minutes there was still no reply.

Does Chance know already?

"Tick fucking tock, Naeema," Mack called from the living room.

What'm I supposed to do?

Fighting back tears she grabbed one of the now empty bags and pushed as much of her stuff into it as she could. It still didn't fill even half the bag. She reached across the bed and pulled the picture off the wall. She pushed it into the back pocket of her jeans.

Where'm I gonna go?

Picking up the bag, she left the room and didn't let herself look back. It wasn't her home no more. Chance just had to find them a new place but Mack didn't want her there no more.

"Yeah, her ass in there packing now. I took care of it," *Mack said, her back to the bedroom door.*

Naeema frowned a little as she paused in the doorway.

"She ain't pushing nobody else's baby off on you."

She felt like all the breath left her body. She went weak at the revelation that Chance knew his mother was putting her out on the street. She forced herself to lock her knees to keep from falling as she walked down the short length of the hall with one hand on her belly. He was by no means her first lover, but once she got with him, he was her one and only. The baby was his.

"Shoulda let me eat dat pussy."

Naeema paused with the doorknob in her hand but she didn't look back at Mack's snide and mocking words. She left the apartment and walked down the hall to the elevator. She wasn't gonna let Mack see her cry, and the tears were about to flow like crazy.

Project life was just as loud as usual but Naeema barely heard any of it as she stepped on the elevator and leaned back against the wall. She closed her eyes just as a tear raced down her cheek.

What'm I gonna do?

"Damn, yo, you a'ight, shawty?"

Naeema nodded, not even bothering to open her eyes

and see who took a moment out of their night to give even a small fuck about her.

"It'll be a'ight, yo," he said just as the elevator gears ground to a halt.

When Naeema finally opened her eyes and pushed off the wall to exit the elevator, she was alone. She walked through the lobby and left the building. It was late September and the air was cool. It pushed right through her short jean jacket without a care. Shivering, she wrapped the bag around her wrist some more and then crossed her arms over her chest.

She had to see Chance and convince him this was his baby. She just knew if she could talk to him to see where that lie came from and then defeat it, that shit would be okay. *I'm'a wait for him to come home,'* she thought, looking around for somewhere to sit.

Naeema moved across the courtyard to one of the benches. For thirty minutes she shivered, watched the endless activity around the buildings, and either called or texted Chance. She was just pulling out her phone to text him again when someone called out, "Yo, Chance. Whaddup?"

She stood up and her head jerked left and right as her eyes searched the scene for a sight of him. Her mouth fell open and her heart sank to see him walking up the street with his arm around a girl she didn't recognize. She stood there feeling like the fool she was as her babyfather and his new boo laughed and played and kissed as they walked into the building together. Naeema knew from the bags they was carrying that he was moving his new bitch in to fill her spot in his life and in his bed.

Naeema and the baby weren't wanted or needed anymore.

"They'll run right through a pretty girl like you."

Her grandfather's words came back to her so clearly.

She started to step to them and fight the girl.

She started to go upstairs, knock on the door, and bust them.

She started to call his phone for the thousandth time.

In the end she reached in her back pocket for the photo and tore it in half before she counted the last of the money she had to her name in the world. Twelve dollars, left over from a twenty she begged out of Chance last week.

Before she got with him she had mad hangout partners that used to let her stay with them, but once she locked in with Chance, she turned her back on hanging out and partying to sit up in that apartment and be his fool while he was out in the world living it up.

"I ain't got nobody in the world. It's just me," she whispered, her voice broken and shaky from the betrayal. The pain. The shame. The fear.

Naeema crossed the street and stood on the corner waiting for the bus. Though her baby kicked and moved in her stomach, she felt so alone. She kept blinking to keep those tears from blurring her vision. She kept sniffing to keep the tears from falling.

It wasn't until she rode that bus downtown and then walked the few blocks to Newark Penn Station to take a seat, with all of her shit in a garbage bag, that her resolve broke like a motherfucker and she cried.

Naeema's heart still stung from the pain of that night. She bit her bottom lip and shook her head at one of her first lessons in how fucked up people could be. How fucked up the world could seem to a pregnant and homeless sixteen-year-old kid.

She never saw Chance or Mack again. Even as she slept in Penn Station at night and begged for money to buy food, she kept minutes on her phone, hoping he would call and check on her. He never did. And her pride wouldn't let her call him.

"Humph," she grunted at the memories.

Naeema could never forget being woken up about one in the morning in Penn Station by an elderly Spanish woman in a McDonald's uniform asking her to understand someday that she'd just been looking out for her and her unborn baby. Naeema had been confused until the two policemen standing behind the woman stepped forward.

She had been pissed but she knew from the jump that the woman had only been trying to help a young homeless pregnant teen taking refuge from the streets in a train station for the last month. To Naeema, the group home where she was placed wasn't much better.

"That's another sad fucking story," she muttered, rising up off the bed at the sound of commotion outside.

She walked over to the window and opened the slats in the blinds. Up the street there was a News 12 van double-parked with the reporter and his cameraman standing in the street. A young girl was standing on the sidewalk cussing up a storm and waving her arms at them. "The fuck?"

Naeema walked over to the door, lifting and pulling it open, to step out onto the porch.

"Get that camera out my fucking face!" the woman yelled at damn near a screech level.

She was surprised to see Sarge at the end of the drive looking up at the ruckus as well. Coming down the stairs, she stepped over the hanging gate to go and stand beside him. "What's going on?"

"DYFUS just left with her kids and she been carrying on with those news people ever since," he said, his eyes locked on the scene.

"Hey, ma."

Naeema looked over at a young dude in an old Honda Accord waving at her from the driver's seat. He smiled as he reached over to turn up the volume.

The chorus to an old Plies song filled the air.

"We fucking or what? Huh? Huh?"

Naeema rolled her eyes and turned her head to ignore him.

"Respect is always deserved," Sarge said.

"We fucking or what? Huh? Huh?"

Naeema looked at Sarge as the music blared on even after the car eventually rolled away.

"But a woman gots to remember that not every man got enough sense to know that. For some respect is given only where it is earned, Naeema," he said.

"I hear you, Sarge," she said.

He was talking about the way she dressed as always. Sarge hated the skintight clothing Naeema favored and she knew his head was about to explode with her outside in just a sports bra and shorts.

"Hearing ain't shit," he said. "Listening and taking heed is what matters."

She reached over to squeeze his beard-covered cheek but he swatted her hand away with an angry turn-up of his lips.

With the music gone the woman's tirade continued loud and clear.

Naeema looked up and down the length of the street to see other neighbors outside coping with the heat to get a better view of the drama. She smiled a little at the sight of Coko sitting on her porch. Her hair was actually combed back in a loose ponytail and she looked sober as she too watched the scene up the street.

Naeema waved to her with a smile but Coko never saw her, as a black-on-black Tahoe pulled up and Coko went down the stairs to sit in the front seat. Soon her head disappeared above the driver's lap.

"I oughta go over and knock on the glass," she said, censoring her profanity out of respect for Sarge. "Mess his good time all the way up."

"For what?" Sarge asked. "To get your head blown off just to keep her from getting high? Shee-it. She got to be willing to face them demons herself . . . same way you trying to face yours."

Naeema spun her head to look at Sarge but he had already turned and headed back up the drive to the backyard and through the rear door to the kitchen. She wondered just what-all Sarge knew about her life. Living in the basement he probably heard any- and everything that went on with her. Hell, she didn't know if he gave a fuck either way.

She leaned back against the corner of the fence feeling confident the police were going to be added to the mix at any moment. At the sound of a car door closing, she looked over her shoulder just as Coko came around the back of the SUV and stepped up onto the curb.

That was quick.

Coko paused and looked at her. Again Naeema raised her hand and waved at her. Coko shifted her eyes away as she waved back and then rushed up the stairs and into her house.

She could have sworn she saw shame on the woman's face.

Bzzzzzz.

Naeema reached in her back pocket and pulled out her cell phone. Tank. She started not to answer him. With a roll of her eyes she accepted the call.

"You home?" he asked before she could say a word.

"Yeah. Why?"

"I got something for you."

"I got company," she lied.

"Tell him to pull it out for a sec, your husband on the way."

He hung up.

Naeema turned to head back in the house but she had just reached the top step when she heard the roar of a motorcycle. She looked over her shoulder and sure enough, Tank turned the corner off Eastern Parkway and pulled to a stop in front of the house. She didn't know if he was coming in or not, so she came only halfway down the stairs.

He looked as good as always and her eyes were locked on him as he took his helmet off and motioned for her to come to him, pulling a manila folder from beneath his shirt, tucked in the waistband of his jeans. He eyed her up and down and shook his head as she walked up to him. "Your man can't control you?" he asked as he handed her the folder.

"He wouldn't be alone . . . 'cause you couldn't either," Naeema said. "And your bitch can't keep you from my house?"

Tank laughed. "Nah, my bitch can't keep me from your house," he said with a smooth lick of his lips, putting his helmet back on. "And neither can your man."

She stepped back as he drove off.

She opened the folder and pulled out the sheets of paper. "Juvenile criminal arrest record of Brandon Mack," she read and then flipped to the second sheet.

Naeema looked up the street just as Tank turned the corner on his motorcycle and disappeared from her view.

Darkness reigned over the city as Naeema pulled up in front of the abandoned two-story home on the corner. It was boarded up and had those yellow signs that the city put on abandoned homes. For three months of her life she lived at the Better Days Group Home for Girls.

She had hated it there. Too many rules. Too many chores. Too crowded. Not safe. No freedom. No privacy. After all that time on her own she had felt like she was losing her mind. She was just sixteen and that or another group home would've been her and her baby's life for the next two years until she turned eighteen.

She couldn't see it then.

Naeema looked up the street, just two houses down, to the small one-story house with dark green shutters and white vinyl siding. She rolled the motorcycle ahead and turned up the driveway. Exterior lights came on. As Naeema got off the motorcycle, lights came on behind the side door just moments before it opened.

She removed her helmet and looked up at Ms. JuJu standing there in her floor-length robe, her silver hair in those old-fashioned foam rollers. "I wondered when I'd see you again," she said before turning to walk back in the house, leaving the door open.

Naeema stumbled back twice before she took a deep breath and steadied herself, then finally walked up the few steps leading into the house.

"Are you drunk?" Ms. JuJu asked, her voice sharp and hard with displeasure.

"And high," Naeema added, pulling back one of the chairs at the small kitchen table to slump down into.

"You trying to kill yourself?"

Naeema let her head drop into her hands as she shook her head. "I'm trying to figure out why you let my son run fucking wild," she said, holding her head up with effort to look across the table at the woman. "I wanted you to make him better than that. And you didn't."

Ms. JuJu leaned back in her chair at the table as she released this heavy-ass sigh. "Get it all off your chest, Naeema . . . and then I gots some things to get off mine."

Naeema wiped her face with her hands and laughed bitterly as her eyes filled with tears that she let fall. "There ain't shit you can say to me . . . that I ain't said to myself. I know . . . I know . . . I . . . I know I ain't shit," she said, her voice breaking. "I know I wasn't good for him. I couldn't provide for him. I picked a 'ain't shit' daddy for him. I know all that. You think . . . you think . . . I don't know all of that?"

Ms. JuJu remained silent, her eyes piercing Naeema coldly.

"But I gave him to you because you were supposed to be better for him but . . . where the fuck were you . . . when he was shoplifting at nine fucking years old, Ms. JuJu? Stealing cars at twelve. Selling and smoking weed at thirteen. Vandalizing. Drinking. Robbing motherfuckers. Where the fuck were you at when my son was in and out of juvie. What, you just got the check and said fuck it?"

"You finished?" Ms. JuJu asked. Naeema just waved her hand like she was shooing away a fly.

"When you out in them streets you loved so much, partying and smoking that weed, I was here doing what you asked me to do . . . what you wasn't *woman* enough to do—"

"I was sixteen!" Naeema roared, slamming her hand down on the table and causing the glass salt and pepper shakers on top of it to rattle.

"And I raised your son for fourteen more years after that with no sign of you," Ms. JuJu said sharply. "You had just started sending money on the regular six years ago."

"You got a check from the state," Naeema said, knowing it sounded selfish and stupid even to her own ears.

Ms. JuJu raised her hands and clapped slowly, meaning to mock her. "That check didn't make sure he was washed and fed and did his homework every night. That check didn't make sure he went to church *every* Sunday. That check didn't throw him birthday parties and give him a good Christmas every year. That check didn't hug and kiss him. And that check didn't mean a thing when he wondered where the hell his mother and father were. The same mother and father too busy being young and dumb in them streets to raise him. The same parents that passed that love of the streets on to their son."

Naeema had dropped her head onto the table, but Ms. JuJu gripped her chin and jerked her face upward so that they looked each other in the eye. Woman to woman.

"I'm sorry, but that boy was just as wild as you, Naeema. I did everything I promised I would do for your boy and more but I can't fight what's in his blood nor what ate him up on the inside because there's nothing like a mother's love . . . and he *never* got that from you," she finished in a fierce whisper before she released her hold on her chin.

Naeema's head hung low and her shoulders shook as she cried. "My boy dead . . . and if I died and went to heaven right now he wouldn't even know me," she wailed as her pain pierced her sharply.

Ms. JuJu came around the table and surprised Naeema when she gathered her into her arms and rocked her. "You did the best you could with what you knew. Ask God to forgive you and move on, Naeema, or you gonna die on the inside from things you can't change."

Naeema nodded in understanding, even though she didn't believe the words. Was God's forgiveness really that easy to receive? *I doubt that shit.*

She allowed her grief to wash over her. It wasn't the first time she'd shed tears over Brandon's death but it was the first time anyone had consoled her. Ms. JuJu was the only person who knew Naeema's truth. She was the bridge between her past and her present. The only person in her life with whom she could say "my son" and not have to offer explanations or apologies.

"I just wish I knew who killed him," Naeema said, long after her tears had subsided and she'd used the damp cloth Ms. JuJu pushed into her hands to wipe her face.

"I wish I knew too, but we have to leave that in God's hands, Naeema."

"I can't," Naeema admitted in a soft whisper.

"You have to."

Naeema didn't bother to change the old woman's mind because hers was already set. "Have the police said anything?" she asked.

"Haven't heard from them in a while. Last I know they were thinking some boy Brandon stole a cell phone from might have did it, but they brought him in for questioning and let him go."

Yet another lead? The copy of the report she had was months old and this tidbit of news wasn't in it. So much was coming at her at one time. She didn't know whether to feel blessed for the knowledge or overwhelmed by so many roads to be tracked for the truth. *What if I follow the wrong lead and the murderer gets away?* "Can I have some coffee? I need to get home and I don't know if I can make it back across town like this," she said. "Shit, I don't know how the hell I made it here."

Ms. JuJu stood up and began moving about her neat kitchen. "You are going up to Brandon's old room and sleep off that drunk before you leave here. And maybe . . . you can look around his room and you can stop hurting from your guilt long enough for me to tell you more about him. If you want," she added gently.

Naeema had first known Ms. JuJu as the woman volunteering at the group home. She came every day with a homemade dessert and was sure to call each one of the troubled teens "sugar" "love" or "baby." And when she got news one of them misbehaved, she would chastise them in a way that evoked guilt and a desire to make her proud. With her came a love that made those who were able to receive it feel warm and welcomed.

During her three months at the group home, Naeema had found herself really looking forward to the few hours a day Ms. JuJu was there. The woman discovered that Naeema loved her banana nut bread and once a week she brought a loaf just to give to Naeema, along with a sweet smile and a soft pat on her rounded belly. And when Naeema found out that the nice older woman from down the street, who she would see from her bedroom window walking to church every Sunday morning, didn't have children of her own, Naeema figured they could help each other.

The one and only time Naeema had been in Ms. JuJu's house was the day she brought Brandon to her and asked her to raise him fourteen years ago. She had been so relieved when the woman had reluctantly agreed to take care of him. Not even when she called to tell her of his death had Naeema come to her home—Brandon's home. "I want that and . . . and thank you. Thank you, Ms. JuJu . . . for everything," she said.

7

One week later

Naeema squatted low and raised her balled fists to protect her face before she jumped up and kicked toward Tank's rock-hard midsection. He blocked her move like it was nothing. Just thorough as hell.

"Good," he said, his bared upper body dampened in sweat. "Again."

Naeema brushed her sweat back with her forearm before she took her position again on the mat of the empty gym. She kicked. Tank blocked it.

"Again," he ordered.

Kick. Blocked.

"Again."

Kick. Blocked.

"Again."

This time Naeema paused and quickly changed plans. She raised the same leg to kick but then jumped down on that one and leveled her other leg toward his side sharply.

Tank caught it just before it landed against his body. He jerked it forward, knocking her off balance, and then dipped low to swing his foot around to knock her other leg from under her. Naeema landed on her back on the mat with an *umph*. One second later he was on top of her and pinning her arms and legs to the mat. He still looked impressed as he smiled down at her. "You woulda fucked up a lesser motherfucker," he said, his face just above her as they both breathed deeply.

"A lesser motherfucker almost did get fucked up," she shot back, trying not to let the feel of his dick pressing against her hip fuck her up.

It wasn't even hard and she was catching hell ignoring it.

"Lesser than who? Your man?" he asked.

Naeema didn't say shit.

"Oh, I mean your imaginary man, Mr. Don't Exist," he teased.

Naeema still didn't say a word.

"Your body soft as a pillow everywhere, Na," Tank whispered as his eyes was all over her face. "Except your nipples. I can feel them pressing against my chest."

Her pulse raced.

"Why I love fucking you so much?" he asked.

Her clit swelled with life and she bit her bottom lip to keep from answering his question.

"Why your pussy so good, Na?" Tank lowered his head and pressed kisses on her neck, his tongue licking her pounding pulse.

She gasped and released a shaky breath before she turned her head and closed her eyes. *Shit.* He just did it for her. Sex wasn't their problem. Never was. It was looking like it never was going to be.

Tank freed her hands and brought his hand down to turn

her face back toward him. The first feel of his tongue stroking her mouth made Naeema wet. With a moan she opened her lips and sucked the tip of it. His dick got harder and longer against her hip and she felt her legs spreading wider so that she could wrap them around his waist.

Once again it's on.

He got up from her body long enough to push her sports bra up above her breasts. He moaned as he sucked one tight brown nipple.

"Lick it," she demanded softly.

And he did, with quick back and forth flickers.

"Shit," she swore, bringing her hands up to lightly dig her nails into his back.

The *Jaws* theme ringtone on her burner cell phone sounded off. Her body went stiff, she knew it was Bas.

Pressing her hands against Tank's shoulder, she tried to free her nipple from his mouth. "Hold up one sec. I got to get my phone," she said.

"Man, fuck that phone."

She freed herself from him and raced across the small garage he'd converted to a gym, to dig the cheap flip phone out of her purse.

"Hello," she said as she pulled her bra down over her breasts and stepped outside the garage into the heat, remembering to use that playful and simple tone to her voice that the crew knew.

"Whaddup, stranger? How's life treating you?"

"Better now," she said.

"Oh, you missed me?" he asked.

"Sum'n like dat," she said.

He laughed. It was low and husky and cocky as shit.

"Keep playing with the snake and you gon' get bit," he warned.

"A snake ain't shit once it fall in the right hole," she shot back—and then wondered if that was too quick on her feet for the role of innocent and naive Queen who just wanted to belong.

"I hear you, Queen," he said. "Come to the spot at ten."

She turned to find Tank standing in the open doorway, his hard dick still hard and fighting to be freed from his jogging pants. "A'ight," she said, before closing the phone and moving past him to reenter the garage.

Tank grabbed her waist and pulled her body up against his. "Who was that?"

Naeema pulled back to eye with lots of attitude. "When I called you and some bitch was in the background, did I ask you about her? Did I give a fuck about her when you was getting this pussy that same night?"

She brushed his hands off her waist and stepped past him. "Won't you try not giving a fuck?"

Tank reached for her wrist. "That's hard to do when you the one always calling me for help . . . for dick."

"I'll make it my business to help you and forget your number," she said. "'Cause if you think I can't, you got me fucked up, playboy."

"Whateva, Na. Keep acting like you so hard and you don't need nobody in this fucking world. Keep believing that shit," he snapped, walking past her to start punching the heavy bag hanging in the corner.

"I wanted to lose weight and working out with you was always good exercise," she said, hoping the piss-poor excuse would ease his suspicion.

"Lose weight where?" he protested, pausing in hitting the bag to look over at her.

She turned and gripped both of her ass cheeks before jiggling them. "So you not gonna help me?" she asked, now standing there with her arms crossed.

"You don't need me, remember?" Tank called over to her as he continued to pound away on the bag.

But she did need his ass.

She was out there confronting people and chasing down her son's killer and she couldn't just rely on her gun. Every situation didn't call for that. Sometimes she just needed to yoke somebody up, and Tank could train her to do that well—or at least well enough not to get hurt.

And she needed him because she knew he would always love her just like she would always love him.

Naeema walked around the mat on the center of the floor and came over to pull the heavy bag out of his reach. Tank dropped his fists and eyed her with those sexy eyes. "What?" she asked softly, pushing the bag toward him.

He easily leaned his upper body out of its way. "That's it for today, Naeema," he said, his voice hard.

She knew he was dead-ass serious.

Coming over to stand in front of him, she tried to wrap her arms around his waist and he blocked her from doing it. Feeling challenged, she stripped before him, tossing her sports bra and leggings aside to stand before him naked. Turning, she wrapped her hands around the chain attaching the bag to the ceiling and pulled her body up, wrapping her legs around it. She had barely done two twerks of her fleshy ass before she felt Tank's hands guiding his hard dick up inside her pussy. She moved down lower on the bag until her arms strained, but the snug fit of all of him inside her pussy was worth it.

"Shit," they both swore hotly as he rocked the bag to guide her back and forth on his hard inches.

The feel of his hard body pressing her body against the leather of the bag as he fucked her was intense. She let her head fall back as she fought not to let go of the chains. "Fuck me, Tank," she begged.

He pressed kisses to her shoulder blades as each of his hard thrusts made her ass jiggle against him. "It's so tight," he moaned against her back.

Naeema pulled up on the chain just enough to swivel her hips as she continued to swing back and forth on the bag. "Oh my God, your dick got harder," she gasped, pressing her face against the bag as she bit her bottom lip in pleasure.

She felt one of his hands move up her spine to tightly grip the back of her neck as his strokes deepened, sending his hard curved inches against the tight and wet walls of her pussy.

Back and forth on the dick.

"Yes, yes, yes," she cried out as his grip on her neck tightened and he reached down to alternate between a gentle push of the bag and a slap of her round buttocks.

"You want this nut?" he asked thickly.

"Please," she begged, letting her head fall back to rest on one of his strong shoulders.

As the thrusts of his dick got deeper and faster, Naeema let the chain go and her upper body fell back on him while he continued fucking her. "I'm cumming," he moaned against her neck.

"Mmmmmm," she sighed, bringing her hands up to

tease her own nipples and massage her soft breasts as her nut exploded, sending her to a world where nothing else fucking mattered at all. She felt each pump of his dick as he filled her with his cum.

She was still shivering when he wrapped his arms around her and turned her body to hold her close. She felt so emotional that she pressed her face against his neck to keep from getting caught up and telling him how much she still loved him.

"We can't keep doin' this, Naeema," he told her.

She knew what he said was money.

They couldn't live with each other but it was clear as day they couldn't do without each other either. And that was the realest shit ever.

"What did you do with your money, Queen?"

Naeema looked over at Bas sitting wide legged in an old office chair, his brown eyes locked on the small television broadcasting video surveillance of their secret entrance into the church. She was the first to arrive and, like he would for the others, Bas had unlocked the door to let her in.

Bas was a thug but he didn't look shit like what most people assumed a thug should be. His hair was cut into a low fade that emphasized the strong lines of his lean face and his full eyebrows. He looked like a model in a fashion magazine. Even now he was dressed in khakis and a white polo shirt with a rich-looking brown leather belt and matching deck shoes. She wouldn't doubt they were Gucci or some other high-end brand. He could've been heading off to a day at college, work at a retail store in the mall, or even church.

But Naeema made no mistake that the fine-ass man sitting in that chair was ruthless. Bas was tall, with the slender but muscular frame of an athlete, but his temper was short. He was one of those motherfuckers that skipped the arguing and just straight put hands on someone challenging him.

Did Brandon piss him off? Did the boy far too young even to be in the company of a twentysomething crowd of thieves become a nuisance to their shit?

Did you kill my son?

She looked away from him as her hand itched to grab his throat and choke the truth out of him. *Chill, Naeema.*

"Nothing yet," she said, sipping from the shot of Henny he had poured for her into a plastic cup.

"You still scared?"

She glanced over at him. "I wasn't scared," she said.

He laughed and even that sounded laid back. "Oh, you was scared as hell and you still scared but don't worry. We won't get caught. I'm too smart for them motherfuckas."

But not too smart for me.

Naeema just shrugged and took another sip. "I ain't gon' front. I don't want to do that shit again," she said with a giggle meant to come off as silly.

"Nah, you good. Once was enough to show and prove," he said, rolling across the dusty floor in the chair to pick up the bottle of Henny sitting atop the large safe.

"Prove what?"

Bas uncapped the bottle and took a sip directly from it, his eyes locked on her as he swallowed the brown liquor. "That you can be trusted," he said, before wiping his mouth with the back of his hands.

Just like I thought.

"You can trust me, Bas," she said softly, cutting her eyes up at him with a smile.

He shrugged before he stood up and walked over to pour more liquor into her cup. "Nothing happens that I don't want to happen," he said.

Including murders?

She tilted her head back to look up at him.

"If I told Viv not to fuck with you like that no more she wouldn't," Bas said, still standing over her until his height cast her in the shadow.

Naeema couldn't front. She felt afraid. Right then she realized it was silly of her to be clear as fuck that he wasn't to be trusted but then move about them with no weapon. What if something—*anything*—happened and he flipped on her? It was risky to get caught with the gun but even riskier to hear people keep saying his temper was legendary and trust he would never flip on her. She decided right then not to be around him without her piece.

"Why would you do that?" she asked.

He laughed and backed away from her. "My bad. I said that shit fucked up, yo," he said, turning with one hand in his pocket, pulling his khakis tighter across his firm ass.

Naeema patted the front of her hair where the glue she used to attach her cheap reddish brown lace-front wig was irritating her skin.

"I meant that I like your look. I told Viv to keep bringing you around," he said, turning to flop back down in the chair. It rolled back a bit from the sudden weight of his frame.

Where is the rest of the crew?

Where the fuck is this shit leading?

What the fuck does he want?

"For real?" she said, keeping her voice light and flirty.

He nodded and put the bottle of liquor on the faded carpet by his feet before he pressed his elbows on top of his knees. "You ain't what you seem, Queen . . . just like me," he said, his eyes locked on her.

Oh shit.

Naeema forced herself not to flinch, blink, or break his stare.

"I been watching you. You come off stupid but there ain't shit dumb about you, Queen," Bas reached in his pocket and pulled out a small vial of cocaine. He looked at it and shook it to make the powder fly inside the glass but then he shook his head and pushed it back into his pocket.

"I like it but I don't love it," he said when he saw her eyes dip to take in that move.

"What do you love?" she asked.

"Money," he answered without hesitation.

Naeema pretended to sip the liquor. She was trying not to get faded in case he flipped and she had to try to fight her way out.

Bas turned and looked at the small screen, some two-hundred-dollar setup from Walmart or Target or something. "What do you love?" he asked, as he kept studying the movement of trees on the screen.

Naeema earned time by taking another fake sip. He was in a talkative mood and she wanted to lead him in the right direction. Discover something. Any fucking thing. "I love loyalty," she said.

Bas slowly turned in the chair to eye her as he nodded his head in agreement. "And money can't buy it. Best believe that shit," he said with a tinge of anger in his husky voice.

"Sometimes when I find out somebody I trusted stabbed me in the back, I be wanting to fuck shit up," she said, looking away and pretending to be embarrassed by her words. He'd called her out on her charade of playing dumb but she was sticking to it. This shit was poker and he could be bluffing to force her to show her hand. Fuck that, no haps, motherfucka.

"Sometimes people got to be dealt with. Period," Bas said, his voice as cold as the iciness of his stare.

"You ever had to deal wit' somebody?" she asked.

Did you kill my son, motherfucker?

"Why?" he asked.

She shrugged and looked apologetic, feeling her fear of him return as he eyed her. "We was just conversatin'."

"Yeah, but keep it about shit that concerns you," he said.

"I'm sorry," she said as Queen, making her voice soft and repentant.

Man, triple fuck you.

Bas turned back toward the surveillance TV and then stood up to disappear through the office door. Naeema felt relief that they were no longer alone. She turned to fling the rest of the liquor in her cup in an empty corner before ramming the plastic cup inside the fake Coach crossover bag she wore. As always she was mindful of not leaving her fingerprints or any DNA behind at the church. If the police ever caught up with the crew for their crimes she didn't want them to trace any evidence foolishly left behind back to her.

Soon voices led the way for the rest of the crew to walk into the office behind Bas's tall figure. Naeema eyed each of them as they walked in laughing and joking with each other.

Red looked ready as ever to kick ass with his muscled arms showing in a tight black wifebeater and black Dickies uniform pants. Vivica was right behind him in a tank top and jean skirt, her bright pink hair now in a fresh bob. Nelson, like Brandon, didn't belong in their company at only nineteen, but there he was climbing his short, thick body up onto the safe to sit with a forever-present blunt blazed between lips darkened by chronic use of chronic. Hammer strolled in last in a plaid shirt and a new pair of dark denims with matching Jordans.

She eyed his boyishly handsome face marred by three red puffy scratches on his cheek. "Damn, Hammer, what cat fucked you up?" she asked.

He shrugged and smiled, forever in a good mood. "Pussy problems," he said, grabbing a cup and pouring himself a double shot of the Henny.

Hammer stayed in the midst of pussy problems because he couldn't stay out of the middle of so many pussies. He already had six kids by five babymamas that he was still fucking, plus whatever new cutie caught his eye. His ass was always in some drama.

Looking down into the brown liquid of her cup, she swirled it until the center looked like the eye of a hurricane. She wanted to get this process moving. Find out just what motivation any of them had for killing her son and deal with the culprit. She wanted her life back and her son's death avenged. She wanted out of their midst.

So Naeema decided to shake shit up a little bit. "I never met him but Viv told me a little bit about him and he seemed like a cool kid so I'm'a pour a little Henny out for y'all friend that's not here. For Brandon," she said, keeping her voice light as she poured a little liquor onto the carpet.

The room got quiet as shit, Naeema pretended to take another sip but eyed everybody over the rim of the cup. They all shifted their eyes to Bas, who was looking at her with a deep frown that made his brows pull together.

"I was just sayin' how much we all missed him," Viv explained, shifting her eyes to Red for his forgiveness.

He just looked away from her. It was clear he had no forgiveness to give.

Naeema's heart was beating fast but she played it cool. "What? What I say? I said something wrong?" she asked, faking like she was concerned.

Fuck all of 'em.

Bas picked up the bottle of liquor and threw it against the wall with a vengeance. The glass shattered and the liquor did a wall slide down the fake wood paneling. He turned and walked out of the office with long-ass strides.

"Bas . . . wait," Naeema called out, standing up like she was going to follow him.

Vivica reached out and held her wrist. "Don't fuck wit' that," she warned with a shake of her head.

"My bad. I thought he was y'all friend. Wasn't he cool with y'all?" she asked as her eyes locked on everybody.

Hammer released a breath and shook his head, looking the most serious she had ever seen him.

Nelson jumped down off the safe and left the room.

Red walked over to a small cabinet in the corner and pulled out a fresh bottle of Henny.

"Bas don't let us talk about him but yeah, he was our

friend . . . but don't fuck with that no more, Queen. Like for real, for real," Vivica said, gripping Naeema's wrist tighter to get her attention.

She looked down at her.

"Okay?" Vivica asked, her eyes serious.

"Okay," she agreed.

What the fuck is that shit all about?

8

"*That's* the best you got, Rico?"

The naked teenage girl spread eagle on the bed and the thin dark-skinned dude with his head buried between her thighs both looked over at Naeema as she leaned against the wall of the motel room with a key in one hand and a billy club in the other. It wasn't hard to get the key when she lied and told the desk attendant that the girl in Room 308 was an underage runaway and she was the girl's older sister ready to call the police.

"Who the fuck are you?" he asked.

The girl covered her face and upper body with a flat pillow as Naeema walked up to tap Rico's flat ass with the billy cub.

WHAP. WHAP.

"Up and at 'em, lover boy," she said, picking up his T-shirt on the floor to toss at his crotch when he turned over and sat up on the edge of the bed.

"So . . . why'd you do it?" she asked, pulling out the stained chair in front of the desk to sit down in front of him.

His eyes darted down to his jeans and Naeema pressed the tip of the billy club between his legs as she reached for his jeans with her free hand. A .357 fell to the floor with a solid THUD.

Naeema looked over at him. "Damn . . . you was gonna shoot me, yo?" she asked, sitting the club on her lap long enough to remove the magazine and slide it into her other back pocket. "I promise you it's not *even* that serious."

Rico lunged for her and landed a blow against her chin that caused her to sway sideways out of the chair and to the floor.

"You short-dick motherfucker," she said, tasting blood in her mouth. She raised her leg and kicked him first in his swinging nuts and then solidly in the center of his chest, sending him flying back onto the bed.

His boo cried out.

"Shut *the* fuck up," Naeema snapped as she jumped to her feet.

Bzzzzzzz.

She pulled her cell phone from her back pocket as she eyed the stocky dude straight mean mugging. "Hello," she said.

"Where you at, Queen?" Vivica asked.

Naeema heard the steady bass of music and loud voices in the background. "I'm on the way. Be there in ten," she said.

"That's right. Turn down for what!"

Shaking her head, Naeema ended the call and pushed the phone into the back pocket of her low-slung jeans. "Since you can't get your act right on, then let's do this your way, young boy," she said, stepping over to nudge his forehead with her index finger.

Knuckling up, she delivered two quick blows to his nose and then one to his stomach. He buckled over with an *umph*.

BAM.

Another blow to the back of his head.

He rolled off the bed to the ground.

THUD.

A kick to his side.

"You don't put your hands on a female. That's a bitch move," she said, squatting down to press her finger against his forehead again as blood began to seep from his nose and from a small split in his lip.

"I just wanted to ask you a question and you had to make this whole interaction go to the left," she said.

"Who are you?" he asked, still with too much attitude for someone who just got fucked up.

"Why did you set Brandon Mack up to be killed?" she asked.

"Who?" he asked.

Naeema rolled her eyes before locking them on his face again. "The kid Brianna was talking to, the one that whooped your ass at school," she explained.

"Who is Brianna?" his boo thang asked.

Rico tilted his head back to look at her. "The little shawty I had way before you, Pilar—"

"Oh, 'cause—"

"Eh eh. Hell no. Are you two motherfuckers kiddin' me?" Naeema asked, her face incredulous as she tapped the gun in her hand. She pointed the nozzle toward her. "Pi-lar . . . Piper . . . Pipsqueak. Who gives a fuck? Shut the fuck up. Rico, turn your little ass this way and answer my question."

"I'm not trying to go to jail behind no bitch and behind no fight," he said. "And he didn't whup my ass, he held his own for a young kid. That's all. And that's too different things, shawty. You can ask anybody 'round the school. It ain't even go down like that."

Naeema kept her eyes trained on him and his gaze never wavered from hers. "So what was on WorldStar?"

Rico made a face and shook his head. "Little dude got in a good punch or two and that's the part of the fight this kid posted online. Now I fucked that kid, Bilal, up for that bullshit move."

Naeema believed him. "I'm gonna ask around, and if I find out you lyin' I will find you again and next time I ain't asking no questions." She turned and stepped over the chair on the floor.

"What about my fire?"

"Is it registered to you?" she asked without looking back as she opened the door.

"Huh?"

"Deuces," she said, slamming the door closed behind her.

As soon as the taxi pulled to a stop outside Club Infinity, Naeema held down the hem of her jean skirt as she climbed out beside a bright red Jaguar. There were plenty of eyes on her as she walked up the length of the long line waiting to get into the club. She knew the combination of her body and her outfit would make just about everybody pause . . . in admiration, in lust, or in hate.

Her denim skirt rode low on her hips and high on her thick thighs. She'd paired it with a crisp white tee with a jagged edge that left her flat caramel belly exposed. She topped off the casual outfit with a bunch of fake pearl and diamond necklaces in varying lengths and a short off-white fur to fight off the chill that crept into the September air late at night.

Naeema raked her fingers through the loose curls of her long jet-black wig as she walked up to security at the door. The tall bouncer dressed in all black didn't try to hide that his hazel eyes were locked on her legs. She curved her gloss-covered lips into a smile and looked at him through her dark shades. "How you doin'? I'm Queen," she said, tucking her replica Marc Jacobs clutch under her arm.

"Last name?" he asked as he leaned back inside the doorway to retrieve a clipboard.

"No last name. Just Queen," she said.

He gave her a once-over that was slow, thorough, and meant to show his appreciation. "As in 'All hail the . . . '"

Naeema smiled. "You tell me."

He just smiled.

Club bouncers—especially sexy ones—got thrown plenty of pussy on the regular. Unfortunately, she knew this for a fact from the days when she first met and started dealing with Tank. Although Tank rarely worked at clubs and instead focused mostly on security details for East Coast celebrities, Naeema's fiery jealousy in their marriage was bred off women at clubs always offering her man the goodies.

This bouncer stepped aside from the door and raised both of his large hands to playfully bow to her. "Enjoy," he said.

She moved past him, and the music that was just a steady bass line outside became louder as she stepped inside the club. The heat of the gyrating bodies pressed nearly wall to wall forced her to remove her fur. As more of the men in the club noticed her, they made room for her to walk past until there was a clear path ahead of her.

Power of the thick thighs and a fat ass.

She had to sidestep a few brothas that tried to get hands

on but finally made it to the rear of the club. Red was sitting alone in a booth dressed in all red with a fresh pair of white kicks on. She was surprised to see him. He rarely ever hung out with them when they had a girls' night out.

She sat in the booth, placing her clutch and coat on the space between them. "What it do, Red?" Naeema asked, leaning over so that he could hear her over the steady pulse of Kid Ink's "Show Me."

Red gave her a nod and barely looked her way as he reached for his drink.

"Where's Viv?" she asked.

"Bar."

This Tiny Lister–looking asshole.

Naeema had to give herself a three count to check her own attitude as she felt the one he was straight up giving her. She never got the chance to catch Red alone and she couldn't let a chance for even a few minutes of convo with him pass her by. She scooted over on the semicircular padded bench. "Are you mad at me?"

He frowned and cast her the briefest side-eye that was dismissive as hell. "For what?"

"Because I brought up that kid . . . Byron," she said, reaching for one of the bottles in the bucket. It was empty. She wasn't really thirsty and when she went home to get dressed she'd hit some fabulous loud called Girl Scout Cookies that her connect Mook blessed her with. She was already mellow as a motherfucker.

"Brandon," Red corrected her before he took another sip.

Naeema forced herself to stop staring at his profile. "I guess I was kinda scared, you know," she said.

"Scared of what?"

Naeema shrugged one shoulder. "Maybe whoever killed him will try to come for one of us too?"

Red balked. "I doubt that shit."

Because one of you did it?

"Why?" she pressed.

"Ain't nobody crazy enough to fuck with us."

"But they fucked with him and he was one of y'all," Naeema said with simplicity.

Red turned his head and looked at her full on. "You a punk?"

Naeema's eyes searched his in the dimly lit club just as colorful lights flashed across the ceiling. She was looking for some sign of crazy but mostly she felt a coldness in the brown depths that sent a yellow streak down her back. She opened her mouth but not a damn thing came out.

"And it won't stop, stop, stop . . ."

They both looked away as Vivica came to stand at the table in a white studded catsuit with a drink in each hand as she sang the chorus to Sevyn Streeter's "It Won't Stop" louder than anyone else in a ten-foot radius of their booth.

Red stood up so that Vivica could ease her way past him to sit. She kicked off her heels and stepped up onto the leather banquette seat, bringing her breasts level with his eyes. She pressed her hands to the back of his bald head and stroked his tattoo as she danced and sang to him. Red stood right there. He didn't smile or dance back or even look that fucking happy . . . but he didn't stop her and he looked her in the face the whole time she performed for him.

"When you give me thunder you make my summer rain," she sang as she leaned in to press kisses to his stern face.

Naeema eyed them as she pressed her back against the

banquette. They actually looked in love and cute . . . but that didn't have shit to do with her putting a bullet in both of their asses if she found out they were in on Brandon's death. She'd kill both their cute asses and keep it moving without a moment's regret.

She reached into her purse for her phone. She was disappointed there were no missed calls or text messages from Tank. When he gave her that thunder on the heavy bag earlier that day he made *her* summer rain. *Shit.*

It had been intense.

It wasn't that they talked every day because they didn't. Since their separation they sometimes went weeks without any communication, but today had been a game changer. They either had to work it out or leave it alone because that middle ground was a mind fuck.

An intense mind fuck.

And it won't stop . . .

Naeema bit her bottom lip and scrolled to a folder within a folder within another folder, where a lone picture sat there waiting to make her salivate in full creep mode. Tank was naked and lying in the middle of their king-size bed atop black silk sheets with his king-size dick in his hand—hard and ready. Everything about it was good. From the serious *come fuck and suck me* expression on Tank's face to the soft, fine hairs covering his muscled chest.

Just sexy.

The pic was a relic from better days in their past.

"What was you and Red talkin' 'bout while I was at the bar?"

Naeema jumped in her seat from the sudden closeness of Vivica. She felt the woman's breath breezing against the side of her face. She was so caught up in Tank's dick pic that she didn't even notice that the club dj's remixed version of one of Lil' Kim's 1990s bangers was playing and Vivica's serenade to Red was over. He had left the booth.

"Huh?" Naeema asked as she locked her phone's screen.

"Red went out the way with you?"

Naeema frowned as she scooted over enough to look Vivica in the face. She was surprised to see that her faux friend was dead-ass serious. *Play your position, Na.*

"Girl, stop playing. Plus, Red wouldn't fuck with that. Would he?" she asked with a doe-eyed shocked expression.

"I don't put shit past him," Vivica said, turning her head. "It ain't like I ain't never caught his ass fuckin' around before."

Naeema followed her line of vision and it landed on Red in the distance as he moved through the crowd. Vivica's eyes followed him until he walked into the men's bathroom.

"Get the fuck outta here," Naeema said, feigning surprise. "Well, let me get this straight 'cause I don't want you feelin' some type of way about me. I was apologizing for bringing up Brandon the other night."

Vivica raised up off the seat long enough to reach across the table for her drink. "Some bitch off Tremont Avenue was sending Red pussy pics," she said as she stirred her drink. "Payback is a bitch."

Naeema was only half listening to "The Days of Vivica's Life with Red" as she gently pulled her fur from beneath Vivica's ass. *Man, who gives a fuck?*

"I used to laugh at his ass every time I thought about Brandon eating me out."

Naeema froze. *Say hunh?*

"Right in the church too. Trust and believe I ain't the bitch to sit back and let a negro play me."

Brandon hadn't been but fourteen and barely that. Vivica had to be in her early twenties. *Was this bitch crazy?*

She felt her anger snap on like a light switch and her fingers curled into a fist so tight that the semipointed tips of her stiletto nails dug into the flesh of her palm. She wanted to box that bitch upside her head until it was lights out for her ass. She pressed her hand between her folded legs to keep from doing it.

"You let a kid eat you out?" Naeema asked, feeling the heat of her anger in her chest.

"Shee-it. Kid? He was taller than me with a light mustache. And it wasn't his first time. Best believe that," she said and then raised her glass in a little salute as she giggled.

This bitch dumb as hell.

Naeema gripped her thigh until she had to wince at the pain of her nails in her flesh. *The bigger picture, Na. Don't forget the bigger picture.*

"Just that once though to pay Red back."

Red.

Naeema's mouth opened a bit as she gasped lightly. Had Vivica's payback been enough to send Red into murderous rage? Naeema wouldn't doubt it. He walked around all day every day like he stayed on one and would shoot up the world over nothing.

Another dude messing with his woman. A younger dude? A younger dude he used to chill with?

She caught a flash of bright red from the corner of her eye and turned her head just as he made his way through the crowd toward their booth. Her eyes squinted and she knew if looks could kill she would've dropped that fool before she could blink.

With her eyes still locked on him, she leaned over to Vivica. "Did Red know?" she asked in her ear as the other woman swayed in her seat to some Young Jeezy banger.

"Fuck no," she emphasized.

Someone stopped Red and he turned to look back at them. The club's colorful laser lights flashed again and highlighted the tattoo KILLA on the back of his head.

Murder was all about motive, and now she knew Red had had one.

Naeema felt overwhelmed.

When Brandon first died, there had been nothing but dead ends surrounding his murder. Now she was standing at a fork in the road and there were so many paths to his possible killers that she felt like she was sinking in all the info. For the first time she felt like everything was over her head. She was playing out of her league. She wasn't no vigilante. No modern-day Foxy Brown, Cleopatra Jones, or some shit.

"Fuck," she swore.

She walked out of the club and the cool fresh air felt like salvation. She took deep gulps of it as she leaned against the building and wiped the sweat from her face with both hands.

"What the fuck am I doing?" she asked.

"You tell me."

Naeema peeked through her fingers to find Bas standing before her. She started and pressed her fat ass back against the building, her heart pounding in surprise. "What you doin' here?" she asked, taking in how good he looked in an off-white thin silk sweater and linen pants.

"I came to pick you up," he said in that low and husky voice of his.

Fuck. She looked left and right and then past him to see a dark gray convertible Maybach double-parked. *"That's your whip?"* she asked.

"Nah," he said with a smile.

Naeema wasn't sure she believed him, and there was no way in hell he'd robbed enough banks to buy a fucking Maybach—even one that was a year or two old. "Where we going?" she asked.

"Your crib."

Fuck. Fuck. Fuck. "I don't wanna go there." She lied, because there was nothing she wanted to do more than go crawl under the covers of her bed and sleep off the anxiety rising in her. "I live with my mother."

"Then come ride wit' me, Queen," Bas said, turning to stride away with this cool-ass swagger that would make Diddy rethink his whole way of being.

Naeema pushed up off the wall and followed his path across the sidewalk and into the street, where he stood with the passenger door opened and waiting. Naeema thought she was older than him by a few years but he had this confidence and suaveness that made him seem older. Still fly as fuck . . . but older.

A'ight, Naeema. This fly and suave motherfucker is still on your list of suspects.

What surprised her was the smallest bit of hope that Red had acted alone.

That brought on guilt.

She slid onto the smooth leather seat of the ultra-luxury vehicle and eyed him through the windshield as he came around the car to slide into the driver's seat. The engine purred so smoothly that she didn't even realize the car was already cranked and running. He checked for oncoming traffic and pulled off down the street.

"Where we headed?" she asked, reminding herself not to give a fuck that she was riding in a vehicle worth two or three of her homes.

He shrugged and glanced over at her. "I told Red to shoot me a picture of you, and that outfit made me take a detour from where I was headed a little while ago."

"And where was that?"

He just laughed low in his throat and sped down the nearly empty street.

"We going to your place?" she asked.

"Nah, I got a little situation at my place," Bas said.

"A permanent situation?" she asked, playing the role.

He looked over at her. "For now," he admitted.

So Bas had a woman.

"Sound like her problem. Not mines," she said, not looking away from him.

"Queen, Queen, Queen," he said before focusing back on the road.

She appeared cool but on the inside both her mind and her pulse were racing. Was Bas trying to finally have her pay up for the months of flirting . . . tonight?

She eyed his profile before she turned and looked out the window as he sped through the streets of Newark. She had just remembered how angry he got at the very mention of

Brandon's name. There had to be an explanation for that and anger at her son wasn't to be overlooked.

At all.

She felt like she was sinking in the minutiae again.

She closed her eyes and let her head fall back against the headrest.

Fuck me running.

She squeezed the bridge of her nose.

"You a'ight?" Bas asked, placing his hand on her bared thigh.

It was warm. Too damn warm.

He stroked circles against her soft skin.

And that felt . . . too damn good.

"Yeah. I'm good," she said, looking up at him in surprise as he ascended the levels of a parking garage until he came to a stop on the top.

With one last soft pat Bas removed his hand and climbed from the car to lean against the wall that came to his hip. *Now what?*

Kicking off her heels, she climbed from the car and came around it to stand beside him. They had to be in or near New York because the Newark skyline was laid out in front of them. The lights of the buildings across the Hudson River glowed against the ebony backdrop.

Being a city girl, Naeema had always loved photos of a city skyline. It was even better in person.

"That shit looks so dope, yo," she said.

"Yup," he agreed. "Dope as hell."

She glanced at his profile.

"That's Newark. A city where you can find low-income apartments or million-dollar homes . . . it all depends on what part of town you want to bust your ass to be in."

That was true.

"You can live or die in that city at a moment's notice," Bas continued, the lights of the poles on the top level of the parking deck reflected in the brown depths of his eyes.

Naeema forced herself to look away. Was that a threat or was he just reflecting? "Are you ever afraid that because you live by the sword, you will die by the sword?" she asked.

Bas stood up tall and shifted over to stand behind her. With his hands on her shoulders, he turned her to face him. "Never be afraid to die," he said.

She felt a chill.

He raised her chin and pressed his cool lips to hers with just the right amount of pressure. Feather light. Barely there.

She was glad when he shifted his attention back to the skyline.

She was confused when she wanted more.

Shit.

$\mathcal{N}$aeema was surprised when they drove back out of New York and he eventually pulled in to the covered garage of the Hilton next to Newark's Penn Station. She was even more surprised when they headed straight to the tenth floor. "You just keep a hotel room stashed for emergencies?" she asked as he pulled out a key card and unlocked the door, stepping inside to raise the lighting.

"I told you that dress caused a detour."

"Well damn . . . just how much pussy do you have lined up, Bas?" she asked as she followed him inside and looked around the suite. The decor was dope. Lots of neutral colors and deep chocolate leathers with small pops of bright colors. If she ever got her financial game up enough to renovate her house, she wanted it decorated just like it.

"I don't like talking about one situation with the next," Bas said, turning to stand before her. "But I come here alone to chill."

"So I'm next?" she asked, looking up at him.

"I like to give people what they want . . . if I can," he said, cocky as fuck.

She gave him a once-over as she stepped past him. "Me too," she said over her shoulder. "*If* I can."

With her back to him, Naeema released a nervous breath.

She was alone with a man she believed capable of murder. A suspect in the very murder of her son.

He grabbed her wrist and gently pulled her back in front of him. "Whassup, Queen?" he asked, holding her hand.

"You the boss," she said. "You tell me whassup."

"I'm feelin' you. I want you," he said low in his throat as he pulled her body closer and grabbed one of her plump buttocks in his hand to massage.

Think, Naeema. Think.

"I don't like dipping in other people's *situations*," she said, reaching up to stroke his face.

Bas backed her up until her ass and shoulders pressed against the wall next to the front door. "Just looking at you got my dick hard," he said, taking her hand to press against the length of his hardness.

Naeema's eyes widened at the feel of his dick print. *Nice.* "Uhm . . . I don't like sharing. Too much dick drama."

He smiled and pressed kisses along her jawline as he reached behind her to grip her ass and jerk her lower body against his. His dick pressed against her stomach as he gently sucked her bottom lip into his and pressed his tongue smoothly inside her mouth.

Naeema brought her hands up to the back of his head and massaged his neck, moaning in the back of her throat and returning his slow kisses. Her eyes popped open in surprise when she felt her clit jump in reaction to him gently sucking the tip of her tongue.

Damn.

He eased the hem of her skirt up and massaged her thick thighs as he freed her mouth. "Let me just put the tip in," he said and then smiled.

Naeema was panting and she wished she could push him away and free up some space between them. Some distance. Some coolness.

Shit.

She lowered her head to his shoulder and the scent of his warm cologne was in his clothes. "I'm not nobody's side bitch, Bas," she said, trying to remember her stall tactic as she felt her nipples and clit aching. "I ain't know you had a situation or I wouldn't have even played Bonnie to your Clyde."

He stepped back from her and held up his hands. "I understand," he said. "You want me to take you home?"

She opened her mouth to say yes but then pressed her lips closed. She couldn't let him nowhere near her house. "No, I can take a cab," she said.

"It's three a.m.," Bas reminded her, reaching in his pocket for his vial of cocaine as he moved across the room to sit at the wooden table by the balcony.

Stay here and risk being fucked or get dropped off and really be screwed when he discovered she wasn't who she said she was?

She watched him as he drew up his line and split half for each nostril.

"I'll tell you what," he said, pinching his nose and sniffing. "I need a little time to take care of some shit. You stay here 'til I do," he said, spreading his legs wide as he settled down in the leather club chair.

His dick was still hard and ready between his thighs.

She shifted her eyes up from it. "I can't—"

"Come here," he said with a sniff.

Bas wasn't to be trusted on any given day, but for sure

she was not feeling like angering him while he was on powder. She walked over to him. "Sit here," he said, swiping away any coke residue before he tapped the table.

"Bas—"

"Sit down," he shouted, his eyes freezing over. "Damn, Queen. You said no pussy and I ain't even pressing you. Sit the fuck down."

Play your position, Naeema.

She eased up and back onto the table. Bas gripped her thighs and pulled her forward until her ass was on the edge of the round table. He spread her knees. "Just let me smell this motherfucker or somethin'," he said.

She frowned and tried to close her knees. "I been in the club all night, Bas," she protested.

"I know the difference between sweaty pussy and funky pussy," he said, pushing her knees apart again.

She was sitting up on the table and looked down as he leaned in to press his face against her thighs. She looked heavenward and rolled her eyes in irritation. She had barely blinked before he swooped her panties to the side and stroked his tongue up the middle of her pussy. She pressed her hands against his forehead and shoulder while he locked his arms around her waist and sucked her clit deeply into his hot mouth with a moan.

Shit.

He had this wicked one-two pull followed by a tongue lick that made Naeema pause as white shots of electricity coursed over her body. She couldn't front. She was already hot from the kiss and now this.

"No, Bas," she said again, sounding weak as hell to her own ears.

Pull. Pull. Lick. Pull

Shit.

The old Naeema that had zero fucks to give emerged and she fell back against the table, arching her back as she gripped his shirt in her fists and circled her hips up against his mouth.

Pull. Pull. Lick. Pull.

He ate her pussy like he was trying to save the world by making her cum. "Yesss," she moaned, her eyes closed as her hard nipples pointed to the ceiling and rubbed and stretched against the lace of her bra.

Pull. Pull. Lick. Pull.

She thought of Tank being the one to eat her and she really felt her freak level rise.

"Shit," Naeema swore, pressing her heels into the table top as she arched her hips forward. "I'm about to cum."

He locked his arms around her hips tighter and sucked her clit between his lips until she was shivering, crying out, and fighting to free herself from the insanity of him continuing to suck her now ultra-sensitive clit.

Bas stayed locked on it even while her hips arched in jerking motions as she tried like hell to back away from the pressure of his lips. He didn't free her until her entire body went slack and head dangled backward off the table as she fought to breathe at a normal rate.

"Look," he said thickly.

She fought for the strength to raise her head just in time to see him jack his thick dark dick until cum fired from it like bullets, landing on her stomach, chin, and near her eye.

If he was Tank, she would have squatted before him and cleaned his dick up with her tongue.

But he was not Tank.

I ain't that cumstruck.

Brrrnnnggg.

Naeema jumped up in the middle of the king-size bed at the sudden high-pitched shrill of the telephone. She swiped some of the tousled wig hair from her face as she got her head together. She was still in bed alone and assumed Bas was still on the couch where he slept off his nut and his high.

Brrrnnnggg.

Naeema reached for the telephone but then pulled her hand away. *This ain't my room so that ain't my call.* Dressed only in the plush cotton robe she put on after her shower, she flung back the crisp cotton covers and left the equally stylish bedroom, only to find the living room of the suite empty. *Brrrrnnnggg.*

There was a room service cart next to the table in the dining area. She scratched at her wig as she moved to remove the metal lids and found a stack of pancakes with fresh berries and another plate with home fries, eggs, and bacon. She picked up the glass of orange juice and took a sip.

Brrrnnnggg.

Naeema looked over her shoulder at the phone sitting on the cherry end table between the sofa and the love seat. Popping a blueberry into her mouth, she walked over to pick it up but didn't say one word.

"Good morning. This is your nine a.m. wake up call. Have a good day," said an automated female voice.

Click.

Placing the phone back in the cradle, she walked back

through the open double doors leading into the bedroom to pull her clutch from underneath the pillow. She dug out her cell phones.

No missed calls on either one.

Damn, Tank. Well fuck you too.

Her thumb floated above the keypad ready to dial 69 on her speed dial. She dropped the phone back into her handbag instead and moved back to the table to tear down on the food and took up the remote to turn on the flat-screen television on the wall. She turned it to *LIVE with Kelly and Michael.* She loved that corny-ass show and it gave her an hour not to think about anything important.

Knock-knock.

Naeema looked away from the blond actress from *Revenge* talking about the new season of the show. She had never seen it but she was thinking it was something she could relate to and get into. *Sometimes a bitch gotta do what a bitch gotta do.*

She ignored the knock and turned back to the television. *Not my room and not my visitor.*

"Queen, it's me . . . Vivica."

She rolled her eyes and wished she'd jetted as soon as she woke up. Her plan was to fuck the breakfast up and then get dressed to catch two different cabs back to her house to get ready for work . . . not to fuck around with Vivica's cradle-robbing ass.

Hell, her child-molesting ass. What makes her any different than Mr. Warren? Not a damn thang.

"Open up, Queen."

Knock-knock-knock-knock.

Naeema jumped up in aggravation and walked over

to the door, forcing herself to swallow back her desire to straight whup her ass as she let the woman in. She had to admit she looked cute in print leggings and a bright yellow blazer that didn't clash too badly with her pink hair. "Chill, Viv," she said. "I was in the bathroom."

"My bad," Vivica said, opening her Michael Kors bag to pull out a stack of money. "Bas said to take you shopping 'cause you didn't have clothes with you."

Naeema didn't take the stack. "I got clothes . . . at home . . . where I'm going in a little bit."

Vivica pushed the money into Naeema's hand before she strolled around the suite. "Well, Bas seem to think you moving in here for a few days," she said, peeking her head inside the bedroom. "Shit, not bad, bitch."

Nothing happens that I don't want to happen.

Naeema chose not to trip off that bit of info with Vivica. She was clear that in this virtual chess game Vivica was a pawn and her loyalty was to the king, not Queen.

Besides maybe I can slow-stroke this bitch for more info.

Vivica dug in her tote again and pulled out a white plastic CVS bag. "I figured you needed underwear and a toothbrush," she said, handing it to her. "You only a little bit bigger than me everywhere but that ass . . . so I guessed on the size."

"Thanks," she said.

"Sooooo . . ."

Naeema eyed her as her faux friend/real foe looked at her expectantly.

"I didn't think he was going to slay that bougie dragon princess but here you are. Boss bitch status," she said.

"And who is the bougie dragon princess?" Naeema asked,

coming over to sit down on the opposite end of the couch from Vivica. "And why you ain't tell me about her before . . . *friend*?"

"That's Bas's business to tell, not mine."

"So why tell it now?" Naeema asked, wondering how much more of Bas's business she was keeping.

"'Cause I know that you know a li'l somethin' about it now."

She needed a break from Vivica and her secret-secret bullshit. She grabbed her handbag and walked back through the double doors to the bedroom. It was then she saw the paper on the nightstand. She crossed the room to pick it up. "See you later tonight," she read.

Rolling her eyes she balled it up and tossed it over her shoulder. She had just turned on the shower when she backtracked and entered the living room. Vivica was still on the sofa flipping through the TV channels. "Viv, I can't go shopping. I gotta get home," she said. "I'll holla at you later."

"You want a ride home?" she asked.

"Can you drop me downtown?" Naeema asked, already planning to catch a cab from there to get home.

"A'ight, but Bas not gon' like you changing his plans."

"I'll make it up to him," she said over her shoulder as she walked back into the bathroom that was filled with the steam from the running shower.

Naeema slipped a shower cap over her wig and then dropped the robe to the floor before stepping into the shower.

She would play Bas's game of hideaway but first she was going home to get the gun she took from Rico.

Bas didn't come back to the suite for three days. No call. No show.

I coulda been making money.

And her boss, Derek, wasn't happy at all that she'd taken more time off indefinitely. Still, she knew that as long as she was the lone female in the shop, kept her body right and tight, and gave her boss, coworkers, and customers plenty of eye candy, her chair was waiting on her return.

Vivica played the go-between just enough to be bait to keep Naeema on the hook for Bas to reel her in when he was ready. When she wasn't sneaking off for a couple of hours every day to look for the identity of the vic of the cell phone grab Ms. JuJu had told her Brandon did, she ordered room service, played Candy Crush Saga on her phone, wondered why Tank had yet to call, mourned her son, and plotted on just how she planned to kill whoever murdered him. All while she waited on Bas to make his next move.

Bzzzz . . . bzzzz . . . bzzzz . . .

She leaned forward on the sofa to pick up her burner cell phone. It was Bas. Naeema set it back on the table. She was playing the role of Queen, who would've jumped at a call from him, but Naeema decided to make him wait. She set the phone back on the table and picked up the remote to turn up the volume on an episode of *The First 48*.

Bzzzz . . . bzzzz . . . bzzzz . . .

Naeema turned the volume up higher and ignored the phone. Finally it stopped vibrating. She was already regretting not bringing some of her weed stash with her. Still playing the game of "just in case," she didn't want Bas to be able to trace back to her real identity through her weed connect. Not everybody sold underground medicinal weed and sometimes the very strain of weed let you know who sold it. Still, she was ready to get fucked up, and the bottle of Absolut vodka and cranberry juice she'd brought wasn't doing it.

Click.

She looked over her shoulder at the sound of the door lock detaching. Moments later Bas's tall figure filled the doorway. He was dressed in all black but the look on his face was darker . . . especially when his eyes shifted to her cell phone sitting in plain view on the table next to her drink.

"Hey, stranger," she said, reaching for the snifter to take a sip of the vodka and juice.

Bas walked over and snatched it from her hand, spilling some of it onto her, before he turned and threw it against the wall. THUD. The glass bounced off the wall but didn't shatter and the red liquid drizzled down the walls to seep into the carpet.

The fuck?

Naeema eyed him. She couldn't front that his action had made her pause like a motherfucker. She had made a calculated move that didn't play well. Her anger at him for not showing her respect was the move, the nerve, and the grit of Naeema . . . not Queen. Somewhere the line had blurred for her.

"Go get dressed," he said before he dropped down on the love seat.

"I am dressed."

"In something besides all that stretchy shit you wear," he said, his tone rude as hell as he eyed the black- and gold-striped leggings she wore with a white tank. "Hell, I knew how fat your pussy was before I ate it the other night."

"I thought you liked it," she said, slipping back into the role of Queen to help calm his anger.

He didn't say anything else and Naeema stood up to head into the bedroom.

"I missed you, yo."

She stopped and looked over her shoulder at him. His eyes were still locked on the television screen and his fists were clasped together under his square chin. She didn't say a word as she moved on into the bedroom.

Naeema emerged a half hour later freshly showered, makeup beat, and dressed in a white off-the-shoulder spandex top and a long fitted skirt that exposed her flat stomach. In her purse she had the gun she swiped from Rico. "More stretchy shit," she said, doing a slow turn beside where he still sat.

"Queen, next time I offer you a shopping trip, please go," he said, sounding more chill as he reached out to slap at her ass.

Naeema looked over her shoulder as she made it clap for him.

Bas slapped it again. WHAP!

"So . . . did you get everyone *situated* while you were gone?" she asked.

Bas stood up and moved toward the door. "Almost," he said, holding the door open for her.

"Must be a serious-ass situation," she said as she passed him to walk down the hall to the elevator.

"Right?" he agreed sarcastically.

Once they were on the elevator he stepped behind her and then pulled her back by her hips to settle her ass against his groin. He pressed a kiss to her neck. "You smell good," he whispered against her pulse.

It was pounding.

Get your shit together, Naeema.

She stepped up from him and shimmied his hands off her hips with a back-and-forth motion. "Don't want to get into another serious situation before you handle the other one," she said, her eyes on his reflection against the metal wall of the elevator.

"I get what I want . . . *when* I want it," he said.

They strolled off the elevator together and crossed the lobby of the hotel. Naeema paused at a bright red Porsche Panamera sitting curbside. When Bas stepped forward to open the passenger door for her, she knew he was somehow involved in a stolen car ring or some shit. There was no way to explain his having access to luxury vehicles worth half a million dollars or better.

What if I get pulled over in this stolen motherfucker?

The stakes kept getting higher and higher.

"This your whip too?" she asked, looking up at him as she slid into the passenger seat.

"Somethin' like that," they said in unison.

As they were cruising through the steady traffic on the downtown streets of Newark, Bas turned on the music. Soon the sounds of "Crooked Smile" by J. Cole filled the interior of the car. Naeema snapped her fingers and moved her hips in the seat.

"When this song first came out last year I had just—"

Bas looked over at her as she bit back the rest of the words. "Just what?"

Shaved my hair off.

But she wasn't sharing with him that the idea of a closely shaven head with her features had nagged at her until she finally tried it and said she would just grow it back if the shape of her head was lumpy or whopped. In the first hours after the deed was done she had regretted shaving off her shoulder-length hair, and listening to that song made her finally say "fuck it" and embrace the change.

"I had just got fired," she lied.

She was glad when he let the subject drop.

Naeema looked out the tinted window as the landscape changed from the tall buildings surrounding Penn Station to the storefronts of downtown to residential town houses. Soon the streets were lined with more lots where houses once stood than actual homes. Whether from the riots of 1967, the demolition of the high-rise projects, or natural disasters, there were still areas of certain wards of the city that couldn't seem to recover.

Naeema loved her hometown and she wanted the best for it.

"Shit," Bas swore as a man stumbled back into the street.

He slammed on his brakes and their bodies jerked forward. Naeema reached her hands out and pressed against the dashboard to stop herself from lunging forward any further without her seat belt on. She cried out when the body fell back against the top of the roof.

BAM!

Two women came running into the street to start throwing hard blows against his body. One woman's shirt was torn in half and her bra was down under one of her breasts, exposing a big and bumpy brown nipple. One of them punched at the man's head as he tried to curl his body into a ball and her hand missed his head and slammed against the windshield.

"Ah, man, fuck this shit," Bas spat as he reached for the door handle.

Naeema reached over and pressed her hand against the horn as Bas climbed from the car.

They seemed to fight the man even harder.

As she watched Bas easily remove each of the women from atop the man and the hood of the car, she knew two women straight fucking up a dude was nothing but pussy problems and dick drama. The man jumped to his feet once he was free and the headlights spotlighted the scratches on his face, the swelling of his bottom lip, and his clothes, nearly ripped to shreds on his body. As Bas spread his arms wide to try to hold back both of the women from jumping on him again, the dude turned and took off running up the middle of the street. His knees damn near touched his chin, he was booking it so hard.

Naeema laughed.

The women both pushed Bas out of the way and he stumbled back as they turned on each other and started fighting while the man's figure receded with each bit of distance he put between them. As they pulled at each other's hair and tugged like crazy, they both fell back between two cars parked in front of a large bank.

Naeema laughed harder.

Bas studied the hood and the windshield before he finally got back into the car. He glanced over at Naeema covering her mouth as she continued to laugh. "That shit is not funny," he said, sounding irritated as he steered the car around the fighting women and the crowd surrounding them in the street.

Naeema fought like crazy to swallow back her laughter. "Is the car okay?" she asked.

Bas shrugged one broad shoulder. "It don't matter. It's getting chopped up tomorrow."

Stolen car. I knew it.

Naeema shook her head at the whole encounter they'd just had. *The streets of the hood stay popping with some mess. Big tittie just flopping around like a fish out of water.*

When they had driven fifteen blocks or better and past the man, *still* running up the middle of the street like he knew hell was on his heels, Bas and Naeema glanced at each other and then they both broke out laughing.

10 //

Two weeks later

"So, you avoiding me?"

Naeema froze in the doorway of her house with her hands still on the knob as she looked at Tank sitting on the edge of her bed. She leaned against the door and let her eyes take him in. Still Laz Alonzo–level fine, in a navy V-neck that pressed against his muscles and looked so good against his brown complexion. His elbows were pressed on his knees and his hands were loosely clasped in the space between them. She lightly shook off that intense initial reaction she had at the sight of him. "You haven't called me either, Tank," she said.

"You left me," he said.

"A year ago," she shot back as she finally stepped into the house and closed the door. "And in that year we talk sometimes and sometimes we don't."

"And we fuck sometimes and sometimes we don't." His eyes were bright with something. Some emotion.

She couldn't identify it.

"True," Naeema finally agreed. "But that doesn't give you a right to do a B&E."

Her eyes shifted to the large plastic container her TV sat on. Inside it was a smaller container with everything in the world she had of Brandon's.

"Sarge let me in . . . after he called me to say you went missing for two weeks," he said, looking down at his hands, then at her as she stepped into the living room and dropped the Louis Vuitton garment bag she was carrying over her arm.

"Sarge?" she asked in disbelief.

"That's right."

She looked up as her elderly tenant—who paid no rent—stepped into the living room from the kitchen. That was a first as far as Naeema knew.

So this little mini-intervention is serious as hell.

"You all right?" he asked, those sharp eyes on her as he scratched his scruffy beard and shifted back and forth in his boots like he wasn't comfortable being in her space.

Naeema opened her mouth.

"You all right," he said again, this time as a declaration, before turning to shuffle back into the kitchen with a rough wave of his hand.

Naeema closed her mouth and arched her brow.

She wasn't surprised when the door leading to the basement slammed and echoed through the house.

Tank stood up and his presence seemed to make the room smaller. "I think we need to give each other some space," he said.

"You mean some *more* space," she said as he walked over to her.

"What kind of games are you playin', Na?" Tank asked. "I told you we needed to do something and then your ass disappear for two weeks?"

Naeema reached up and stroked the side of his face as she closed the gap between them. "Tank," she whispered up to him.

"Nah," he said, leaning back from her touch and sidestepping the feel of her breasts pressed against his chest.

She got stiff with anger, feeling rejected. "So you not feelin' me now?" she asked, pointedly reaching for him.

"So you want me to use you for sex? You want me to chop you down like any other bitch in the street and then walk away before I even zip my dick back in my pants?" He grabbed her by the waist and then gripped the back of her neck to roughly bend her over before him. With her ass spread before him in the maxi dress she wore, he ground against her, his arm stretched as he kept gripping her neck to hold her down. "This what you want, huh?"

Naeema looked at him over her shoulder. "Fuck me," she said, grinding back against him.

Tank's face became cold as he roughly pushed her from him.

She stumbled forward and almost hit the wall. Reaching out with both hands, she blocked the fall then stood up to slowly turn and face him.

"If you lookin' for dick on demand, then buy you a dildo," he said, striding to the front door.

Naeema leaned back against the wall and looked over at him. "Don't leave me, Tank. I need you. Don't walk out that door," she said, reaching up to remove the black wig she wore. She flung it across the room.

Tank froze at the door.

She felt those invisible waters rise again, covering her

and drowning her. Her eyes filled with tears and she felt her anxiety literally make her skin itch. Tank was her drug and she needed a hit. She jerked the straps of her dress down and pushed it over her hips and ass to puddle around her feet.

His back was still to her and she walked up behind him to press herself against the length of him as she dragged her hands down his chest.

"I'm not feeling this shit no more, Na," Tank said, reaching up to catch her hands before they slipped inside his pants to stroke his dick.

She laughed as she freed her hands and pushed him back against the wall. "Yeah, right," Naeema said, her voice slightly mocking.

He grabbed her hands again.

She looked into his face.

"Where you been the last two weeks, Na?" Tank asked.

Her eyes shifted away from him. "I was—"

"Don't lie to me," he ordered in a hard voice.

I was laid up with a thief who might be the murderer of my son.

"I took a little trip and I shoulda let somebody know. My bad," she said.

Tank still held her hands in his as he stared down into her face. His eyes opened wider in a sudden awareness. "You rawin' that dude?" he asked, his hands tightening on hers.

"I'm not fucking nobody else, Tank," she told him honestly. And she wasn't.

Most of the time she sat around that suite alone waiting on Bas. His situation at home kept him busy and she was

more than fine with that. They were still playing the flirting game. But she knew she had to find out the truth soon
or risk blowing her cover when he did make a play for more
than just flirting. That shit was stressful and she truly could
use a little Tank in her life to make her forget for a while,
the way only he could, physically and emotionally.

He released her hands and brought one of his up to
grip her chin tightly as he tilted her face upward. Her eyes
studied his and she saw the conflict within him rage in the
brown depths. She gasped as her chest radiated with pain.

She loved this dude and he meant more to her than a
fuck.

Tell him.

Something must have shown in her eyes because his face
changed quick as hell.

Tell him.

She shifted her eyes away and he jerked her face to make
her lock her gaze with his again. Tank released her face and
stepped back from her. He looked pained that she was keeping something from him.

He knew her better than anybody else in the world.

He knew her and he loved her. She had no doubts
about that. But she couldn't face telling him the truth and
seeing disappointment in her for not stepping up to her
responsibility or anger at her for lying to him and keeping
her son a secret. She couldn't do it. Especially not right
then, when everything else seemed to be weighing her life
down.

Shaking his head, he reached past her to open the door.
She didn't reach for him. She didn't stop him.

And just like that he was out.

She slid down the wall and pulled her legs to her chest as she rested her head on her knees.

Hours later, Naeema left her bathroom with her damp body in a plush black robe that she'd swiped from Tank when she left him. She picked up her TV from atop the plastic container to remove the lid and pull the smaller container from inside it. With it tucked under her arm, Naeema turned her fan on low and let it rotate, even though the house wasn't hot. Climbing onto the middle of the bed, she set the container before her and opened it.

Right on top was a big eight-by-ten-inch photo of Brandon when he was in first grade. The night she went to Ms. JuJu's to check her—and wound up getting thoroughly checked her damned self—the woman had blessed her with photos of Brandon she'd collected during the years Naeema had missed.

She smiled a little as she touched his face before she set it down and picked up the next. Photo by photo, she saw her son grow year by year until his eighth-grade graduation photo was the last of the pile. "Damn," she swore at the senselessness of it all.

Brandon had been a hustler like his daddy—making it do what it do by whatever means necessary—and although he didn't sling dope like his daddy he started out hustling backward just like him. Wasting a lot of time out of his life appearing busy and gaining not a motherfucking thing but a police record. Ms. JuJu was right. She did her best but Brandon needed somebody wise to the streets to see that hunger in him and kill it.

He needed us.

Getting up from the bed she dug her purse out from beneath the garment bag and pushed aside that same wad of money from the robbery and removed the gun she took from Rico, unloaded it, and set it in the container next to her 9mm. That gun was in her name and it woulda been dumb as hell to kill someone with it. She smiled, thinking of the days when Tank took her to the range and taught her to shoot after he bought it for her.

She felt so alone in her search for her son's killer, and she knew Tank would've had her back if she'd had the balls to reveal her truths to him. He always had been her protector and if he knew she was in the streets of Newark straight running up on fools and being undercover with a gang of thieves, he would've flipped the hell out.

More and more she was feeling like she needed someone to talk to about it. Someone to run shit by to make sure she was seeing everything clearly and not getting caught up in her own head. She opened the file again and pulled out the notebook she kept with it. Under her list of suspects she scratched off Rico, put bold-ass stars next to Red, a question mark next to Vivica, and a circle around Bas. That left Hammer, Nelson, and the dude Brandon stole the cell phone from.

A look at the updated police report would help but she wasn't trying to ask Tank for more help with it. She tried to find more info within his juvie record but that was one of the crimes not listed in his report.

It was time to put more pressure on the Make Money

Crew because Naeema was ready to get it handled and leave them the fuck behind.

Especially Bas.

Her eyes shifted to the Louis Vuitton bag on the floor. He gave it to her along with the clothes inside it. If her fireplace was working she would light the bitch and shove the bag into the flames. Not that she didn't love authentic Louis . . . she just didn't want it from Bas.

She didn't want a damn thing from him but the truth.

But what if he's not in on it? What then?

She pushed away that doubt. It didn't matter.

And the fact that he probably gave her the best pussy licking of her life didn't matter either. "Whoo," she said, fanning herself.

Frowning she instantly felt fucked up for her hope that she didn't have to kill Bas. Good candy licker or not, if he was behind Brandon's death, then she had no mercy for his life.

Naeema looked down at her notepad and tapped her pen directly between the names Hammer and Nelson. *I need to get them alone.*

Hammer the Lover and Nelson the Kid.

She didn't have phone numbers for either one, so even if she came up with a scheme to meet up with them, she would need Vivica to execute it. She wasn't trusting that.

"Man, shit."

She needed a break from thinking. Sometimes when you set a problem on the "shelf" and walked away from it—forgot about it—the answer would just appear. She needed one of those moments big-time.

Shaking her head, she closed the container but kept the

ring on her finger as she replaced the containers and the TV. She turned on the radio, took out her weed pipe, and packed it as she swayed to Faith Evans singing "Soon as I Get Home."

"Baby I'll do what I gotta do," Naeema sang off-key as hell in between inhales and exhales.

BAM-BAM-BAM.

Naeema kept on singing as she raised her foot and stomped back in response to Sarge's nonverbal complaint.

STOMP-STOMP-STOMP.

Humming along to the song, she took another toke from the pipe. "Sing, Faith," she said, feeling herself get emotional as she thought of Tank.

The weed and the music were fucking with her.

Being free from a hotel suite (aka high-end jail cell) was fucking with her.

Living a double life was fucking with her.

Knowing old crabby Sarge in the basement cared about her was fucking with her.

Seeing those pictures of her boy was fucking with her.

She used to be surrounded by friends and partying nonstop but she preferred being a loner—except when everything was coming at her at once.

"Shit," she swore, sitting the dick pipe down and picking up her cell phone to call Tank's phone number.

It rang once and went to voice mail.

Was he serious about pulling away from her? She couldn't believe that his words the other night were nothing more than just that. Actions trumped everything.

There's no way Tank is done. No way in hell.

Naeema opened her robe and lay back on the bed to

spread her legs wide like propellers and used one hand to spread her lips down below and the other to take a picture that she sent to him along with the text COME AND GET IT . . .

She dropped the phone and put her arm over her eyes as she heard gunshots in the distance. She was feeling the weed and getting lost in the slow jams as she lay in the middle of the bed and stroked the soft hairs covering her fat mound.

Good thing too or Bas woulda seen my tat.

Only Tank's dick game was strong enough to make her put his name on it.

She bent her leg and swayed her knee back and forth as she picked her phone up from the bed. Nothing from Tank.

He was her constant.

Even after she left him he was always there when she called. Always.

"I'm not feeling this shit no more, Na."

Did she underestimate him?

She dialed his number again and it just rang endlessly this time.

Naeema called again. And again. And ten times more.

"You have reached an automated voice mail system. Please leave a message after the tone."

Naeema paced back and forth across her living room.

Beeeep.

"Fuck you, La-va-ri-us," she said, using his first name because she knew he hated that. "I ain't the one to play with and you know that. You got me mixed up with them little tricks in the street that's blowing up both your heads. Don't call me no more. And look for them divorce papers."

Naeema ended the call and flung the phone back onto the bed as she continued to pace. It wasn't like Tank not to answer her call. For any reason.

"I'm not feeling this shit no more, Na."

She remembered the night she went with him to the club and he walked up just as some random dude brought her a drink. That led to a discussion of his woman being disrespectful by accepting a drink—which he said was basically an "I want to fuck you" calling card. That discussion led to a heated argument that led to them yelling in the street outside the club and ended with her trying to run him over with her car.

And when she called him an hour later and told him to *come thru* they had the most explosive sex ever on the hood of that same car. He fucked her so fast and furious she thought she saw Tyrese, Ving Rhames, and the ghost of Paul Walker applauding from the sidelines.

But he still had answered her call.

What if something happened to him?

And just like that her anger turned to fear.

She snatched up her cell phone and called his phone again. It went straight to voice mail.

"You have reached an automated voice mail system. Please leave a message after the tone."

Naeema's heart was pounding like crazy.

Beep.

"Tank, it's not like you not to call me back . . . not to answer me. Hell, are you okay? Just call or text me that you're okay. Please?" she said, not caring that she was pleading.

She dropped down onto the bed and covered her face

with both of her hands. She hated not knowing. Who wanted to be angry at someone who was laid up in the hospital or worse? And she hated to worry about his ass if he was just ignoring her calls.

"Lawd Jesus, all these emotions while I'm high," Naeema wailed, throwing her hands up to the ceiling before she flopped back onto the bed.

Knock-knock-knock.

Naeema tilted her head up and looked toward the entrance to the kitchen. She couldn't see any of Sarge but his arm stretched across the doorway as he rapped on the frame. "Yes, Sarge," she said, sitting up and feeling her upper body sway.

Yo, I am soooo faded right now.

She fought the urge to giggle.

"Tank a'ight," he said, never moving past that point behind the wall that kept him from seeing into the living room.

So he called Sarge and not me. Oh, okay.

"Oh, so you *can* answer the phone I bought," she snapped, shooting her anger in Sarge's direction.

Moments later the door to the basement slammed shut. WHAM.

So they both mad at me.

And her mood swung from fear and anxiety back to anger and then nonchalance. *Fuck it.*

Good weed kicking in had that effect.

"And they both will be *the fuck* a'ight," Naeema said, leaning her head back to look up to the ceiling. "O-*kay.*"

Bzzz . . . bzzz . . . bzzz . . .

Naeema picked up her cell but it wasn't vibrating. She

reached in her purse for her burner cell phone. It was Bas. She sucked air between her teeth. "*This* motherfucker," she muttered.

She had freed herself from the hotel suite and told the front desk he checked out before she caught two different taxis to bring her tired black ass home. She was sick of waiting on him to spare her twenty minutes and a phone call every day. She'd meant to shake him up by leaving because she couldn't accomplish a damn thing roaming around a suite all day. It was seriously time to shake shit up. So she ignored his call and lowered the volume to silent before dropping the cell onto the middle of the bed.

Besides, there was no way in hell she could talk to him so high. Naeema wasn't *even* trying to trust that shit.

Naeema stayed up all night enjoying the effects of the weed and then getting smoked up all over again as soon as she felt even an ounce of clarity. At nine p.m. she grabbed her wedding ring from its jewelry box and tossed it into the ashes of the unlit fireplace. She dug through those same ashes ten minutes later to find it and then called and cursed Tank out via his voice mail again. At ten o'clock she watched the news while sitting butt naked on the edge of the bed crying. At eleven she baked a batch of brownies packed with walnuts and then ate damn near the whole pan while she blazed on. At 1:00 a.m. she sang along to the entire *The Miseducation of Lauryn Hill* CD at the top of her lungs as Sarge continued to bang on the ceiling below her. At 3:00 a.m. she walked through every room in the house for no reason at all. And at five she tacked the mug shots or photos of the

Make Money Crew to the wall and pretended to blast shots through the dome of each one. At six she fell face forward onto her bed and slept.

Naeema's eyes fluttered open and with each blink of her eyes her vision, focused on the doorway leading into the kitchen, was now covered with a dark gray blanket. It wasn't definite whether the gray was dinge or not. Raising her head from the bed she looked around the living room. She arched her brow at the photos torn in half on the floor like big-ass pieces of confetti. It took a minute to remember being the one to rip them and throw them up in the air.

Groaning as she backed up off the bed, she smacked her lips and frowned at the nasty taste in her mouth. The combo of morning breath, brownie, and weed had to be worse than dog shit. Naked, with her breasts swaying in countermotion to her hips, Naeema walked to the bathroom. She paused at the entrance and whipped her head to look over her shoulder at the blanket.

Her eyes squinted.

Vaguely she remembered the sound of hammering last night during her adventures. She was quite sure Sarge must have accidentally caught sight of her naked ramblings around the house. "Oh Lord," she drawled, feeling her face flush with embarrassment.

Bzzz . . . bzzz . . . bzzz . . .

She turned and walked back to the bed to search the covers for her vibrating phone. "Hey, Bas," she said into the throwaway phone as she strode back to the bathroom.

"I'm coming to scoop you up."

She paused with her mouth open as she searched for a lie. "I'm at the dentist."

"I wanted to show you my new crib."

"New crib?" she asked. "What happened to that old crib . . . and that old situation?"

He laughed. "I told you I was taking care of that."

"The old folks say even a slow and steady drip can make an impact and the tortoise beat the rabbit and all kinds of shit to back up you slow rolling on this," she teased.

"You comin' to see it or not?"

Naeema bit her bottom lip. *There is no way I'm passing on that.* "Uhmm . . . well, can you pick me up downtown? I should be done in like . . . thirty minutes."

"A'ight. Where?"

"Just come to Broad and Market."

"Bet."

"What you driving?" she asked.

"It'll stand out."

What's next, a fucking helicopter?

"A'ight," she said.

Naeema called for a cab as soon as he hung up and then rushed to the bathroom.

"What city is this?" Naeema asked as she continued to look out the passenger window of the metallic orange BMW Z4 roadster.

Glancing over at him, she saw the look of confusion on his face as he shifted gears. "We're still in Newark," he said, as if that shit should've been obvious to her.

It was her turn to be confused. The long suburban streets lined with either mansions or mini-mansions with manicured lawns and towering trees looked like something on television and nothing like the Newark where she was born and raised. Nothing at all.

She was used to the towering office buildings and the old-looking buildings housing the museums and churches downtown being so different from her hood. And her hood, made up of small homes or three-family apartment buildings, differed from the projects where she used to roam as a wild teenager . . . but this was like nothing she knew existed in the city she loved.

"Yo, you never been out the Central Ward?" Bas asked, smiling over at her.

She might as well have been the naive Queen she played so well for him. She just held up her hand and shrugged before raking her stiletto nails through her black lace-front wig.

"This is the Forest Hill section of Newark, Queen," he said, like he was talking to a toddler or some shit. "It's supposed to be the city's like richest neighborhood . . . on the books anyway. But this is where you'll find all the nice-ass cribs built back in the 1920s by rich white folks. Some of the houses are historic landmarks—that means you can't fuck with 'em, without permission."

Naeema's interest wasn't faked and her eyes shifted to take in each home as Bas drove up the street past them.

"Some of these joints 'round here are worth a million dollars."

"Newark is way bigger than I thought," she admitted.

"Word."

He pulled up alongside a huge stone mansion that sat high above the street on manicured grass and was surrounded by a stone wall topped with black wrought iron. "I used to live there," Bas said.

Naeema turned and looked at him in surprise.

"And I'm going to live there again."

She saw the determination in his eyes even with just the light from the towering streetlight above to illuminate the interior of the car. "What happened?" she asked, deciding to feed her curiosity even though she knew she shouldn't give a flying fuck about his story.

"This my hood," he said, flexing his shoulders. "Little private school kid with the prep school flow. My father was a surgeon."

She stayed silent. *Was?*

"We lived here until I was in college at NYU and my father . . ."

"Your father what, Bas?" Naeema asked softly.

"He passed away," he answered her, suddenly accelerating forward away from the house.

"Wow. I'm sorry, Bas," she said, her eyes on his profile. There was more to the story. Her gut told her that. "That must've been hard on you and your mom."

Bas's jaw clenched. "Don't mention her," he said, his voice hard and angry.

Another order from him on a person he didn't want to discuss.

"Did your moms die too, Bas?" she said, meaning to nudge him. Bait him.

He slammed on the brakes, bringing the car to a stop in the middle of the street. Thankfully it was quiet and no other cars were behind them. He released the wheel and grabbed her chin. She stiffened as the pressure of his fingers deepened.

Just as quickly he smiled and released her. "Yeah, she's dead," he said.

Her heart was pounding and she was ready to reach for the gun she carried in her purse, but she didn't fall back. "What happened to them?"

"Don't fuck with that, Queen," he said, his voice low and filled with warning.

She let it go and settled back against her seat but she set her pocketbook on her lap and patted her piece inside it just in case the motherfucker flipped. Besides, his parents' story really wasn't any of her concern. She was on the hunt for her son's killer and the only thing she could promise Bas was that he would see both his parents sooner than later if he was the one who did it.

11

///

$\mathcal{N}$aeema's eyes widened a little bit in surprise
when she first stepped inside Bas's house. She hadn't really
paid much thought to where he lived, but the small two-
bedroom brick structure with bright yellow shutters didn't
seem to fit him . . . especially after hearing more about his
high-saddity upbringing in a house that looked like a mansion to her. "Where's your situation?" she asked as she took
in the contrast between the outdated house more suited
to an old woman and the leather furnishings and high-end
electronics more suited to him.

"Out of town."

*She stepped in front of a large framed photo of Bas and
a slender dark-skinned woman.* If you didn't know any better, they looked like Mr. and Mrs. Suburban Black America. Only thing missing was the two kids and a fucking dog.
Bunch of bullshit.

"I wouldn't want no other bitch in my spot while I'm
gone," Naeema said, sitting down on the rich-looking brown
leather sofa with metal studs lining the edge.

"I wouldn't worry about the next bitch," he said. "Plus
this ain't her spot. It's mine. This the house I grew up in
before we moved to the other one."

Here we go with his past again. Naeema bit her lip to keep from expressing how little she gave a fuck.

"My dad killed himself."

She was studying her nails but she looked up at him as he dropped that info like it was nothing serious. "Damn. For real?" she said, not sure what to say.

Bas walked into the kitchen and came back with two bottles of Heineken beers. He handed her one. "Getting cheated on, put out the house you love and bust your ass to pay for, not able to see your son and then sued for major alimony after getting lied on was too fucked up for him to deal with, I guess."

Naeema didn't miss how he told the story of his parents without directly mentioning his mother. She looked at him over the bottle as she took a sip. This shit was too weird for words.

"That's when I learned to never trust a bitch."

"You can trust me," she lied.

Bas stepped over her legs to sit down by her on the couch. "For your sake I hope so," he said, glancing over at her as he picked up the remote and turned on the television.

Naeema set her pocketbook beside her and felt a little safer with the heavy weight of the gun leaning against her thigh.

Bzzzz . . .

He glanced at the front of his cell phone before swiping his thumb across the touch screen. "Yo, whaddup," he said, rising to his feet and stepping past Naeema again to walk out of the living room.

First Brandon and now his mother? What was he avoiding by not talking about them?

"Queen, I gotta make a quick run," he said, already striding his tall figure to the door.

"Okay," she said.

The door slammed before she could fully get it out.

Naeema hopped to her feet and walked over to one of the windows flanking the door to watch as the orange soul car pulled down his drive and turned to speed down the street.

She started searching every damn thing, not even sure what she was looking for but not wanting to miss any chances while being in Bas's crib alone. The hallway closet. Every kitchen and drawer in the Suzie Homemaker kitchen. The living room.

She moved quickly but didn't find much to speak of. The only thing she knew for sure was that a woman definitely lived there with him, they kept a clean house, and the house was old but he—no, *they*—liked nice shit.

There were three bedrooms and two were filled with boxes of all kinds of electronics. Bank robberies. Car thefts. Now stolen goods. *This motherfucker dibble and dabble in all kind of shit.*

The last bedroom was the master and she left the door open as she moved past the king-size bed that dominated the room to pull open the bedside dresser drawer. She frowned at the pink rabbit vibrator and lubricant before slamming that shut and coming around the bed to pull open the top drawer of the other.

WHAM.

Oh shit.

Naeema eased the drawer shut at the sound of the front door slamming closed. She looked around like her ass could hide somewhere or leave the room quick enough not to get caught. *Think, Naeema, think.*

And her pocketbook was still in the living room.

Shit, shit, shit.

She quickly pulled off her clothes and lay across the bed in nothing but her lace bra and thong just as his figure filled the doorway.

His eyes searched the room before they rested on her curvy frame half-naked on the bed he shared with another woman.

"Surprise," she said, keeping her voice light and flirty. Just beyond him she could see her pocketbook sitting on the sofa. That motherfucker was of no use to her from there. "You said not to care about the next bitch . . . but I can get up."

"Nah, fuck that," he said, dropping something from his hand onto the bed.

She looked. It was a bag of powder. At least a half ounce. Definitely the kind of weight to be flipped by a small-time dope boy and not snorted. *Fuck around and have a coronary.*

Powder changed Bas and she did not want him snorting that shit with her so far from home and her piece.

She got up on her knees and pressed her hands against the deep curve above her hips. "You can handle all this?" she asked, feeling nervous about the situation she was in.

This man was not to be trusted and she already knew he didn't trust her.

Bas locked his intense eyes on hers as he unzipped his jeans and freed his dick from his boxers and zippers. It was long, thick, and a few shades darker than his medium-brown complexion. "What you think?"

"You straight," she said with a lick of her lips.

Well damn . . .

Naeema had seen and done a lot in her younger days. A one-night stand hadn't been shit for her. And there had been plenty of times the dick was so whack that she faked it or just lay there thinking of other random shit until he was done.

She was attracted to Bas but her wild days were a long time behind her and she didn't want to give up the goodies to Bas. No matter how fine and how promising the dick looked.

And it did look promising.

He stepped up close to the bed and cupped her breasts in his hands like he was weighing them as he stroked her nipples through the sheer lace. "Touch my dick," he said, his voice dark and low and even huskier.

She did, feeling the heat under the smooth skin as she massaged the length of that hard motherfucker from the base covered by thick hairs to the smooth tip. Back and forth.

Very damn promising.

Bas arched his narrow hips forward as he eased her bra strap off her shoulders. "I didn't bring you here for this, you know," he said as he pushed her down onto the bed to lie beside her.

Naeema felt a thrill at his touch but she made her mind go blank. She knew how to do it well. Having a lot of sex didn't mean it was always a lot of good sex. She gripped the back of his head and arched her back as he sucked her nipple through the see-through material but her eyes were open and staring at a long, deep crack in the ceiling.

Bas lightly bit the sheer material between his teeth and worked it down to expose her full breast. She felt his breath blow against it just before he circled her areola around the dark brown edge and up until the tip of his tongue dragged against her nipple.

Naeema's eye shifted to the open closet door even as she felt a slight tremble of pleasure course over her body. *I should have checked this . . . this . . . this . . .*

She gasped and closed her eyes as he shifted to kiss the warm crease under her breast. *Now that's some new shit. Damn.*

Naeema's fingertips lightly dug into his lower back as he sucked the flesh just above the crease. He pulled her thong to the side and stroked her pussy from the moist opening and up to her pounding clit. Her eyes opened in surprise at the feel of his touch. She tried like hell to focus on something—any motherfucking thing—in the room and not the feel of Bas's tongue, lips, and fingers on her body. *Shit.*

She locked her eyes back on the crack in the ceiling but when he shifted his body to pull the cup of the bra down to free her other breast and gather them together to lick at both her nipples at the same damn time, her eyes crossed until everything was a blur.

It was nothing like the fiery chemistry she had with Tank, but there wasn't shit lacking in Bas's skill to get a pussy primed for fucking.

"You like that?" he whispered against her wet nipples.

"Do it again," she said, pulling the edge of his shirt from his jeans to stroke the smooth flesh of his back. Soon she felt tiny bumps under her fingertips as he reacted to her touch.

Bas pressed his dick against her hip as he moved his

tongue back and forth from one aching nipple to the other before sucking one deeply into his mouth.

"Ah," she cried out, cupping the back of his head as she trembled.

Bas moved from licking the crease under her breast to kissing a trail up to the taut nipple to suck it deeply into his mouth before he did the rotation all over again.

Naeema reached for his dick, rubbing her thumb across the smooth tip as she lightly squeezed until he dripped. He rolled away from her and stood at the foot of the bed to snatch his shirt over his head and lower his denims and boxers down to his ankles. She closed her eyes and reached her arms above her head to grip the covers on the bed as she felt his hands on her thighs as he jerked her body to the edge.

That first lick of his tongue against her pussy made her thick thighs come up to cup his ears as she circled her hips up against his mouth.

This motherfucker can eat some pussy so good.

He put some serious attention on her clit until she was so horny that she cupped her own breasts and teased her nipples as she rocked her hips back and forth, bringing her clit against his tongue. "Yesss," she moaned. "Shit. Eat that pussy up. Eat it."

Bas used his finger to open her lips wider and expose all of her swollen clit for him to suck deeply into his mouth. "I'm cumming," she cried out, a fine sheen of sweat covering her body as she opened her eyes wide like she was truly free-falling.

He did not let up.

Naeema's upper body jerked up like she was doing sit-ups as she fought to push against his head to free his mouth from her pussy as she came.

He roughly brushed her hands away and kept on sucking and wildly licking and pushing her straight over the edge until her throat was dry from crying out so much.

Finally, Bas moved away from her quivering body.

She opened her eyes just enough to see him roll a condom onto his dick before he grabbed her legs and pulled them apart wide as he pressed one knee onto the foot of the bed and guided his dick inside her, gripping one of her ass cheeks. She was wet and he slid inside her with one hard thrust of hips.

He looked down at her as he fucked her with long strokes.

They'll run right through a pretty girl like you.

Naeema closed her eyes, not believing it. Not only was she fucking Bas's crazy ass, but she was enjoying it. Her instinct was to fuck back but she wasn't trying to make him fall in love with her pussy and Naeema knew she could make a dude's head be gone. No, she let him do all the work. Her participation back would take shit straight to a whole other level.

Naeema was the type of chick that said fuck it all when she was throwing her pussy game. Nothing was off-limits.

Bas pulled her legs together and then pushed them down until her ankles were by her ears and her ass up in the air. His dick was planted in her pussy as he lay atop the back of her legs and kept thrusting like a fucking horse trying to get across the finish line.

Naeema reached behind him to feel the clench and release of his tight ass as he fucked her good like he had something to prove and nothing to lose, until he moaned and cried out hoarsely with his own nut.

I fucked Bas . . . and I think I liked it. It will be a damn shame to kill him . . . but I can. Fuck that.

He rose up and freed his condom-covered dick from her. Turning, he flopped back on the bed next to her. "Damn that killed me," he said, putting his forearm over his eyes.

Nah, bitch. This gun gon' kill you if you killed my son.

Naeema rolled off the bed and eased her ass out the door to the living room, where she picked up and unzipped her pocketbook. She slipped her hand inside and felt the cold metal as she made sure the safety latch wouldn't keep her from putting it to work.

She walked back in the room, pretending to check her cell phone before she set the pocketbook on the bed between them. She lay down on her side and propped her head on her hand. "Can I ask you something?"

"That's up to you."

"Why don't you like talkin' 'bout dead people?" she asked, trying to outthink his ass.

Bas glanced over at her before closing his eyes again. "Talking about it ain't gon' do shit to bring 'em back."

"No but it helps you remember the good times."

"Maybe there wasn't none," he said, his tone short as fuck.

Say what, motherfucker? Her anger popped off and she slid her hand into the bag and slid her finger against the trigger. "So if I get killed out here you gon' act like I didn't just give you all that bomb-ass pussy?"

"My mama and Brandon ain't never give me no fucking pussy because I know that's who you talking about."

Wait. Hold up. His mama was killed, or did he just mean dead? Naeema focused her thoughts. "Okay, I kinda took Brandon's spot. If something happens to me you just gon' forget about me?" she asked, leaning down to press kisses to his chest to distract him.

"Nobody could take his spot," Bas said, sounding angry.

Naeema's heart was pounding harder than it did when she came. "What did he do to make you mad?" she asked, her eyes calculating as she pressed kisses to the side of his face and massaged his chest.

"Die."

Naeema froze. "Huh?"

Bas sat up on the edge of the bed. "I first met him when I caught his little bad ass throwing rocks at the windows at the church. I was going to go out there to fuck his little ass up but he stood up to me like he was really ready to get at it with me, you know."

She took her finger off the trigger and moved to kneel behind him, pressing her breasts against his back as she wrapped her arms around his neck. She looked off at some indiscernible spot as she visualized Bas's words. Her boy was a tough one. *Just like me.*

"Just a dumb little kid that didn't even know—or give a fuck—that he was going head up with a crazy mother-fucka like me," Bas said, shaking his head. "I kinda took him under my wing. Wanted to look out for him. He would come around damn near every day fuckin' with us. Wanting to get put on to whatever we was getting into."

Naeema closed her eyes behind Bas.

"I felt sorry for the little dude," Bas said, his shoulders getting stiff. "He told me how he didn't even know his mother or father. That shit was really fucking with him, you know?"

She dropped her head as pain radiated across her chest. She had to release long breaths through pursed lips that she kept as quiet as she could, and she fought not to let one damn tear fall. "It hurt you when he got killed," she said softly in revelation.

"Still fucks with me sometimes," he admitted.

"I bet it does," she said, thinking of her own grief.

It was ironic as hell that one of her prime suspects for the murder of her son was claiming to be in just as much pain as she was about the murder. *Ain't that a bitch?*

She felt overwhelmed again, with every shift in her footing. Every end to a road she traveled upon. Every addition or subtraction of a suspect from the list. *I don't know what the fuck I'm doing.*

Bas stood up and walked with his jeans still around his ankles as he left the bedroom. The sex haze was over and she had to stay on point about why she was so deeply entrenched in Bas's world that she just gave up the goodies to him.

But he claims that he almost offered Brandon protection of sorts.

She got up from the bed and straightened her bra and thong on her curves as her thoughts raced like crazy.

Would his protection be enough to keep Red from killing him?

Naeema had just picked up her pocketbook to put on the safety when she heard the toilet flush. Seconds later the sound of the shower spray echoed.

Was he lying? Because the only thing I know for sure is my son's dead.

"Not much fucking protection," she muttered under her breath as she rolled over on the bed to reach and open the bedside dresser's top drawer.

"Yo, Queen!"

She looked over her shoulder toward the bathroom when he hollered to her. With a roll of her eyes she searched through the drawer. Nothing but condoms, some receipts that she checked for anything relevant, and a picture of a couple with a small boy; the woman's face was burned out. She recognized the stone house in the background and knew it was Bas and his parents. In the photo his mother was a dark-skinned slender woman with style. Naeema's brows dipped as she lightly rubbed her thumb across the charred film. *Well, damn.*

Naeema turned the photo over. "Malcolm and Olivia Jones. 1995," she read before she put the photo back.

That shit was so disrespectful, especially knowing her life had been taken.

She closed the drawer and pushed her pocketbook on the floor just under the bed.

"Queen!" Bas called again.

The sex session had loosened the glue of her lace-front wig and she shifted it a bit on her head as she left the bedroom.

"Who the fuck are you?"

Naeema looked up to see the woman from the first picture standing in the open doorway with a Louis Vuitton garment bag over her arm and an evil look in her eye. *See, all this bullshit is so motherfucking extra.*

Naeema shrugged and sat her still damp ass on their leather sofa and crossed her leg as she used the pointed tip of one nail to clean under the others.

WHAM!

Naeema heard the front door slam closed just as the sound of the shower got louder. Bas's boo was striding across the room just as he stepped into the living room, butt naked and still sudsy and wet from the shower. His eyes went from Naeema straight chilling on the sofa while his boo was coming straight for him with one hand already raised to slap the fuck out of him.

"Don't start nothing you can't finish, Kelly," Bas warned.

"How could you, Sebastian?" she screeched as she slapped his face.

WHAP.

Sebastian?

Naeema winced as he gripped her around the neck and lifted her up off her feet. It was mad crazy for him to get mad at her for his ass getting caught. And she felt bad for the girl too, but sympathetic chick wasn't the role she was there to play and she didn't want to be a witness to shit just in case he did something to cause the police to be called. "Excuse me," she said, as she moved past them to walk into the bedroom and pull on her clothes.

"You tried to send me out of town to bring this ghetto trick in our home, Sebastian?"

Hold up. What?

Naeema peeked her head out the door. Bas had her pressed up against the wall with her hands held in one of his. Tears streamed down her eyes. "Don't start nothing with me you can't finish, Kelly," she said, playing her role even though she could see the pain and betrayal in the woman's eyes.

"Oh, go straight to hell," Kelly snapped.

Naeema rolled her eyes and walked back into the bedroom. She sat down on the bed and slipped on her shoes before she pulled her cell phone out of her pocketbook. Using the GPS, she pulled up the address and then the nearest cab company. She was making her request when she heard shit hitting the wall and then something crashing and breaking. *I am tapping out on this bullshit.*

Her foot sent the bag of cocaine spiraling across the floor. She walked over to pick it up and then slid it into her purse. *The last thing that fool needs is to get high and hurt that damn girl.*

She left the bedroom and acted like she didn't see them sprawled across the couch fighting. Putting their drama behind her, Naeema walked out of the house to wait on the sidewalk for her cab headed back to her side of the city.

Bzzz . . . Bzzz . . . Bzzz . . .

Naeema didn't bother to pick up her vibrating cell phone. She already knew it was Bas calling. Between him and Vivica, her burner cell phone had been going off all day since she left him and his drama behind. *Handle your handle, bruh . . .*

She wasn't ignoring him because she was mad or jealous or hurt. Not at all. But she was glad for him and Vivica to think otherwise.

Naeema tilted her chin up and released a thick stream of smoke through her pursed lips as she lay in the middle of her bed. She didn't know if there was enough cannabis planted in the world to relax and calm her anxiety.

A simple internet search had revealed more about Bas's story than she ever thought she wanted to know.

Not only had his father killed himself but he had murdered his wife as well. Their story had been prominent in the news and the bloody crime scene was one of the reasons the house had sat empty for years.

No wonder Bas's ass is so damn serious.

But that's not all that dominated her thoughts and fucked up her head space. For months she'd been so sure that Bas was behind Brandon's murder and now that belief was shakier than a motherfucker. To her surprise she welcomed that idea.

Did she have feelings for Bas? And if she did, what did that mean about all of the love she *knew* she had for Tank?

"It's time to bring this undercover shit to an end," she said, closing her eyes as she shook her head at the shame of it all.

$\mathcal{N}$aeema was at the barber shop sitting in her chair and looking out the window at all the comings and goings of the liquor store next door and trying to ignore the usual loud and rowdy politicking of the shop when she spotted Tank on his motorcycle pulling into the parking lot. She tapped her fingernail against her teeth as she tried to make out his sudden reappearance in her life. Climbing from the chair, she smoothed her hands down her hips in the low-riding skinny jeans she wore with a white shirt tied at the bottom above her belly button and the top buttons left open to expose her smooth cleavage.

She had just exited the shop as he climbed off his Harley looking finer than ever in a V-neck gray tee and gray jeans. Her heart was pounding like crazy and she knew there would never be another man that she loved like she loved him.

He removed his helmet and eyed her from her freshly shaven head down to the hot-pink polish on her toes in her high-heeled sandals. "What are you up to, Naeema?" Tank asked, his voice hard and his stare even harder.

He was pissed.

She froze as she was about to lean in and kiss his smooth cheek. "Well, damn, hello to you too," she snapped.

"When you start lying to me?" he asked with a frown.

Naeema forced herself not to flinch or look away but she said not one word. He was shitting her.

"You can tell me *anything*. You can ask me for *anything*," Tank told her as he stepped forward to stand closer to her.

Naeema closed her eyes and released a breath as she let the closeness of his presence wash over her, energize her, and tantalize her. Turn her the fuck on. "Tank—"

He pointed his finger against her chest. "You are my wife, and I don't give a fuck if we never live in the same house again, there is never a time you can't put your burdens on my back for me to carry."

The thing was, he didn't have to tell her that because she already knew it. If there was nothing else in life she could depend on, she knew that Tank would *always* have her back.

Naeema glanced down the street to break their gaze. "What's this about, Tank?" she asked, looking back at him.

"Your son."

She felt her breath catch in her chest as she licked her lips and crossed her arms over her ample chest and shifted her stance. Tears welled up and she tried—and failed—to smile through the sadness that washed over her. "I, uhm . . . I didn't . . . I didn't know how to tell you about him," she admitted, her voice soft as she released the lie and the secret that she had kept from so many people over the years.

Tank reached out to swipe away a tear from her cheek with his thumb.

"I never knew him," she said, closing her eyes to drift back to a moment she had revisited so many times in the days after learning of his death. "I ain't laid eyes on him since I gave him away."

"You could have told me, Na," he insisted.

"Who the fuck wants to tell their husband—who wants you to have a child—that you had one and gave it away and you don't think it's right to have another because you didn't do right by that one," Naeema said, feeling pain in her chest like her heart was truly breaking. "You don't get do-overs with being a mother, Tank. I had my chance and I fucked it up because I wanted to rip and run."

"Go get your stuff," Tank said, turning to climb back onto his Harley. He pulled a spare helmet from the rigid saddle-bags on either side of the rear tire and patted the passenger seat. "Come ride wit' me."

Naeema paused for just a few seconds. She needed to work and make up the money she lost during the two weeks she spent at that hotel waiting on Bas. The money from the robbery was still untouched and she wasn't accepting anything from Tank.

Still, she turned and went inside, grabbing her shades and fake Michael Kors bag. "Tell Derek I had to leave early, but I'll be in tomorrow," she said to Loc, the second-in-command when Derek was not in the shop.

"Everything a'ight, Naeema?" he asked, his eyes moving past her to Tank awaiting her outside.

She smiled at the older dude with the bald head who resembled a smaller version of Suge Knight. Everyone knew Tank was her husband but they also knew they weren't together anymore. "I'm good," she said, noticing the sudden quiet in the normally noisy surroundings. All eyes were on them. These fellas were her boys. Her brothas. They were concerned about her being missing in action a lot.

That made her tear up. Sometimes she needed a reminder

that she wasn't as alone as she felt in the world. Turning, she left the shop before she started straight bawling. She made sure her own bike was locked and secured before she pulled the helmet on, pushed her bag into the other saddlebag, and climbed onto the passenger seat behind him. At first she reached behind her to hold the bar running along the top of the backrest, but looking at the wide expanse of Tank's back, she wanted to feel his strength. She leaned forward and wrapped her arms around his waist.

Naeema didn't give a care about where Tank was taking her as they sped through the streets. She just closed her eyes and enjoyed the ride. It wasn't until he pulled to a stop that she opened her eyes and looked around her. She smiled at the royal-blue canopy of the house on the corner of South Eighteenth Street and Madison Avenue that housed D & J Country Cooking, or Dick and Judy's as everyone called it.

Best soul food in the city, hands down.

Naeema's stomach grumbled at the smell of food in the air as they climbed off the motorcycle. "How you know I needed some good food in my life?" she asked as they walked to the corner entrance.

Tank just laughed as he opened the screen door for her. "I ain't forgot you can't cook," he teased her.

"TV dinners don't count?"

"Hell no."

Dick and Judy's wasn't big. There were just four small booths and a counter with seats, but what it lacked in size it more than made up for in good down-home cooking. They served everything from homemade biscuits to oxtails with everything in between and all the Southern sides a mouth could water for. The heat from the kitchen filled the restaurant and made you feel like you were in the South during a heat wave. The only thing it was missing was a jukebox playing good hole-in-the-wall music like Tyrone Davis and Marvin Sease.

She ordered lemonade and smothered pork chops. Tank got sweet tea and the oxtails. Their meals came with white rice and they decided to split a side of macaroni and cheese.

When the waitress left with their order, Tank looked at Naeema across the table. "I wouldn't have judged a decision you made when you was just a kid, Na," he said, his eyes serious.

She glanced out the window at the large yellow apartment building across the street. "Plenty of teenagers raise their kids, Tank," she said. "I brought him into the world, somebody else raised him, and some scroungy motherfucker took him out."

"And you're trying to find out who killed him."

She shifted her eyes back to him. "How'd you find out he's my son?" she said, purposefully avoiding his comment.

He shrugged one broad shoulder. "'I have my ways. You was too caught up in his murder, and that last night we spent together, when you was waking up in dreams yelling out his name and shit, I decided to see just what was going on. Since you wouldn't tell me."

She sat back as their drinks were set before them.

"Anything else you want to tell me, Na?" he asked.

She shook her head and opened the straw to slide into her lemonade.

"Naeema."

She locked eyes with his.

Tank pressed his elbows on the top of the table and

leaned in toward her. "Let the police handle this before you get yourself into a situation you can't get yourself out of."

Situation?

Naeema shook her head at an image of Bas's tongue licking her nipples. Guilt flooded her for fucking Bas, but she pushed that aside because she knew Tank *had to be* fucking somebody. His sexual appetite was ferocious. It was nothing for them to go at it two or three times a day and he stayed ready. There was no way in hell he was running around without pussy on deck.

Shaking her head again, she ran her hands over her closely shaven head. "Tank, stop lecturing me," she said, sounding exhausted.

"Stop lying to me, yo," Tank countered.

"I know how to take care of myself."

He captured both her knees between his under the table. "Because I taught you . . . and you're not ready to be out here playing vigilante or Foxy Brown or some shit. This real life."

"Foxy Brown is a bad bitch," Naeema said, thinking of the sexy heroine from one of those 1970s blaxploitation films her grandfather used to watch all the time.

"You do know I mean the chick from the movie and not the rapper, right?"

She rolled her eyes and looked up as the waitress brought their steaming hot plates of food. "Stop. Playing," Naeema said, moving her glass out of the way.

"That report I gave you isn't up-to-date," he said, not even glancing down at his food before him. "And the info that's in there now I wouldn't give to you knowing you on the manhunt for a killer like you're a marshal or some shit."

Naeema dropped her fork and the chunk of pork chop on it. "What's in it?" she asked, her mind already spinning with the possibilities.

"Na—"

"What's in it?" she repeated, her voice cold as she stared down at some spot on the table that she never really focused on. She was trying like hell not to flip on Tank's ass in public. The more he held out, the more the countdown continued. Slow but steady.

Tank picked up his fork.

Naeema yanked his plate from in front of him.

Tank sat up straight and yanked it back, his face lined with annoyance.

"He was my son and I ain't never did shit for him," she stressed.

"And what purpose would dying for him serve?"

Naeema pressed her hand to her chest as she spoke. "I just want to know what happened to him," she said, switching gears on him.

Tank sat back in his seat and eyed her. "They were looking into a cell phone grab your son did a few weeks before his death," he said. "But the body of the dude who owned the cell phone has been in the morgue unidentified since about a week after the robbery."

One less motherfucker to hunt for. Good.

"What else?" she asked.

"Nothing else. Not yet," he said.

Bullshit.

Naeema focused on her food even though her appetite was gone.

"At least let me help you, Na," Tank said.

She took a bite of the macaroni and cheese. "I got something that needs your help," she said, meaning to flirt to get him off her trail.

Tank swiped at his mouth with his napkin. "I didn't come to see you about that."

"So you don't want it no more?" she asked, her eyes on him as she chewed slowly.

"I'll always want it . . . but I don't need it, yo," Tank's eyes dipped to her cleavage exposed by her shirt.

"And it don't need you," she shot back smooth as hell. *Dicks are a dime a dozen.*

Naeema looked away as she drifted back to the moments of her ass high in the air as Bas tore the pussy up.

"Here," he said.

She looked over at him as he held his palm out with a bulky gold ring in a small plastic bag.

"It's your— It's Brandon's," Tank explained.

Naeema gasped a little as she took it and pushed the bag from the plastic. She slid it onto her index finger and held up her hand. It was real gold but the diamonds were fake. Not even cubic zirconia. More like tiny rhinestones or some shit. It couldn't have cost more than fifty dollars, but for a fourteen-year-old kid with no ends that must've seemed like a million bucks.

"It was in evidence."

She dropped her head and pressed her lips to it, feeling just a little bit closer to the child she'd selfishly left behind. "I thought I had time to fix shit," she admitted, her voice broken.

Tank reached across the table and stroked her free hand with his thumb.

She met his eyes. "Thank you so much. I don't even deserve anything of his. But thank you."

"Stop beatin' yourself up, yo. You gave birth to him. You chose to carry him and give him life and that ain't no little thing, Na. For real, yo," Tank said. "His father ain't even done that."

Naeema looked up. "You know who his father is?" she asked, surprised.

Tank shook his head. "Nah. I just assumed if you gave him up for adoption, that fool wasn't no help to you."

Naeema forced a smiled that instead came off sad. "No he wasn't. I ain't laid eyes on that motherfucka since before the baby was born."

She took a deep breath and for the first time ever told someone else about the pain and shame she felt that night she was put out on the street pregnant and broke. It felt like a weight off her soul to speak on her struggles being homeless and pregnant.

She wasn't surprised to see the anger in Tank's eyes.

"Chance Mack, huh?" he asked, already pulling his iPhone from his pocket and walking out of the luncheonette.

Naeema didn't bother to stop him. She had enough battles to fight and was fine with Tank taking on that one. What Chance and his mother/father did to her was fucked up.

She looked down at the ring. If it was in the police's possession, then he was wearing it the night he was killed. She didn't even realize she was crying until the tears blurred her vision.

Naeema knew she had to finish what she started and find her son's killer. She was determined to question Hammer and Nelson once and for all but she knew she couldn't make a sudden reappearance without getting shit straight with Bas first.

Swiping away her tears, Naeema reached for the burner cell in her pocketbook and powered it on. She ignored the alert that she had a dozen or more voice mail messages on the five-dollar phone. She pulled up Bas in her contact info and dialed his number while she looked out through the mesh of the screen door at Tank's imposing figure pacing back and forth on the street as he talked on the phone.

"So you all right now, Queen?"

"You called me?" she said, surprised that the sound of his voice in her ear excited her.

"You got jokes?"

She used her thumb to circle the ring around her index finger. "That hot-ass mess that went down with your *situation* was pretty fucking funny, dude."

"I didn't want to hurt her like that," Bas said, sounding less than pleased.

"Or me either, right?" she asked, faking like she was upset.

"You know that."

"No, I don't. I told you I don't like sharing dick, Bas," Naeema said.

"You not."

"So what happened?" Naeema took a bite of her food.

"She left. I didn't stop her . . . but I wish I did because she took my powder."

"No she didn't," Naeema admitted around a mouthful of mac and cheese.

The line went silent.

"I didn't know you fucked with blow," he said.

"I don't. I just didn't want it to hype up an already

fucked-up situation, you know?" she said, her eyes zoned in on Tank.

"I need that package."

"Don't need it. Want it," she said in between bites of food. *Lawd, these people can cook.*

"Don't *fuck* with me about it," Bas said, his voice filled with all kinds of threats.

And just like that all the niceties were shot. "My bad," she said.

"Hold on to that until I get back in town."

She watched Tank end his call and turn to walk back inside Dick & Judy's. "When will you be back?"

The screen door opened and slammed closed.

"Next week sometime."

"Can I holla at you when you get back?" she asked.

"We gon' do more than that," Bas promised.

Not if I wrap this shit up before then.

Tank already had her dick-struck and mind-fucked. She didn't need another dude—especially a coke-sniffing thief—fucking with her emotions. She was ready to slip back into her life and a world where Bas Jones did not even exist.

"My birthday is next week, so bring me back something good," she lied.

"What you want?"

"Let me call you right back," she said before snapping the plastic phone closed and silencing the ringer.

Tank reclaimed his seat and began shoveling into his food.

"Did you find him?" Naeema asked.

"Not yet."

"And what do you plan to do with him when you do?"

He didn't answer her.

Naeema left it the fuck alone. Tank was cool as hell as long as he wasn't crossed. Chance Mack didn't know it yet but he'd just made the shit list for something he did fourteen years ago. *Fuck him.*

They ate their food in silence. Naeema spent most of her time looking out the window at the traffic-free street and wondering what Tank really thought about her now that he knew the truth about Brandon.

"Do I need to check if those dudes Brandon was friends with are still alive?" Tank asked suddenly.

Naeema stiffened and she avoided his all too knowing eyes. "I'm not a killer, Tank."

"Oh, you not?"

Naeema closed her eyes as a vision of a bloodied body with a neck slashed by a razor blade flashed. A scene from her past. She blinked and shook her head before she locked eyes with him. "That was different," she said, angry that he'd brought up a secret she shared with him.

"Murder is murder."

That is a story for another time.

"Take me back to the barbershop," she said, jumping to her feet and damn near flipping her plate.

"Sit down, Na," he said, calm as hell as he kept on eating his food.

"Or?" she snapped, her temper turned up.

"*Or* . . . sit down, Na," Tank repeated like he was speaking to a child.

Ignoring his demand, she crossed her arms over her chest and turned to lean against the frame of the window as she looked out of it.

Tank just chuckled at her.

"Don't bring it up again," she said, glancing back at him over her shoulder.

He said nothing.

Looking back at the window, Naeema was surprised to see a black SUV with the darkest tint ever on its windows pull up and park on the street right outside the large bay window.

Tank's cell phone began ringing just as the rear doors of the SUV opened. She recognized the damn near seven-foot dude who climbed out on the street side. He was Grip and he worked for Tank doing security. She squinted her eyes as someone else tried to leave the vehicle but Grip reached in one strong arm and mushed whoever it was before solidly closing the door.

Naeema took a guess.

"You have to let it go, Na," Tank said, as he pulled out his phone.

"Says the man who just had my babyfather, who I haven't seen in fourteen years, brought to me."

Tank stood up and pulled a thick wad of money from his pocket. He unpeeled a fifty-dollar bill and dropped it onto the table. "Let's ride."

Naeema followed Tank out of the luncheonette. She couldn't believe she was about to come face-to-face with the man who once was the boy who broke her heart. *My baby-father.*

She glanced at Tank as they walked up to the SUV. *I wonder what the fuck goin' thru his head.*

Grip stepped aside as Tank opened the rear passenger door and motioned for her to step forward. She did.

"Naeema . . . you behind this bullshit move right here?"

She looked into the face of Chance and felt none of the love her young and dumb ass *thought* she had for him back in the day. Life had tapped his ass a little bit because he looked way older than his twenty-nine years. His eyes were yellow and glassy and she knew some addiction had a grip on him. "It don't come close to that bullshit move you and your fucked-in-the-head-ass mama pulled on me that night," she said, feeling her anger slowly get stoked.

"Don't talk about my mother—"

Her lips became a thin line as she reached in and slapped him two times. Fast and hard.

WHAP-WHAP.

"Yo, *fuck* that bitch," Naeema said, her tone snide as fuck.

"You dumb ho," he roared as he lunged for her.

Tank reached right in, smooth as hell, and gripped him around the neck with one strong hand.

Naeema turned and strode over to the motorcycle. With jerky motions only hinting at her rage, she unzipped her bag and removed the gun, quickly prepping it to be shot without hesitation. She quickly walked back to the truck.

Grip got the fuck out of the way.

Naeema reached past Tank to press the barrel to Chance's head. "Call me another, motherfucker. Huh? Huh? I dare you."

"Na," Tank said.

Chance's eyes got so big that there seemed to be nothing but white.

Naeema nudged him with the gun, her finger steady on the trigger. "This ain't the pregnant kid you and your dickless mother threw on the street, you slack-ass motherfucker. So I dare you to call me another one."

Chance swallowed hard past Tank's hand holding his neck in a vise.

He was between a rock and a hard place.

Naeema didn't give a fuck.

"There were times I was so fuckin' hungry but *so broke* that I started to eat food out the damn garbage because you found a new bitch and didn't want to lay family no more." A tear raced down Naeema's cheek as her eyes glittered brightly with her anger.

She gritted her teeth and pressed the gun against his head so hard that it tilted back against the seat. "Do you know our son is dead? Huh? And . . . and . . . and I oughta do you a favor and kill your bitch ass. Then you can lay eyes on your seed for the first time on the other side."

Her hand began to tremble as his eyes went dull.

His shock at the news wasn't nearly enough.

"Lie now and say he wasn't yours, motherfucker," she said in a whisper as she fought the urge to shoot him and leave Tank to clear away his dead body.

"Naeema," Chance said, "I—"

She flipped the gun, pushed the safety latch, and started straight pummeling his face and head with the butt of the gun. She even climbed up onto the seat to really nail his ass good. Not even the sight of his blood seeping from breaks in his skin stopped her. Not even the loud crack of whatever bone she fractured.

Tank wrapped an arm around her waist and jerked her out of the vehicle so roughly that her shoulder slammed against the frame. "That's enough, Na," he said, holding her body close to his.

She let her head fall onto his shoulder and her hands drop to her side.

"It's okay," he kept whispering to her even as someone took the bloody gun from her.

Naeema just gave in to all the emotions inside of her, sinking below that now all too familiar wave as she cried and gave in to his strength.

13

One week later

BAM-BAM-BAM.

Naeema was holding paint swatches up against the flowery wallpaper of the living room when a sudden loud noise from the kitchen scared her. She turned and crossed the room to push past the blanket covering the opening to the kitchen. She leaned in the door frame and looked down at Sarge hammering on a door.

He barely spared her a glance.

BAM-BAM.

"This will look better than that blanket," he said.

She saw him pause with the hammer ready to strike more blows. He was giving her a moment to protest. "It sure will, Sarge," she agreed.

BAM-BAM-BAM.

Naeema didn't exactly know which room he borrowed the door from or if it would be a good fit, but she let him roll with it. *It couldn't be any worse than the semipro job on the front door. So fuck it.*

"Are all your kids alive, Sarge?" she asked, grabbing one

of the chairs that used to surround the table she'd shot to smithereens while playing target practice with the photos of the MMC. She took a seat and crossed her legs in the hot-pink yoga pants she was wearing with a matching long-sleeved jacket that zipped to the neck.

"No," he said, grabbing the counter with one hand and standing with effort. "Both of 'em gone on before me."

She stayed silent. The thing about Sarge was, if he felt like going deeper about a topic then he just did, but if he had nothing else to say on a subject then a dozen questions or comments wouldn't change his mind.

"Both of 'em overdosed," he said, lifting the door to lean next to the opening. He removed the blanket, and light from the living room flooded the kitchen. "I wasn't here enough for them. Off saving the world and no one around to save my kids."

Naeema lifted her leg to press her foot against the seat as she rested her chin on her knee and wrapped her arms around her legs.

"Once I came back from all that shit in Vietnam, I was so fucked up I didn't want them to see me that way." Sarge stopped and stared off into the distance. "Seen way more shit than I shoulda."

"Do you think being around would have changed the kind of people they became?" she asked, risking him shutting down and quieting up.

He looked over at her. "I don't know that about mine . . . and neither do you about yours, Naeema," he said, before turning to align the door with the frame.

So Sarge knew.

Naeema wasn't surprised. There wasn't much he could miss just one floor down and barely ever venturing outside.

"Let it go, gal," he said, glancing back over one of his bent shoulders at her.

"Tank said the same thing."

Sarge frowned. "You tell him?"

She shook her head. "You?"

"Ain't my business to tell."

She believed him. Releasing a heavy breath, she rose and walked across the kitchen to the back door.

"Bullets don't care who they kill, Naeema," he said sharply.

She paused for a second but she continued out the door, closing it softly behind her.

I'm in too deep.

Tank was confident she was off the trail of her son's killer, because she had been hanging around home a lot this week when she wasn't working. He was wrong as hell. Bas got back in town that night and she had spoken to him every day that week getting back in his good graces after snubbing him. He was even planning to take her out for dinner for her fake birthday. She convinced him to include the crew. It was enough of the pussyfooting, because she wasn't giving up any more pussy to Bas. She had every intention of catching Hammer and Nelson alone and straight up asking them about Brandon. Plus she wanted to know if they were up on Vivica using him to pay Red back for his cheating. If they knew Red knew it too. *That brick head motherfucker did it.*

Was she scared of Red? Without a gun? Hell yeah. But a gun would equalize shit. She just wasn't sure if she was going to take Vivica the fuck out too for instigating the bullshit.

Naeema pulled her gold chain from inside her fitted

jacket and looked down at her son's ring hanging from it as she crossed the yard to her motorcycle. *I done sacrificed too much to let this shit ride now. I'm too fucking close. I can feel that shit.*

She dropped the chain back inside her jacket and opened the doors to her garage. She knocked the kickstand up with her foot and climbed onto the black leather seat, loving the feel of the entire bike vibrating between her thick thighs as she turned the key in the ignition. Rolling across the small backyard and then down the paved driveway, Naeema looked to the right to check for oncoming traffic. "Oh shit," she exclaimed behind the visor of her pink helmet when she spotted her neighbor Coko passed out on her front porch. *This girl keep chasing death.*

Naeema hopped off the motorcycle and turned the key in the ignition all the way to the left to lock the wheels before she rushed down the street and took the steps two at a time to bend down next to Coko. She frowned at the fresh scent of vomit blending with her body odor. "You okay?" she asked, lightly shaking her shoulders.

No response.

Naeema turned her over onto her back and she went cold at the woman's eyes rolled up into her head and her tongue sticking out of the side of her mouth as she drooled heavily. "Shit," she swore, unzipping her jacket and snatching it off to ball it up under Coko's head.

Naeema stepped over her to enter her house. "Phone, phone, phone," she said, wishing she had brought her cell and not wanting to leave her alone too long.

When she turned and entered the living room, that stench that clung to Coko's body filled the air. The red and black decor fucked her head up for a second. The room looked like the pit of hell, with its black walls and floors and red furnishings, along with an eerie red light beaming from the lamp. She spotted a cordless phone on a low round table next to a bright bloodred leather sofa, but when she saw the back and battery were missing, she threw that useless motherfucker against the wall.

She was just turning in a circle in the middle of the room among the clothes and papers scattered everywhere when she spotted a cell phone on the mantel of the black-painted fireplace. She ignored the open baggie of off-white powder next to it, knowing it was heroin.

She called 911.

Naeema assumed most people fucked with pills or coke. Pedope, the cheaper form of heroin, was what everyone was sniffing back in the 1990s. *Heroin? Who the fuck wanted to shit up themselves if they couldn't cop a hit soon enough? Child, please . . .*

Walking back onto the porch, she was shocked to see Coko struggling to rise to her feet. Naeema stepped forward to help her, holding her breath to keep from inhaling her scent.

"What the fuck you doin' in my house?" Coko asked, her words slurring.

"What the fuck you doin' passed out on your porch?' Naeema shot back, sick of her attitude every time she tried to help.

Coko leaned against her heavily and Naeema had to damn near drag her inside the house and across the black floor to let her body slide down onto the sofa. "I called an ambulance," she told her.

"I don't need no ambulance," Coko snapped as she

scratched at her skin with nails that needed a fill-in bad. She had at least an inch of new growth.

"Yes the fuck you do and a bath, like . . . yo," Naeema said, walking over to the window to unlock and open the bitch wide.

"Bitch . . . fuck you," Coko said, covering her face with her hands seconds before she turned her head and threw up on the floor.

Naeema cringed. "That shit killing you," she said, shaking her head.

Coko wiped her mouth with the back of her hand. "I don't give a fuck if I die," she said, closing her eyes.

That's a fucked-up place to be.

"They killed the man I loved."

Keno wasn't no angel.

"My bitch left me."

That freaky bitch needed to go.

"My moms act like I should kiss her ass for paying my bills."

I did wonder how a junky paid a mortgage.

"But she stole my son, so *fuck* that and fuck *her*."

Naeema walked across the living room, being sure to miss the vomit, and looked first before she entered the kitchen. The red, white, and black decorations continued, but you could barely tell from how nasty it was. The sink and kitchen table were filled with dirty dishes and the garbage can was overflowing. Roaches were everywhere like she loved their asses. The floor hadn't been mopped in weeks— maybe even months.

She searched like hell for a clean glass and opened the freezer for ice. Wasn't a damn thing popping in *that* bitch but ice.

She poured her a glass of water and grabbed a stiff dish towel then headed back to the living room. She pushed the glass into Coko's hand and covered the throw-up the best she could with the towel.

"Your son worth you getting it together," Naeema said, looking down at her as fresh wind finally blew through the sheer black and red curtains at the window.

Water spilled out of the glass as Coko struggled to sit up on the sofa. "What the fuck you know?" she asked, before taking a deep sip of it.

I know you need to wash your ass, Naeema thought, eyeing the dirt under her nails and on the bottom of her feet. *This glass probably the only water her ass been around in a minute.*

"I know I'm about to tell you something that if you pop off at the mouth I will pretty much fuck you up," Naeema said.

Coko leaned back and looked her up and down with her yellowy eyes.

"My son was killed," Naeema said and then gave her face that was filled with *Now fuck with it.*

Coko just sipped her water.

"Look, I didn't raise him and now I don't have a chance to get to know him," Naeema told her, reaching up to grip the ring dangling from the end of her chain. "It's the worst feeling . . . so if you can pull your shit together and get your son, you should."

The sounds of the siren in the distance filled their silence.

"Trust me, I ain't judging you. I'm not in no position to look down on you about your son," Naeema added.

Coko eyed her over the rim of the glass. "Sure don't fucking sound like it," she said with a twist of her mouth.

No, this bitch didn't?

"Keep sucking random dicks and fucking for dope, bitch. Live your life," Naeema said before she reached over and knocked the small bag of heroin from the mantel to spill onto the floor.

Coko threw the glass at Naeema. It flew barely a foot before it dropped onto the floor and crashed. She was too weak to do any better.

Naeema just waved her hand, dismissing her, before she turned.

"I'm sorry."

Naeema was at the open front door. She stopped at Coko's softly spoken words. The red lights from the ambulance reflected in her eyes as it double-parked in front of Coko's house.

"I'm sick of living like this," she said.

The EMTs hopped out of the ambulance and came up the stairs just as she heard Coko vomit again behind her. "She's inside. She's up now but she's real weak. I found her passed out and damn near foaming at the mouth," she told a thin Puerto Rican dude with curly black hair.

Naeema started down the stairs as they rushed inside but she stopped. *This smart-mouth bitch don't deserve no help.*

She stood there having an inner battle while neighbors either peeked out the window or boldly walked down the street to see up close what was going on.

But her son deserves a mother—his mother—just like mine did.

Turning, she jogged back up the stairs and stood just outside her living room as they ran tests on her. "You want me to call your mother?"

Coko looked up at her and shook her head. "She would use it against me with my son," she said, tears forming in her eyes as she hung her head. "I don't have nobody."

Naeema remembered saying those same words to herself many a night when she was pregnant and homeless. It was the worst feeling in the world.

When the EMTs loaded Coko into the back of the ambulance on a stretcher, Naeema made sure her door was locked and pushed her motorcycle back into the garage before she climbed in the back with her for the ride to the hospital.

Naeema had been at the hospital all morning and early into the afternoon with Coko before she finally left and made her way home. Coko was admitted to the psychiatric ward for them to begin her detox before she entered a rehab facility. Getting clean off drugs was tough. Getting clean off heroin was one of the toughest. Naeema sent prayers up for her recovery.

She smiled at seeing the door now filling the entrance to the kitchen. As she undressed she walked across the room to push it open. "Well, I'll be damned, Sarge," she said when it swung back and forth smoothly. "Gotta find some other shit for him to do 'round here."

Naeema stepped out of her pants, leaving them on the floor, as she sat on the edge of her unmade bed and pulled the original wad of stolen cash from her bag. She rolled it between her fingers and tossed it up into the air to catch. *If*

Bas was innocent, did that take the stain of my son's blood off of it?

She dropped it back into her bag atop the gun she'd taken from Rico, then she removed her lingerie and walked into the bathroom for a hot shower. She stood under the spray, letting the water rain down on her head as she wiped her face with her hands.

Naeema had a craving and it was really fucking with her.

She'd been fighting it since the day before and it hadn't edged off yet. "Shit," she swore, tilting her head back so that the water flowed down her neck and onto her breasts.

Her nipples hardened.

She turned and pressed her head against the wall, letting the water slide down her back and onto the rounded top of her buttocks. *He got me fucked up.*

She had dick on the brain. One dick especially. It felt like no matter what she tried to do, there was a male voice in her ear taunting her: *"Come get this dick. Come get this dick. Come get this dick.*

She wanted it. She needed it.

Naeema turned again in the shower and reached for her lavender bathing gloves and her bottle of body wash, but the feel of the slick soap against her body wasn't doing shit to cool it down. *Don't call. Don't call. Fuck that.*

There was so much other shit she could be thinking about besides the feel of his dick inside her as she came. But there it was.

Come get this dick. Come get this dick. Come get this dick.

Big, long, hard, curving, throbbing dick.

She leaned forward to cool down the water some and rush through the rest of her shower. Grabbing a towel, she dried off and wrapped it as tightly as she could around her body as she stared at her reflection in the steam-covered mirror.

Go get it.

She shook her head.

Leaving the bathroom, Naeema padded into the living room and used the remote to turn on the television. She settled on a marathon of *I (Almost) Got Away with It* on the ID channel. She was determined to get dick off her brain.

It didn't work.

She dug around in her Michael Kors for the baggie of Canna Sutra. As she prepped her pipe, she smiled at the label on the bag. "Good for bronchial dilation," she said. Naeema didn't have asthma and she doubted any of her contact's clients did. Although the first medicinal weed shop opened in Jersey in 2012, her connect Mook still brought his shit straight from a shop in Los Angeles.

"California . . . knows how to party," she sang the chorus from 2Pac's "California Love."

As she blazed Naeema lifted the TV just long enough to open the container and pull out her "Brandon file" to look through for the hundredth time or better. Her towel fell but she didn't bothering covering up as she took a toke from the dick pipe and settled on the bed to look through the police file.

Through the thick haze of smoke she released from both sides of her mouth she looked at the police photos of the crime scene. She tried to pay attention to everything, even the fucking trees lining the street. Brandon's body in the street. His bones protruding oddly from his slender teen-aged body. His eyes vacant with death. His neck slashed.

Blood pooling around him. The tire tracks of the car blackening the shirt he wore. The spit in the street and against the side of his face. *What the fuck am I missing?*

Her *Jaws* ringtone on her burner phone sounded off.

Then her other cell phone started vibrating loudly.

She set the picture down and dug both phones out of her handbag. She knew one was Bas calling. She looked at the other. Her heart pounded hard. Tank. She smirked as she looked down from one hand to the other with both phones going off.

Come get this dick. Come get this dick. Come get this dick.

From which one?

Naeema dropped both phones onto the bed and got up to grab one of the containers lining the wall, pulled out leggings and a long-sleeved fitted tee in black. Not bothering with underwear, she got dressed and slid on riding boots. She grabbed her keys and rushed across the room and through the kitchen to leave the house and reach the garage.

Naeema rode her bike through the traffic of the Newark streets until she pulled up outside Tank's house. There was a small yellow car in the drive that she didn't recognize but she parked behind it and walked across the front yard to jog up the stairs and knock on the front door.

The day she'd packed her shit and left him, she had left her keys to the house on his pillow in their bedroom along with a note saying she was sick and tired of being sick and tired of arguing.

She turned at the sound of the door opening. *What the . . . ? Wait. What?*

Naeema eyed the full-figured dark-skinned cutie answering the door to the house where *she* was legally still the queen. And from the look in the woman's eye, she knew damn well about her continuing reign.

Making a face like *bitch please,* Naeema brushed right past her and stepped into the living room.

Tank came out of the kitchen wiping his hands. "Who is at the . . ."

"She just brushed right past me, Tank."

Naeema looked over her shoulder and gave the woman a nasty up-and-down. "You lucky I didn't walk right over you . . . after I knocked you the fuck out."

"Na," Tank snapped, coming over to stand in between them.

Naeema nudged the back of his head. "Oh no, mother-fucker, you don't ever give *me* your back," she snapped.

He turned to eye her hard. "Yo, why you actin' like this?"

"Like what?" she snapped, keeping her eyes locked on his. "Childish."

Naeema leaned to the left to look past him at the other woman. "Better child-*ish* than whor-*ish*," she said with another wicked up-and-down look.

"But you the one in the funky spandex," the woman snapped, hostile as hell.

"Tina," Tank said, placing a restraining hand on her waist.

Naeema's eyes dipped down to take in the more than comfortable move. It hurt her. The dick had been calling her and she raced her ass across town to get it and there might as well have been a damn OCCUPIED sign hanging from the tip. That shit hurt like a motherfucker.

His good deed from the day before of ensuring her baby-father, Chance, didn't press charges was forgotten.

"I just came for the updated police report," Naeema lied to save face. "You couldn't sit here and wait for number one forever so I understand settling for second . . . or third . . . humph . . . maybe *fourth* best."

Yes, she was being childish as hell and she knew it.

"Tina, excuse me for a second."

She came around Tank and rolled her eyes at Naeema. "Yes, please do handle *that*."

Line crossed.

Naeema reached out quick as shit with her right hand and brought it down on the back of the woman's head. She cried out as she fell forward onto the floor. "The police report," she said coldly, ignoring Tank stooping down to help her to her feet.

"Yo, you got a fucking hand problem, Naeema," Tank snapped. His date or whatever stood swaying on her feet as she cupped the back of her head.

"And she got a mouth problem. Let's see who fix their problem first."

Tank came over and grabbed Naeema by her upper arm to steer her back onto the porch. "Why you actin' like this, yo? You left me."

"The police report," she repeated, not even looking at him.

"I told you, I'm not giving you the report to go out there and get yourself killed."

She shook her head as she finally eyed him. "Well, if I'm dead you don't have to worry about a divorce where my childish ass could yank this fucking house we used to live in *together* . . . where you are now fucking new bitches," she said, holding up both her hands. "So give me the police report."

"Man, go home with that nonsense, Tina," he said.

"Tina!" she snapped, not thinking it was possible for her to feel more hurt and more anger . . . until he called her by the other woman's name.

Tank's face filled with regret. "Na," he began. "I didn't mean to—"

"Fuck you, Tank," she said, turning to walk down the stairs.

He reached out and gripped her wrist. Naeema snatched away from him. At the bottom step she looked back and laughed. "What's so crazy is while she in there tryin' to play my position we both know if I told you to send her ass home you would."

She stormed across the yard and climbed onto her motorcycle.

Tank turned and walked back inside the house.

Naeema climbed her ass right back off the motorcycle and raced down the drive to Tank's garage. She entered her birth date on the keypad to unlock the door and slipped inside using the flashlight on her phone to keep from turning on the lights. In the corner was his desk and she headed straight to it. Right on top of the stacks of papers and receipts was the file.

By the time Tank reached the end of his drive to catch up to her, Naeema was turning her motorcycle and racing away up the street with the file safely tucked in her waistband.

Naeema hopped out of the cab and came up the walkway to the front door. Before she could knock on the front door it opened and Bas's tall figure filled the frame. She flipped her long black weave over her shoulder and opened her wrap dress to show him she was as naked as the day she was born.

"Damn, Queen," Bas said releasing a long-ass breath that had to be him letting off steam.

They'll run right through a pretty girl like you.

Naeema shook her head to clear it. *Not now, Grandpa Willie. Not right fucking now.*

She smiled as she grabbed the front of his V-neck tee and roughly pushed him up against the wall, then she kissed him deeply and stroked his hardening dick. She'd sworn never to give Bas her all when it came to sex, but it was his lucky night because she figured the very best way to say "fuck you" to Tank and take care of her own needs was to thoroughly fuck the hell out of Bas.

$\mathcal{N}$aeema smoothed some of her jet-black wig behind her ear as she waited for Bas to come around the vehicle and help her out. The wig was twenty-four inches with a natural-looking part down the middle, giving her a Pocahontas vibe, and it was the perfect hair to match the dress she wore.

The Lamborghini door opened and she smiled up at Bas looking fly as he held his hand out to her. She smoothed down the hem of the custom B. Allen bandage dress she wore. The mesh gave away plenty of her brown skin but each three-inch strap of leather was perfectly placed to hide her nipples and the vee above her thighs. It fit her curves like a second skin and she had to admit that although Bas purchased the dress, she loved it.

Wearing it was supposed to be a part of her role as Queen but the fit was everything she loved as Naeema.

"Can I get a repeat of last night?" Bas whispered in her ear as they walked inside Club Platinum Plus in Manhattan.

"You couldn't handle it," she teased, smiling off the uneasy she felt.

She had most definitely given Bas too big of a peek into her freaky side. She'd tried to go home but he insisted she stay. They fell asleep together and he tried to spoon all night. They had breakfast at a diner in Maplewood and then he took her on a birthday shopping spree.

She couldn't deny that a part of the reason she went so wild was him putting in work as well. Still, she had no intention of keeping any of what he told her to "throw in the bag" like Fabolous. Her affiliation with him had nothing to do with that—or the good sex, really.

The walls and floor of the club were painted dark blue but everything else was silver (or platinum as they were trying to insinuate) and the place radiated. The music was loud as ever and people seemed to be in modes of either chilling or partying.

Naeema had to admit she liked the upscale vibe. *Maybe I'll come back on my real birthday in a few weeks.*

Bas spoke briefly to the bouncer, who then said something in low tones on his headset before he directed them away from the flow of traffic in and out of the two-story club to a small lounge area to the left of the door.

"I know I'm'a have to kill a fool behind your ass in that dress," he said, reaching over to press his palm to her thigh as they sat on one of the silver banquettes lining the wall.

Naeema only smiled because she doubted he was playing.

A double door on the other side of the small area opened and a petite Latina with reddish blond hair came to stand before them in a white bodysuit.

"Hello, Mr. Jones, and happy birthday, Queen, I'm Ashia, your personal hostess for the evening," she said. "Right this way." She waved them into the elevator first.

Naeema wasn't used to this shit. Not even when she partied hard had she hit the door of a club on this level. The elevator was glass and they were able to look down at the large club and the partygoers as they reached the second level, which was strictly VIP. *My my, damn.*

As Ashia led them to their section, Naeema's eyes widened when she spotted rappers, singers, and popular radio dj's she recognized, all enjoying their bottle service and special treatment. She felt like she was filming an episode on a reality TV show because that's the only time she came even close to something as dope as Club Platinum Plus. *Fucking* Lifestyles of the Fly and Fabulous *or some shit.*

She wouldn't doubt there was a minimum just to book a VIP station. *Bas spent a grip for this shit.*

"Happy birthday, Queen!"

She held her hands over her gloss-coated lips at the sight of the crew plus a few more all seated around a cake in the shape of a royal crown with tall sparkles surrounding it.

"Happy birthday," Bas said with a press of his warm lips against the corner of her mouth before he pulled her closer to the semicircular booth to sit.

"Thank you," she said.

She didn't have time to feel even half a second of guilt about her lies to these people. Her son's murderer sat among them. She knew it in her gut.

Her eyes shifted from Bas's profile. To Hammer. Nelson. Red. And Vivica.

Party or no party. Gifts or no gifts. She was not Queen.

She was Naeema. Brandon was her son. One of them was going to die.

Period.

Over the rim of her flute of Armand de Brignac (or Ace of Spades) champagne, as they overlooked the crowd below, Naeema eyed Hammer dancing behind his date. She didn't know if the cute girl with a spiky short hairdo was one of his babymamas, one of his girlfriends, or a brand-new recruit, but Naeema was ready to chat it up with the playboy.

"Queen, you are slaying us with that dress, bitch. It's everythang on that body."

Naeema set her flute down and smiled at Vivica looking Rainbow Bright as ever in a multicolored bodysuit and matching Chinese bob weave. "Thank you," she said.

"Bas did it baller status for you, girl," Vivica said, reaching for the gold opaque champagne bottle in the bucket of ice to refill her glass before she moved from her seat across the table next to a solemn-looking Red to sit beside Naeema.

"I guess he making up for his girl catching us in their house."

Vivica side-eyed her. "I heard about it," she mouthed before she took a sip.

Naeema eyed Nelson asking their hostess a question when she brought a new round of drinks and glasses to their table. She followed where Ashia pointed something out for him. The restrooms. *Young dude gotta pee-pee.*

"I'll be back," Naeema whispered to Bas before Nelson could even make his move. She picked up her black ostrich feather clutch and shimmied by Vivica to make her way past each VIP station to the restrooms.

Her jam, "Drop It Low" by Ester Dean was blaring and people were getting off. Naeema had to fight the urge to "drop, drop, drop" right in front of a famous New York rap icon and his whole entourage.

Before she walked into the bathroom she glanced over her shoulder to make sure Nelson wasn't strolling his behind over. She entered but kept the door cracked to catch him just before he pushed open the men's bathroom door across from her. "Hey, Nelson," she said, stepping out into the short hall and pretending to air-dry her hands.

"Whaddup, birthday girl," he said, smiling and causing his already tiny eyes to seem to disappear behind his chubby cheeks.

The smell of weed was heavy as hell around his short and thick figure, like the dirt cloud around Pig-Pen from the Charlie Brown cartoons. "Yo, you stay faded. You got something on you?"

"You know that," he said, patting the pocket of his pink and gray paisley print shirt he wore with dark denims.

"Shit, let's blaze," she said, turning to push back against the men's bathroom door.

Naeema just laughed when he tried to stop her. She checked each stall before sitting up on the granite countertop of the sinks. Nelson eased in as she crossed her legs and set her clutch on her lap.

"We can't smoke in here," he said, reaching in his pocket for a box of Newports. He pulled out a blunt. "It'll set off the smoke detectors and shit. You keep that."

Naeema took it and slid it inside her clutch. "What was

up with that kid Brandon?" she asked, pulling out her lip gloss and playing with it nonchalantly as she turned on the counter to put it on in the mirror running along the entire length of the wall.

Nelson looked down at the floor, pressed his thick lips closed, and shook his head.

"Y'all was cool, right, or . . ."

"Nah, we were straight," Nelson said, motioning with his pudgy hands. "We was the closest in age so it feel like I lost a little brother."

She rolled the cap back on the tube. "The way he got killed it's like somebody was mad at him like . . . yo."

Nelson frowned. "You heard about it?"

"Bas told me," she lied.

"Bas talked to you about Brandon?" he asked, sounding disbelieving.

Naeema nodded. "Yeah, he told me all about how the little boy was tossing rocks at the window in the church when he first met him," she said, glad for the tidbit of truth to feed back to him to ease his doubts.

Nelson visibly relaxed. "Yeah, Bas took him under his wing and shit. Just like he did me. You know?"

"I'm surprised anybody could be *that* mad to risk pissing off Bas to hurt him. Right?" she asked, meaning to sound naive and nosy instead of calculating.

"Nah. Bas woulda fucked somebody up behind Brandon," Nelson said.

If not Bas, then who? Maybe you?

"Yeah, but he must've pissed somebody off," she said with a shrug. "I mean, he couldn't have been perfect, you know? He had to work somebody's damn nerve. He ain't never pissed you off?"

"Dude was fourteen, maybe fifteen," Nelson said.

Fourteen, you fat fuck.

"What could he possibly do to make somebody wanna kill him?"

"Your girl is cute," Naeema said, meaning to change shit up on him.

Nelson strolled over to the urinals. "She just some bitch who got lucky for the night," he said before he unzipped.

Naeema hopped down off the counter and left the bathroom. She crossed over to the women's bathroom and walked into one of the stalls to flush the blunt he gave her.

I don't smoke shit I ain't seen rolled, motherfucker.

People were lacing their weed with dope, crushed pills, or coke—if they could afford it. She'd heard too many stories about dudes popping Xanax and straight passing the fuck out while they were walking. OxyContin, Percs, dippies, sticks. Fuck all that. Naeema wasn't interested in shit but her semi-government-regulated marijuana.

"Naeema . . . you still in here?"

Inside the stall she rolled her eyes at the sound of Vivica's voice echoing in the large bathroom. "Yeah," she called out, turning so her toes pointed forward toward the stall door.

She reached behind her to flush and waited a few seconds more before she finally walked out and washed her hands at the sink. Vivica was touching up her mascara.

Let me try this bitch again. What the hell?

"Bas told me why he don't like talkin' about your little finger fucker," she said, drying her hands under the automated blower.

Vivica looked confused.

"Brandon," Naeema reminded her.

"My little finger fucker, huh? Queen, you crazy," she said with a laugh. "And pussy eater too. Don't forget *that*."

Naeema forced a smile but her eyes glittered coldly. "If I was a teenage boy that got to play in a grown woman's pussy I woulda told *some*body."

"I lied and told him he could do it again if he didn't say nothing—"

Bullshit.

Naeema turned and left the restroom as it hit her that she knew exactly who a young boy trying to fit in would tell his dirty little sex secret too. She came back to the VIP section and moved right on over to Hammer and his boo-thang for the night still looking down at the club below as he grinded on that "good-good."

"Y'all having fun?" she said to the girl, not to seem out of pocket.

"Yes. I can't wait to tell all my friends about it," she said, pulling out a cell phone and posing for a selfie.

Both Naeema and Hammer stepped out of range of that shit.

She typed something on her phone and hit Send. When she put the phone away they both stepped back.

"That's nothing. I was just talking to K. Michelle in the bathroom, girl," Naeema said all breezy and easy before she turned away and started dancing like it was nothing.

"I'll be back, boo," the girl said over her shoulder to

Hammer before she took off to the restroom, already digging her phone back out of her purse.

"What about you, Hammer?" she asked as that Robin Thicke banger from last summer, "Blurred Lines," began to play. "You having fun?"

He shrugged. "I'll be having more fun with that fly honey, though," he said, pointing down below.

Naeema followed where he pointed to a white chick with a deep tan in a strapless bodysuit, her long ash-blond hair flowing down her back to the top of her ass. "All pussy black in the dark, huh?" she leaned over to ask him.

"Exactly," he said, his eyes locked on the girl down below.

Naeema had to admit that White Girl had soul and was getting it *in* on the dance floor.

"Did you tell Red?" she asked.

"Did I tell Red what?" he asked, distracted by the Great White Power.

"About Viv and Brandon."

Naeema didn't know if she had truly seen someone shocked until that very moment. He gave her a chastising look before he glanced around to make sure no one had heard her. *It feels good to be right. Who better to brag to than the biggest dick slinger you know?*

"Man, leave that shit alone before you get Viv fucked up real proper. Real real proper."

"Like Brandon?" she asked.

Fuck it. I'm sick of this shit.

Hammer frowned. "Nah. They ain't fuck with that."

"I'm not saying shit but I could see if the man did. That's fucked up. Right?"

Hammer looked down at her. "How you know?"

Naeema made a face like *Who you think?*

He nodded in understanding. "Little man couldn't have come to this but he woulda been to the church first thing asking us about what all went down," he said, looking down into his glass of brown liquor before he downed it in one gulp. "It don't be the same around the church without him there fucking with us."

"Y'all were like his family," she said, giving in to the truth.

"And we let him down," Hammer said, walking back over to the table to re-up his drink.

As soon as Hammer moved away, Bas moved to her side to take his place and stood behind her with his arms on either side of her body as he gripped the railing. "You look good in that dress . . . but you look better out of it," he whispered just below her ear before he lightly bit her neck.

Naeema shivered and leaned back against him because he expected her to make such a show of her possession of him. On the real, her thoughts were heavy because everyone was fronting like Brandon was truly one of their own and they wouldn't hurt him.

Had his death been a random act of violence?

Did she just waste precious months out of her life going down a dead-end road?

Or . . .

She glanced over her shoulder at Red. She felt a true chill to find his eyes were already locked on her and Bas. She gave him just as hard a stare back before turning to press her hand against the side of Bas's face and kissing him. "Thank you," she said against his lips before she kissed him again.

"Those lips. Those lips," he said. "Them some bad mother-fuckers."

Naeema blushed because she knew exactly which heated moment he was referring to from the night before. "Later," she promised.

Bas smacked her ass before he moved back over to his seat. She looked on as he and Red lowered their heads together to talk.

"Excuse me."

Naeema turned to find their personal hostess, Ashia, standing behind her with an empty tray in her hand. "Yes?"

"Hello, Queen. There's a gentleman downstairs who keeps asking to be let up. He says he knows a Naeema that's in your VIP section," she said.

Oh shit. Oh shit. Oh shit. Fuck! I shoulda known I would run into somebody in one of these damn clubs! Fuuuuuuuuuuuuuck!

Her heart was pounding so fast as she looked down at where Ashia pointed. *Motherfucking Mone. His yellow ass gon' get both of us killed.*

Naeema reached into her purse and pulled out a fifty-dollar bill, then slipped it to Ashia. "That's for you," she said. "He has me mistaken with someone else but I will tell him that myself so that he stops harassing you."

Ashia slid the folded bill into her pocket. "He's no problem."

"I'll tell him. Let's go," she said, already turning to walk away.

"I'll be right back," she mouthed to Bas as Ashia hurried around her to lead her to the elevator.

They rode the elevator in silence and Naeema fought to

stay calm. She wouldn't put it past Bas to come behind her or send Red to see what she was up to.

Ashia led her right to him and then walked away.

"Naeema," Mone shouted, a big goofy grin on his face. "I thought that you with all that ass."

She grabbed his arm and pulled him behind her toward the exit. "Mone, shut the fuck up and listen to me. You got to get your ass out of here quick or you gon' get both of us fucked up," she said, her voice urgent.

"Yo, Naeema, you need me to flex on a fool?" he asked, jumping around and air-boxing.

She glanced up and saw Bas and Red standing at the rail looking down at them. "This ain't no fucking joke, Mone. Damn," she said irritated as hell.

He got serious at the look on her face. "Yo, you a'ight?"

Naeema pressed her hand to her chest. "I'm a'ight and you gon' stay a'ight if you get the fuck out of here right now," she said, pointing to the exit. "I'm dead-ass serious. If you don't leave and get the fuck away from this entire club quick as fuck you gon' be a dead ass. Don't even wait for a cab out front. Go!"

She looked again and Red was no longer standing by Bas. She knew he was on the way down.

"I'll tell you all about it Monday at the shop. I promise," Naeema said.

Mone looked conflicted as hell but at the look she continued to give him, he turned and rushed through the bodies. Her eyes followed him until she saw him disappear out the front door.

Naeema turned and waved up at Bas with a smile. He didn't wave back.

"I love your dress," she said to some random girl standing by her. She was stalling from going back upstairs and possibly missing Red try to go behind Mone.

"No, your dress is *beau*-ti-ful," the girl gushed.

"Thanks," Naeema said, spotting Red stepping off the elevator into the lounge area/waiting room for the VIP section.

She moved past the woman and stepped in front of Red. "Bas said this dress would be trouble," she said, shaking her head as she raked her fingernails through the long inches of her weave.

"Who was that?" he asked.

"My cousin," she lied. "He wanted to join the party upstairs. Didn't want him to overhear the wrong shit. Right?"

She eased past him and then purposely tripped and fell.

Red stepped over and held out one big hand to help her up.

"Thank you," she said. "No more champagne for me."

He turned and walked out of the lounge.

Naeema followed him but as soon as he stepped out the door, it seemed he turned and came right back in just as quickly.

Mone's ass had to be gone. Thank God.

She walked back to the lounge and summoned the elevator. The door opened as he stepped back inside next to her.

They rode back upstairs in silence.

They got back from the club in the early hours of the morning. Naeema feigned being drunk and was glad Bas went straight to bed too. As soon as she heard the steady in-and-out breathing of his sleep, she climbed out of the bed and went into the bathroom, locking the door behind her. She wished she was home in her own bed. *My own life.*

Although she'd already been over the updated police file a dozen times, she knew she would have to look through it again to see if she was wrong about nothing being different but the info on the cell phone vic, just like Tank told her. There wasn't shit else.

A waste of fucking time.

The police were doing worse than her in flushing out Brandon's killer.

Maybe I shoulda just put a bullet in each one of their heads and said fuck this espionage bullshit.

But then she shook her head as a tear raced down her cheek because that was not true at all. If nothing else, she knew more about her son than ever. She had his ring, his pictures, she'd met the girl he'd loved. She had more than she knew she even fucking deserved.

Naeema left the bathroom and tiptoed to the bedroom to make sure Bas was still stretched across the bed naked. She walked into the living room and dug her touch-screen phone from inside her pocketbook, where she kept it along with the gun. She swiped to the photos of Brandon she'd saved from his Facebook page. "I'm getting tired," she whispered to a photo of him smiling with his arms outstretched. "I don't know why I thought I could do this."

She stood there in the darkness of the small living room, swiping through each photo and wishing she had stood up sooner and made herself known to the only child she would ever allow herself to birth.

No second chances at motherhood.

Her shoulders drooped as she continued to swipe through each photo. Each one not so different from the last. A smiling teenage boy who seemed to love girls, hip-hop, and . . .

Wait . . . wait . . . wait.

Naeema went through each picture again and each time there was a commonality that couldn't be ignored. Her heart pounded and she felt jittery as she zoomed to one of the pictures and waited for it to become clearer.

The answer to it all had been sitting right there the whole time.

Naeema tapped her nail against her teeth as her mind raced.

"Queen."

She dropped her phone inside her purse and pretended to search through it. When she turned, Bas was damn near standing right behind her. She prayed he didn't see the tremble in her hands. "I wasn't sleepy," she said, forcing her emotions down until they almost choked. "I was looking for the blunt Nelson gave me. I was gonna blaze it for the last hoorah for my birthday but I can't find it."

"Good. Who knows what the fuck Nelson had laced in that shit," Bas said, pulling her against his chest.

Naeema wanted to flinch from his touch but she took a deep steady breath to get her shit together.

It's almost over. A gun will do the rest. Finally.

"*I* just checked, the house is still up for sale."

Naeema looked up at Bas leaning in the doorway to the bedroom as he looked down at where she sat on the edge of the bed. "You really got enough money saved up for the down payment?" she asked, fighting through the numbness she felt.

"Down payment?" he balked. "Nah. Cash deal. In full."

Crime pays.

"Matter fact, the fellas and I are meeting. Time to put in work," he said.

No, it's time to put a body in the ground.

She nodded but she didn't have zero fucks to give about the next move of their little crime syndicate.

"I gotta make a run," he said, scooping up his keys. "You want me to bring you something back?"

Naeema looked up at him and shook her head. "You meeting up with the crew now?" she asked, seeming calm even as one hell of a storm brewed inside of her.

"Nah," he said. "Not 'til tonight."

Damn.

"A'ight," she said.

Moments later he was gone. As soon as she heard the door shut she hopped up to her feet and grabbed her cell.

First she called for a cab and then she called Ms. JuJu, all as she made sure she left nothing behind. Every single thing Bas had purchased for "Queen," including her entire outfit from the night before, she left in a neat pile on his bed.

"Naeema?"

"How you doing, Ms. JuJu?" she asked as she walked to the door and left the house without looking back one last time. *I'm free.*

"My arthritis been acting up and the doctor said—"

"Ms. JuJu, did Brandon have on his chain the night he was killed?" Naeema asked, knowing she was being rude.

"He sure did. I just assumed it was stolen that night."

"It was, Ms. JuJu. It was," Naeema said, as the cab pulled up and she opened the door to climb into the back. "Let me call you back."

"How you been, Naeema?"

"I'm better now."

"Good."

"Bye, Ms. JuJu," she said. "And thank you."

Naeema ended the call as she settled against the backseat of the cab.

"Where to, ma'am?" the driver asked, looking at her in his rearview mirror.

She started to give her own address but caught herself. The charade was over but she still didn't want to be tracked down, especially when Bas realized that she was gone. For good.

Don't lose it, Naeema. Play this shit smart.

"Newark Penn Station," she said.

She had the upper hand and she had to use it to her advantage.

She looked out at the beautiful sprawling homes lining the streets of Forest Hill, but her focus wasn't on them. Naeema was on the hunt for a killer and now she had her focus locked on the right target.

Lying motherfucker.

Last night, for the first time, she had noticed that Brandon wore his ring and a long gold necklace with a lion medallion in every damn picture on his Facebook. Every single one. But the fact hadn't really mattered to her until she realized that she'd seen that same chain on his killer earlier that night.

She dug her fingers into her thigh so deeply that she was sure she left tiny bruises in the flesh.

Lying thieving motherfucker.

As the pieces to the puzzle had finally slid together and locked into place, she had floated somewhere between joy and rage. The shit seemed so clichéd but just when she was contemplating admitting that she had to walk away from the chase for her son's killer, everything became clear as day.

She didn't know whether to cry or laugh.

For the rest of the morning she lay there stiff as a dead body with Bas's arm draped over her while she tried to find a reason for her son's murder. Although her gut had always told her one or all of them was behind it, she just couldn't make sense of why *he* did it.

With the light of day she realized it really didn't fucking matter. *Lying, thieving, bold, murderous, soon-to-be-dead motherfucker.* She picked up her phone and started to dial 69 on her speed dial but she put the phone away again. *This is my fight . . . and I gotta learn not to rely on Tank anymore.*

She didn't allow herself to feel anything about the strain between them right then. She was flooded with enough emotions, and spending time on her disappointment in her husband wasn't going to do shit but fuck up her focus. She'd have to deal with her relationship with Tank another time.

Naeema paid the cabbie once he pulled up outside Penn Station. Her intention was to hop in another cab and head home but first she walked inside and headed for the waiting area where she had once spent so many nights trying to stay warm and off the actual streets of Newark. *Everything looks so different, but my memories ain't changed.*

In those weeks, up until she got placed in foster care, she had done more to nurture her son while he was in her womb than she had once she birthed him. *I did the best I could.*

Turning, she walked back out of the grand-looking building to climb into the back of one of the many waiting cabs lining the streets. As soon as it pulled up to her house, she quickly paid her fare and rushed up the stairs to unlock her front door. With a lift and a push she entered. She snatched off the wig and tossed it into the cold fireplace before she moved her TV off the hard lid of the container and pulled out the smaller plastic box.

Brandon's ring was nestled in the corner. Naeema picked it up. The sunlight beaming through the window made the gold gleam.

She took it off the chain and slid it onto her index finger. Tonight, under the cover of darkness, she would kill the man responsible for her son's death, and then tomorrow she would say good-bye to the wigs, the false identities, and the fake detective work to get her ass up and go cut hair for a living as Naeema Cole.

Tonight all the Foxy Cleopatra Christie shit came to an end.

She was ready.

Naeema sat on her bike in the drive of an abandoned house across from the old church that housed the Make Money Crew's hideout. She wasn't playing like she was one of them anymore. She had finally tossed her burner phone into the fire, although she knew Bas was blowing that number up while he wondered what happened to his Queen.

She never really was yours, motherfucker.

She was glad to be free of him because her mind was saying this could never work between them, but her pussy was a deceitful, no-manners bitch.

With her eyes trained on the overgrown fields surrounding the church she calmly waited. There was a path through the high grass that led to the back of the street behind it. They usually parked their personal vehicles another block over, in the lot of an abandoned supermarket, and walked over to take the path to the side entrance into the church. The entire block was mostly empty and you would never know the abandoned church with its boarded windows was being used.

Some of Bas's clever shit.

Naeema pressed the black leather gloves down onto her hands and zipped her black pleather jacket up to her neck. The sun was gone and there was a slight chill in the early-October air. Winter in the northeast was brutal and she suddenly realized she had to make sure the house had heat. *Fuck around and find Sarge down in that bitch like a big-ass angry ice pop.*

"What's that?" she mouthed as she climbed off the bike and used her foot to put down the kickstand.

The door to the church opened and closed but she couldn't tell who had just entered or left the building. She pulled on her spare all-black helmet and hopped on the bike. As soon as the motor revved she took off, entering the street and then turning the corner by the church and going down to the end of the block to check for oncoming traffic before she sped up the one-way street.

As lights suddenly flashed, she cut through two parked cars and up onto the sidewalk. She slowed down and sat idling as she waited twenty feet down from the overgrown field connecting the back of the church to the next street.

A figure stepped through the break and turned up the street in the opposite direction.

It's him.

Adrenaline made her heart pound.

She waited to see if anyone was coming out behind him before she revved the motor and sped off the sidewalk and back into the street just as he crossed it to reach the lot. Knowing he was strapped, she hit him with the bike from behind, knocking him forward onto the sidewalk. She pulled up and onto the sidewalk, already reaching with one hand, behind her for the 9mm in the waistband of the black jeans she wore like a second skin. She pointed it at him down on the ground as he struggled to rise up to his hands and knees. "Don't do nothing stupid, Nelson," she said in a cold voice, her anger sparking as the chain fell forward on his neck and the lion medallion dangled from the end of it.

She had to maneuver like crazy to back the bike into the parking lot as she kept the gun trained on him, while he looked up at her lost as a motherfucker. "Don't fucking move or I will blow your fucking head off."

Naeema climbed off the bike and walked over to press her boot onto his back and push him back down onto the cold concrete of the sidewalk. She looked up and down the street to make sure no other crew members or random strangers got near them.

"Queen?" Nelson asked as she patted him down.

"Shut the fuck up," she snapped, pulling a switchblade from the pocket of his hoodie.

Naeema opened it. The knife was serrated with tiny sharp teeth along the edge of the blade.

She closed her eyes as she recalled the image of her son with his neck slashed open. The edges of the cut hadn't been smooth. Nelson's knife was just the tool to make the rough cut.

No gun.

She stood up and kicked him in his sides as she pressed her lips into a thin line.

He cried out and rolled onto his side as he brought his knees up to his chest like it would ease the pain.

"Get up," she snapped.

Nelson coughed. His eyes were tightly closed.

She bent over to press the gun to his temple.

"A'ight, yo. Damn," he swore, struggling to lift his portly frame up to his feet.

She backhanded his ass, causing his head to swing to the left as the connection echoed in the air.

WHAP.

Hatred for him and the brutality he put her son through made her growl as she eyed him. "Let's go," she said, coming around with him but never removing his head as the target of her gun.

"Go where?"

Good question.

All her plans to take him to an abandoned building to kill him flew out the window when she chased him. She looked around and then jerked her head in the direction of the trees, bushes, and high grass separating the parking lot from a house hollowed out by a fire in the past.

"Through there," Naeema said, roughly nudging him across the unlit parking lot.

She looked back at the sound of a car starting and Nelson turned and grabbed her wrist. "Silly bitch," she said, not even stressing as she kneed him in the nuts and then roughly pushed him back enough to kick him square in the chest between his fluffy boobs. He fell back to the ground.

"What do you want, yo?" he cried out, sounding tired and worn out.

She pressed the foot of her thigh-high boots against his cheek. It was the car down at the corner, in front of a small house. Still, both Red's and Hammer's cars and a small blue Porsche sat parked next to Nelson's Cadillac convertible. They could be coming out any second. She couldn't fight all four.

"Get up," she snapped again, kicking his thighs when he took too long.

With her gun pressed to his back she led him across the lot and through the high grass to the abandoned house. The exterior walls of what appeared to be the kitchen were missing and she moved him deeper inside the charred mess to the living room. A large rat scurried across the blackened hardwood floors bold as hell.

Is this shit even safe?

Only the streetlight in front of the house lifted the dark shadows of the house as she pushed him down onto the floor.

She finally took off her helmet and dropped it to the floor by her boot.

"Queen?" he asked again, his eyes taking in her shaven head and makeup-free face as he looked up at her.

She shook her head. "That's what your mouth say," she told him, squatting to tap the barrel of the gun against his soft chin.

"You think Bas gon' let you get away with this?" Nelson asked, sounding a little cocky at knowing his captor.

"You think I should just let Bas know you killed Brandon?" she asked, her voice filled with menace as she pierced him with cold eyes.

His round face filled with shock before it changed in an instant with his anger. "Trust me, I know he'd kill me for Brandon. Trust me," he said with attitude. "But I didn't kill Little Dude."

"Liar."

"I didn't."

"*Or* should I go through with my plan to kill your punk ass for taking out *my son*, bitch?"

She didn't know which part of the bombs she'd just dropped on his ass was the cause for it, but it was clear his mind was fucked.

"And then you got the nerve to wear his chain?" Naeema spat as she boxed him in the face. She snatched the chain from his neck and then swung it at him, landing the lion medallion across his forehead, where it broke the skin.

Worse was coming for his ass anyway so oh the fuck well. "That's how I know you did it, dumb ass."

"Me and Brandon both got that chain," he stuttered. "We bought them at the same time."

"Liar," she said.

She'd checked the date on Brandon's Facebook and he owned that chain months before, when Bas told her they first met.

She popped his bottom lip so hard that it bounced up and down. Nelson yelped like a hit dog.

"He was like a little brother, huh?" she said bitterly, tossing back the lies he gave to her the night before.

She boxed him in his gut. "No, he was fourteen years old, you stupid motherfucker, and there wasn't shit in this world he could've done to you to deserve you running him over and then cutting his throat and leaving him in that street to die."

She took a deep audible breath as tears welled up. "I'm going to kill you," she promised him in a whisper that seemed to echo around them.

Fear filled his eyes even as his lips stayed pressed in a straight angry line.

"I am going to leave your dead body here for the rats and the dogs to eat on until you rot and burst from the maggots eating your dead ass from the inside out," she said, stroking his fat bottom lip with the barrel of the gun. A tear raced down her cheek and landed on his chin. "And then I will pray every day that your worthless-ass soul rots in hell."

The smell of his pee filled the air.

"And that's still more than your motherfucking ass deserves."

She stood up and shoved the necklace and medallion in

her back pocket with his knife as she backed away from him. "Why'd you kill him?" she asked, struggling between her heart breaking with sadness and her soul blazing with rage. "Why?"

Nelson said nothing, just closed his eyes and let his head fall back against the charred wood floor.

She looked up as car lights came on and the parking lot got a little bit brighter.

"Help me!" Nelson cried out.

Naeema jumped on top of him and pressed the barrel of the gun between his plump, ashy, quivering lips. "Go ahead, open your mouth. Scream for help like a bitch so I can slide this pistol dick farther down your throat just before I blow the back of your head out." She pushed the gun until it tapped against his teeth.

The lights from the car disappeared and the room darkened just a little bit again.

Naeema climbed off him and backed up with her gun still locked and loaded on him as she looked through the missing rear wall. "They're all gone. Not that they woulda helped you anyway. This jam you in, you dumb fuck, is a rock and a hard place," she said.

She tilted her head to the side as she stepped up and looked down at him.

Trust me I know he'd kill me for Brandon. Trust me.

Naeema shook her head and released a heavy breath as she tried to pull forward a memory. Something else he said. Something that seemed so innocent . . . then.

Bas took him under his wing and shit. Just like he did me.

She stood above him and straddled his thick form. "You killed my boy because you were jealous of him and Bas being close?" she asked, her voice rising with each word to a roar.

Bas took him under his wing and shit. Just like he did me.

"Are you fucking kidding me?" Naeema grunted as she kicked him square in the nuts and then jumped out of the way when his body made like a cheese curl and he hollered out in pain.

Naeema dropped to her knee and pressed the ring she wore on top of the glove against his mouth. "Kiss the ring," she said. "Kiss it and *beg me* not to kill you."

Nelson's face was still twisted with pain as his eyes shifted down to her hand. "Please . . . please don't kill me," he said before he puckered his lips against the gold metal.

She frowned in disgust at the feel of his wet lips and wiped her hands against her jeans. "Did Brandon beg you for his life?" she asked him.

Nelson lay flat on his back. "Nothing I say is gonna keep you from killing me," he said, his voice cold and flat.

"Nothing," she agreed with a sad shake of her head.

She sat back from him. "You recognize the ring, don't you? He was wearing it and the chain the night you killed him," she said. "I guess you ain't had time to snatch his ring too."

"The chain was in the way when I cut his throat."

Naeema took a step back. "Well, ain't shit in the way of this motherfucker."

She fired her gun.

POW!

The kickback knocked her shoulder back a little but she watched the bullet go straight between his eyes. Moments later, thick crimson blood pooled from the back of his head.

His body convulsed twice before the look in his eyes was filled with death.

Her hand dropped down to her side, smoke filtering up from the hot tip of the gun she still held.

She stood there, shaken by it all; she tilted her head back and her chest rose and fell deeply with her heavy breaths.

It was all finally over.

She felt weak and spent and just wanted to crawl into her bed, cover her head with pillows, and sleep. Yes, she had taken a life before but never like this. She was shaken and maybe not as hardcore as she thought. Her anger at his words had fired that gun even more than her will to kill him out of revenge for Brandon.

With one last look back at Nelson's dead body, she left the abandoned house and walked back to her bike, dropping the gun and his knife in one of the saddlebags as she fought not to give in to her tears and the steady trembling of her hands. She climbed onto her motorcycle and was happy to speed away from the scene of her crime.

$\mathcal{N}$aeema sped through the streets of Newark, easily zooming in and out of traffic and taking turns to avoid red lights. She was more running toward home than running away from the murder she'd just committed. Time had settled her nerves because she did what she had to do. Nelson killed Brandon—a fourteen-year-old man-child—over a jealous rage like a man-bitch.

An eye for an eye.

She turned down Eastern Parkway and made the right onto her street. She was just slowing down as she neared her house when she spotted a tall and broad figure with a bald head walking up her driveway. The darkness soon covered his figure but Naeema would recognize Red's crazy ass anywhere.

"Sarge," she whispered behind the visor of her helmet, alarmed that her actions would bring harm to him.

Naeema didn't have time to think of just where she had shown her true hand to them, as she continued up the street and paused at the end of the drive to lay on her horn. Red stepped out of the darkness and came running down the driveway at full speed.

Damn that big bitch is fast, she thought, revving the bike to speed away.

A car's passenger door opened just as she reached it and Naeema screamed out as she tried to brake in time not to collide into it. She felt like her heart leapt out of her chest, while her body was propelled forward over the handlebars of the bike and the open car door until she landed against the asphalt of the street. Her head slammed against the inside of the helmet and her body ached as she rolled to a stop on her stomach.

A pair of deck shoes came to a stop right next to her and Naeema kept blinking to regain clarity.

"Just who the fuck are you . . . Queen?"

Bas.

He tapped his toe against her helmet just before she felt someone lift her up and carry her, then roughly drop her on the rear seat of a vehicle. She winced and lay on her side. She heard the two front car doors close.

"I told you that bitch was foul," Red said. The car lurched forward and he drove away.

She felt a little relief that they were leaving the house and Sarge behind. *And the gun. It's in the saddlebag. Shit.*

"Her mail says her name is Naeema Cole," Bas said, tossing the stack of envelopes over his shoulder onto her like she and it were trash. Obviously he'd swiped it at the house.

Naeema looked through her visor at Red behind the wheel and Bas on the passenger seat.

"You think she's undercover?" Bas asked, glancing back at her, his jaw squared up with anger.

"She's not wired," Red assured him.

Bas tapped cocaine out onto the back of his hand and sniffed it. "Regardless, she know too much."

"True," Red agreed.

What the fuck am I going to do? No weapon. Body bruised and aching. Head pounding. Two men against me. Think, Naeema, think.

"Who else knows?" Bas asked.

"Just you and me."

"Good."

They rode in silence. Naeema didn't know how far they traveled away from her house. The car slid to a stop and Bas climbed out.

The passenger door opened. She looked up as Bas took her helmet off and dropped it in the street. Just behind his shoulder she could make out the garage door leading into the church. His eyes were glassy and there was powder still clinging to the edge of one of his nostrils. He wiped his hands over the top of his head as he looked down at her.

"Nelson killed my son, Brandon. I wasn't coming for you. I don't give a fuck about whatever y'all got going on. I'm not a fucking cop. I just wanted to know who killed my son," she said in a rush, knowing her only chance to stay alive was the truth. She held up her hand and showed them Brandon's ring on her finger.

"Nelson?" she heard Red say in disbelief.

"What sucking my dick gotta do with any of that?" Bas asked with a laid-back shrug.

"Word?" Red asked before he chuckled.

This is the most I ever heard that motherfucker talk. Damn.

"Kill the lying bitch," Bas said cold as fuck.

A chill raced over her body. "Bas," she said, pleading with her eyes as she held her pounding head up from the seat.

He reached in to massage her ass and thighs. "Damn shame. You got some bomb-ass pussy too," he said, before he stepped back and slammed the door closed.

Naeema dropped her head down onto the seat and closed her eyes.

An eye for an eye.

"Oh well," Red said, all motherfucking blasé, before he pulled off and turned up the radio.

She knew things were finally over when she put one in Nelson's dome, but she didn't know this would be her last night alive too. *Fuuuuck.*

Every pothole he hit caused her body to rise a bit and fall back down on the seat, aggravating the injuries she already had from the motorcycle crash.

"Don't do this, Red," she called from the back of the SUV. "It's not worth it."

"I got the last song just for you, *Queen*," he said, as he pushed buttons on the touch screen.

The opening notes of Biggie's "Ready to Die" played and Naeema couldn't front that she was about a second away from shitting herself.

"As I grab the Glock, put it to your headpiece . . ."

Naeema pushed her hands against the seat of the vehicle and tried to sit up. Red looked over his shoulder and then turned back to face the road but reached back to box her with his fist as he rapped along with Biggie: "The Q-45, Glocks and tecs are expected, when I wreck shit . . ."

Naeema cried out from the sharp pain that radiated across her jawline. She cut her eyes up to glare at the back of his head. Killing Nelson had shaken her a little bit and that had been all about revenge. But Red gloating about killing her made her want to put a Glock to *his* dome and fire off all the rounds until everything in the vehicle—including her—was covered in his blood and brain matter. *Ugly motherfucker.*

He turned the music down. "What the fuck?" he snapped as he slammed on the brakes.

Naeema's body rolled forward off the seat and slammed against the back of the front seats just before she heard Red jump out of the SUV. At the sound of raised voices she sat up and looked out the windshield. Her mouth fell open at the sight of one of Tank's SUVs blocking the street.

Red posted up and raised his gun to fire at the vehicle. POW. POW. POW.

"Shit," Naeema swore, her eyes big as shit as she ducked down, trying to avoid the bullets she thought would bounce off Tank's bulletproof SUV back toward her.

When that didn't happen, she peeked her closely shaven head up just in time to see Red turn to stride back toward his own SUV. Naeema eyed the door that was still sitting open. "Oh, no, motherfucker," she said, quickly climbing over the armrest to slide down into the driver's seat and lock the doors.

Red's face twisted with rage as he raised the gun.

Naeema's eyes shifted to watch Tank race from his SUV and come running full speed at Red, tackling him to the ground just as the shot fired.

POW.

The dirt and grass lining the sidewalk next to Red's SUV flew up when the bullet entered it.

Tank and Red both fought for control of the gun until Tank precisely punched Red's inner wrist against the asphalt and his grip loosened around the handle. Tank spared a second to push it away with force before he delivered a round of ferocious blows to Red's face and shoulders.

Naeema's breath was caught in her throat like thick spit as she eyed the gun go spinning down the street like a wild top before it stopped on top of a sewer grate.

Tank cried out.

Naeema shifted in the seat to look through the driver's-side window. Red was pressing his hand to Tank's neck just enough to slide his fist up against his chin. Tank's head snapped back and blood dripped from the corner of his mouth, even as he maintained his death grip on Red's own neck.

Red head-butted him and Tank stumbled back long enough for his opponent to jump to his feet and deliver a blow to the side of his head. Naeema opened the door. Tank was a proud man who wouldn't want her help, but if she had to double-deuce Red from behind to make sure he whipped Red's ass, then she gladly would.

Tank shook the hits off before he stood up tall and walked straight up to Red, avoided the next blow to his face with a swift duck, and grabbed Red's neck and jerked his hands in different directions.

Naeema's mouth fell open as Tank held up his hands and Red's body drooped to the ground with his head twisted at an odd angle.

Yo, Tank broke that fool's neck.

There was no coming back from that.

Tank motioned for her to get out of the truck before he bent to flip Red's body over his shoulder. He walked over to his own SUV. She frowned at the way Red's eyes stared off into space and his head bounced like a bobblehead against Tank's back.

One down. One to go.

Kill the lying bitch.

There was no coming back from that shit either.

Naeema tapped her fingernail against her teeth as she watched Tank toss Red's body into the back of the SUV like he was nothing more than a sack of potatoes. *I gotta do this. That fool ordered me dead.*

She threw the car in reverse just as Tank looked up at her through the windshield.

Naeema didn't stop until she was near the sewer grate. She hopped out quick as hell and picked up the gun before she climbed back in and did a fast K-turn. The tires squealed as she turned the SUV in the opposite direction, back toward the church and as far away from Tank as she could get.

Naeema removed the clip to make sure it was still loaded with bullets as she waited at a red light not far from the church. She took the turns to drive by the parking lot. The only vehicle still sitting there was Nelson's Caddy.

Bas wasn't there.

"Unless he was waiting for Red to swing back through and pick him up," she said aloud.

"I need a gangsta bitch . . ."

Naeema looked down at Red's cell phone at the sound of his ancient-ass ringtone. Still wearing her gloves, she picked it up. On the screen was a picture of Vivica butt naked with her legs spread wide and a lollipop in her ass. *Dumb bitch.*

She took off one of her gloves to be able to swipe and sent Vivica's call to voice mail. "Lawd, why didn't I tell Red that she let a kid eat her out before his neck got snapped?" she asked as she checked his text messages.

Overlooking Vivica's long row of incoming texts steadily asking him where he was, she was checking if he and Bas ever texted.

They did.

Naeema started typing a text to Bas using the same fucked-up lettering that Red seem to prefer but before she could hit Send the phone sounded off with the old-school classic ring. BAS was displayed on the screen, without a picture, naked or otherwise. *Thank God.*

That would've been too suspect and the last thing she needed to top off the night was knowing the same dude that licked her ass was licking his homeboy's too. *O-kay?*
DONE?

Naeema laughed bitterly at the text, wishing she had taken one of the many opportunities she'd had to truly fuck Bas up. "Oooh, motherfucker," she said, backspacing the text she had typed to simply put: ouTsiDE.

She pulled around the corner and parked outside the garage door entrance where Red had dropped his wannabe mafioso ass earlier. He would be able to see the SUV on the surveillance equipment in the office but she already knew the tint was 5 percent and usually used for privacy glass so Bas couldn't see inside. She hoped she'd waited long enough for him to leave the office and be traveling across the church to the garage, then she grabbed the gun and eased the door open enough to squeeze out. Her pulse was racing as she stooped down to wait at the back of the SUV.

The familiar scraping of the door against the sidewalk echoed against the night as she stepped from behind the truck with the gun raised. "Surprise, motherfucker," Naeema said, her voice as cold as the stare she leveled on him while she stepped up onto the sidewalk.

The look on his face was worth a million dollars.

She turned the gun sideways and kept her grip steady as she stood before him and pressed it against his chest. "So . . . my sucking your dick *and swallowing* shouldn't have nothing to do with this right here, right?" she asked sarcastically, motioning in the air between them with her free hand before she backhanded him across his pretty-boy face with it.

He turned his head back slowly to glower at her until his eyes seemed lined with red anger.

She circled his body to pat him down although she knew Bas rarely carried a gun.

"Go inside," Naeema told him. They had all taken too many chances with their violence in the middle of the streets of Newark like there were no witnesses lurking to see their shit.

Bas turned and opened the garage door and walked inside. Naeema kept the gun pointed at him as they made their way through the church and into the sanctuary.

God forgive me.

She pushed him down onto one of the dusty pews.

"Where's Red?" he asked, leaning forward and pressing his elbows onto the top of his knees as he looked up at her.

"Dead as a motherfucker," Naeema said. "Just like Nelson."

He squinted his eyes at that but his face remained expressionless.

She stood in front of him. "I told you I wasn't coming for you. I just wanted whoever killed my son . . . and I got him. All you had to do was go on with your life, but no, you want to be the godfather and order motherfuckers to kill me, right?"

"And you woulda killed me if you thought I killed Brandon."

Naeema nodded vigorously. "It woulda been a waste of good dick . . . but yeah, I woulda."

He eyed her with a deliberate pause at the warm vee above her thighs in her skintight jeans. He shook his head before he hung it with a little sardonic laugh. "You ain't fake all them nuts. That's probably the realest shit I know about you . . . *Na-ee-ma.*"

"Probably," she agreed.

Bas sat up and slouched back against the pew. "So you're the MIA mother not in his life?" he asked with a lick of his lips.

Bastard.

"You don't want to talk about mothers," she shot back.

His entire body went stiff and his coolness evaporated into a look that thankfully had no power to kill. "If you knew the truth about that, you wouldn't have come back for me," he said with a momentary tightening of his lip—an inadvertent reflex of the anger she stoked.

Naeema eyed him as she shifted the gun from one hand to the other, keeping it pointed at his heart. She raised it up until the barrel was pointed at the spot just between his eyes.

More brain matter and blood splatter.

"I would have dealt with Nelson myself if you just told me," he said.

She smiled sadly and opened her eyes wide a few times to keep tears from pooling. "You know what, Bas . . . I believe that," she finished with a softness to her tone that surprised her. "He was jealous of Brandon taking his spot with you."

Again his eyes squinted a bit but his expression never changed.

Her finger stroked the trigger. She came to kill him, not to chat or listen to riddles about his mother's death. *Shoot him.*

His eyes were locked on her. Steady. Unwavering.

Shoot this motherfucka.

Naeema straightened her arm and stroked the trigger again, softly.

He never flinched.

He's a killer . . . but so am I.

"I was right. You wasn't what you seemed," he said, his tone slightly accusing.

You ain't what you seem, Queen . . . just like me.

Naeema walked up to stand before him with her legs spread wide. She put the gun to his head and raised her other gloved hand balled into a fist and displaying the ring. "Kiss the ring and ask me to forgive you for wanting me dead," she said, keeping his steady stare.

Bas pressed his lips to the gold. "Forgive me, Queen," he said.

She arched her brow at his use of her alias. Stepping back from him she shook her head. "For whatever we shared that I know was real," she said. "And for whatever love you showed my son. I forgive you."

Naeema backed away from him with the gun raised.

"Stay away from me and I'll stay away from you. I got just as much dirt on you as you got on me."

She pushed back against the swinging doors of the sanctuary. She gasped when Bas ducked down and pulled a gun from under one of the pews and pointed it at her. *Damn, I led him right to a damn weapon.*

POW!

"Ah!" Naeema cried out as the bullet pierced the flesh of her shoulder and the force knocked her back against the wall, even as she fired back.

POW!

Her aim was better.

The bullet landed in his heart and the force caused his body to curve out as his arms and legs came forward. The gun fell out of his hand and he landed back atop the collection table.

Wincing from the burning pain in her shoulder, she came over to stand above his body. Blood spread across his sweater from just above his heart.

"I forgave you," she said. "But you still were going to kill me?"

Blood filled his mouth. "I killed my own mother."

If you knew the truth about that, you wouldn't have come back for me.

"You really think I ever gave a fuck about you?" he said, the blood in his throat already thickening his words.

His body began to convulse and his eyes rolled back in his head until she saw nothing but the whites.

Naeema raised her gun and shot him in the head.

POW!

She put him out of all of his miseries.

17

Everything feels different.

Naeema raised her head from the pillow and looked over at Tank asleep on the floor in a sleeping bag with one of her pillows pushed under his head. His snores filled the air like a long and loud chainsaw. His mouth was slightly open and she smiled, thinking of a mouse crawling into it.

Tank.

She let her eyes linger over him. Her anger at him had faded last night when he killed for her. Even at the worst moment in their relationship, he had been her savior. She was alive because of him. *And I love him still.*

Her head whipped around at the sound of a short snort. She winced in pain at the soreness of her right shoulder as she eyed Sarge, sleeping, sitting in a chair pushed up against the front door with his arms crossed over his chest and a machete in his hand. He must have come up sometime during the night after Tank had carried her in the house and tended to her bullet wound. Her heart tugged.

My own security team.

Naeema pushed back the covers with her good arm and eased up off the bed. She looked down in surprise to see she was wearing Tank's old football jersey. He had to have put it on her because she didn't remember shit after the pain pills he gave her knocked her the fuck out. She didn't mind the jersey at all.

She tiptoed over to Sarge and eased the machete out of his hand before he woke up and chopped off his own leg or some shit. Sliding it under her bed she reached for the box and opened it to pull out her pipe and the stuffed baggie of weed beside it.

She was halfway across the living room when she turned back for her Louis Vuitton bag. She left the living room and crossed the kitchen, stepping out onto the small porch with its missing step. It was the sight of her motorcycle through the open door of the garage that made her knees weak. She thought it was another casualty of the night before.

The October morning wind was cold as hell against her bare legs and sent her right on back inside to shut the door tight. "Shit," she swore.

Still, if her shoulder wasn't tender she would have dropped everything and hopped her half-naked ass on the bike and rode it around the block to make sure she was truly okay. Just like that.

The kitchen door swung open.

She smiled at Sarge standing there, his eyes still puffy with sleep. "I'm okay," she reassured him.

"It's over?" he asked, the wrinkles around his eyes deepening with concern *and* aggravation.

She loved his old angry self.

"It's over," she promised.

He looked over his shoulder. "It's over?"

She looked past him at Tank rolling up the sleeping bag.

"It's done," he said to Sarge, although his eyes were on her.

Her heart sped up.

"Ain't nothing wrong with normal," he snapped as he passed her.

"Nope . . . nothing at all, Sarge," she agreed.

"The same old same old," he said, his head rocking back and forth like he was preaching or playing a blues guitar.

Tank laughed. "Get on her, Sarge."

"I done did dat," Sarge hollered to Tank.

"Same old same old, Sarge," Naeema promised.

He paused. He turned around. He nodded at her. "You did what you had to," he said before he turned and headed through the door leading to the basement. "But you shouldn't have to do it no more. Right?"

"Right."

Of course he slammed the door shut.

WHAM.

Naeema set her weed and her bag on the counter before she walked back into the living room. Tank looked at her as he picked up the chair Sarge had been sitting in by the door to carry it back into the kitchen. She moved over to her bed to pull back the covers and smooth the bottom sheet before she pulled the top sheet and comforter back up tightly across the bed.

"You'll bust your stitches."

She stood up straight and turned to face him. "I'm okay."

He shook his head and turned his lips downward as he gave her a pensive stare filled with everything he was feeling. "No, you're not. You're stubborn. Vindictive. Dangerous. You *think* you're the baddest bitch born and . . . and . . . because of all that shit, yo, some morgue woulda been calling me to ID your dead body, Na," he said, as he held up his hands.

"I'm—"

"Shut the fuck up, Na," Tank yelled, his voice exasperated.

She couldn't even snap back.

"I don't know whether to . . . to . . . choke you or hug you," he said, his conflict written all over his handsome face as he wiped his hands over his cheeks while he paced.

She opened her mouth and he held up his hand to stop her.

"Just because we can't live together doesn't mean I want to risk having to live in this world without you," he admitted.

Naeema gasped as his eyes got bright. *Tears?* Tank's hardcore ass never cried. Like . . . NEVER.

I will always love him and he will always love me.

The chorus to that J. Cole song came to her.

"Nobody's perfect . . . but you're perfect for me . . ."

But they couldn't be together. They swung between real hot or real cold. Their asses could never find the comfort in the middle. Their love was all about fucking extremes.

"How you find me?" she asked.

"Ain't your ass glad I did?" he barked.

"Tank," she said softly, asking for a break from his anger.

"I figured you were up to something with that crew your son used to hang around and I had my fellas watching all of them. One of my boys hit me up and let me know they had just snatched you up from the house. I told him to go in and check on Sarge and hauled ass to get to you."

"Thank you, Tank," she said, coming over to touch his arm.

"That leaves Hammer and Nelson," he said.

"Hammer doesn't know about me being undercover," she said. "And Nelson is as dead as it gets."

Tank looked at her like *No you didn't.*

"He killed my son," she said with emphasis.

They shared a look filled with understanding.

"Why'd you go to that church alone?" he asked.

"I wanted to handle him myself," she said truthfully.

His eyes bored into her. "Why?"

Naeema's hand fell from his arm. "He looked me dead in the face and told his hit man to kill me," she said.

"And that's it?" he asked.

No more lies.

"If it isn't, you really don't have a right to ask, with your new boo and all," she reminded him gently.

He looked down at her even as the muscles in his jaw worked overtime.

"Nobody's perfect . . . but you're perfect for me."

Tank shook his head and turned away from her like he was trying to break an invisible hold she had on him. His jaw was tight and square as he pulled on his boots and grabbed his keys from the fireplace mantel. "I gotta get to work," he said and walked to the door.

"I wanted you to deny her that night at your house and you didn't, Tank," Naeema said from across the room, causing him to pause in the open doorway. "You wanted me to deny him just now . . . and I didn't either."

"Then I'm glad the motherfucker's dead," he said before he walked out of the house.

Naeema stood there, hoping he would come back, but soon the sound of his motorcycle tearing up the street echoed loudly.

"Nobody's perfect . . . but you're perfect for me."

She retrieved the plastic case holding all of her son's things and removed the police file before walking to the kitchen. She set it on the counter as she pulled a large pot from underneath the sink and then slid the file into it. From her bag she pulled out Red's and Bas's cell phones. When she'd called Tank to tell him where she was and that she had been shot, she had taken the phone from Bas's dead body before leaving the church to wait outside.

Bas's cell phone was locked. She tried his birthday but then gave up when it failed. She threw the cell phone into the large pot and set it back on the counter. She leaned against the counter as she went through Red's call log, a dozen missed calls from Vivica and a dozen more text messages begging him to call her and let her know he was okay.

Naeema felt a little bad for the woman because she had to be worried that her man never came home and never answered the phone. But there was not a damn thing she could do about it. In time it would sink in that he was dead and gone and she would just have to mourn him and move the fuck on.

Just like I am . . . finally.

Scrolling to his older messages with Bas, she could tell they kept it all coded as fuck. She paused her thumb over the touch screen when she spotted her alias, Queen.

"Damn you really love her?" she read out loud.

Bas's reply: HELL YEAH.

Naeema looked at the date. It was during the weeks she spent at the hotel with him.

"You really think I ever gave a fuck about you?"

He'd lied.

She didn't know how she felt about knowing Bas could have possibly cared for her but still ordered her dead.

"I killed my own mother."

Naeema shook her head. Bas was crazier than a mother-fucker.

She tossed Red's phone into the pot as well before she carried the pot outside, being sure to avoid the step with the missing bricks, and grabbed the lighter fluid sitting by the base of the steps. Naeema dropped the pot on the ground and doused it with lighter fluid. She dashed back inside for her lighter and her weed, then came back to set everything in that pot ablaze. The warmth of the fire felt good in the midst of the chilly fall air circling her body.

She hoped flames similar to the one slowly claiming everything it touched burned a million times hotter in the hell where she'd sent Nelson's soul.

"I almost forgot," she said, crossing the yard to open the garage and reach into her saddlebag.

It was empty. She checked the other. Same thing. Nada.

Last night she'd told Tank about the gun for him to get rid of it for her. *He must've taken the knife too. Fuck it.*

Two less things for her to worry about on her road back to normalcy.

She looked down the length of her drive and frowned as Coko came staggering past on her way to her own house. She was obviously out of rehab and fucked up. Naeema didn't move from her spot. She'd done all the saving and revenge-making her ass could take. *Coko gon' have to fight that battle on her own.*

She glanced down at her little bonfire in the pot as she went back inside and away from the cold. In the kitchen she stood at the window inhaling her weed from the dick pipe and stroking her son's ring with her thumb as she watched everything she had connected to his murder go up in flames.

"Did you love him?"

Naeema turned in surprise to find Tank standing in the doorway with one strong arm holding the swinging door open as he leaned his sexy frame against the door frame. Releasing a thick stream of smoke through pursed lips, she locked eyes with him, her heart pounding, her pulses racing like crazy, as she shook her head no.

"Nobody's perfect . . . but you're perfect for me . . ."

He was hurt. Just as hurt as she was that night at his house so she understood completely. But he loved her. He couldn't deny her. And it was the same for her.

Neither one could really take that final step to leave the other alone. It was like the bond was stronger than them and all their issues.

He held out his hand.

Naeema licked her lips as she stepped up to slide hers into it.

As he picked her body up against his and pressed his lips to her mouth, she didn't give a fuck about anything else in the world.

Not the weed burning and wasting away on the counter.

Not even the fire burning in the backyard.

Work. Sarge. The pain in her shoulder. The carnage from the night before. The bitch that was at his house that night.

Not a damn thing.

Tank sucked her tongue into his mouth gently as he backed into the living room to lay Naeema down on the bed. Slowly, like revealing a gift, he undressed her with his eyes, shifting from her hot eyes to the parts of her body he uncovered.

Her bandaged gunshot wound.

Her round breasts and hard nipples.

The smooth skin over her flat belly.

Thick thighs.

The soft hairs covering her pussy.

Tank stepped back from her to pull off his own clothing. "Shave it," he said, with a subtle lift of his chin toward her plump vee as she writhed like a snake and spread her legs before him.

He wanted to see the tattoo of his name stamping her pussy as his and only his.

"I will," she promised.

Naeema gasped at the sight of his chiseled body standing between her legs. His dick hung from his body with weight. She loved how it was several shades darker than the rest of him, with the tip smooth and shining as it eyed her.

With a bite of her lips she maneuvered to her knees before him to lick the deep grooves of his abdomen down to the flat hair surrounding the base of his dick.

"Suck it," he said thickly.

She glanced up at him before she lay across the foot of the bed with her back arched, pushing her hard nipples up high. "Put that dick in my mouth," she said.

Tank stepped down by her head to squat his strong thighs and he pressed his dick down with his thumb until it lightly tapped against the tongue she rolled out. She eyed him as she took the smooth tip into her mouth and sucked it deeply and her tongue cupped it. His face tightened, he released a long breath, and the muscles of his thigh clenched.

Naeema circled him as his hands stroked from her

thighs across her pussy and over her belly before he warmly held one breast and then the other and teased her nipples between his fingers with just the right amount of pressure to turn her the fuck on. She lifted her head from the bed, not giving one care about the strain on her neck, as she took more of his long and thick length into her hot mouth.

Tank pumped his hips, stroking her tongue with his dick as he reached to cup the back of her head with his hand and support her.

They locked eyes.

Even during sex he looked out for her.

She lifted one of her legs and let it rest against his hard chest as she spread the other toward the head of the bed. He didn't waste a second easing his hand from her nipple to cup her core before he slid his middle finger deep inside her to circle her tight and wet walls and pressed down onto her clit with his thumb.

"Tank," she whispered. She arched her hips up off the bed and rolled them as she did the same with her tongue before licking the tip with the flutter speed of butterfly wings.

"Ah," he cried out in pleasure, letting his head fall back as his body went stiff.

He didn't need to warn her that he was about to cum. She felt his dick harden in her mouth, his pulse throbbing against her tongue. Naeema freed his dick, giving him a second to let his nut ease away. Tank looked down at her with a shake of his head in thanks.

They knew each other well.

Rising up, she stood and wrapped her hand around his dick as she pushed down onto the bed with her free hand. She straddled his lap backward and spread her legs wide with heels pressed down into the bed as she bent down to wrap her hands around his ankles.

"Shit," he swore, already knowing what was in store for him as he extended his legs and held on to her hips to help her keep her balance.

Tank looked down as he lifted her and guided his dick inside her.

With a moan at the feel of him deep inside her at last, Naeema locked her legs and began to pump her hips up and down like she had the motion of a jackhammer. She stopped and then did a slow grind down the length of him before she sped up again like she was trying to pump water from the earth.

"Naeema," Tank moaned, closing his eyes, his fingers digging into her soft flesh while she rode him like the motherfucking soldier she was.

She let her head drop down to rest her forehead against his shins and her breasts against his knees.

Naeema brought her legs down and released his ankles to work her way up until her back was pressed against his chest. She shivered at the feel of his lips pressed against her skin as his arms came around her body to place one hand on the opposite hip and the other to cup one of her full breasts. She raised her arms and wrapped them behind his head as her head fell back against one of his shoulders. They both worked their hips slowly, sending his dick in one direction and her pussy in the other.

Just pure fucking goodness as they came together and felt the tiny explosions in their bodies.

It was more than sex.

It was the emotions they shared manifested through the physical they both craved.

There was an energy between them that gave Naeema life. And no one could do that for her but Tank.

No one.

"Nobody's perfect . . . but you're perfect for me . . ."

Naeema climbed from the back of the Tahoe before Grip could leave the driver's seat and come around to open the door for her. She closed the door with her hip and winked at the annoyed look on his face as he came around the truck. Dressed in all black he posted up by the passenger door as she stepped up onto the sidewalk in front of A Cut Above. She hated that she couldn't ride her bike, but tenderness from the wound made it hard to steer. As she crossed the lot, all the fellas loitering on the trunks of cars spoke and waved. She half-expected them to run up to her and question her well-being. Of course they didn't. The fact that she had killed, almost been killed, and witnessed a murder last night was known to very few.

Back in her own life this shit seemed surreal.

The door to the barbershop opened and Naeema paused as Mone stepped outside. His thin face was filled with concern. She gave him a soft smile. He was the reason she came to the shop. *Well, one of the reasons . . .*

"You good?" Mone asked.

Naeema could tell he was just as glad to lay eyes on her as she was to lay them back on him. They both had made it. "Always," she lied.

He nodded and looked off at something in the distance.

"Derek here?" she asked about the shop's owner.

"He just left," Mone said, looking down at her again. "He said he's gone for the day."

"I'll call him," Naeema said, looking over her shoulder at Grip watching them like a hawk.

"You not working?" he asked, pulling the glass door.

The men in the barbershop were as raucous as ever and the sounds of them seemed to fall out the open door to fill the air.

Naeema shook her head. "Nah, not 'til next week some-time," she said, hoping the soreness of her shoulder would be gone by then. "I gotta go."

"A'ight," Mone said.

Naeema loved working at the shop and just being there with all the fellas talking shit about any- and everything, but she had a lot on her mind and their noise was a distraction.

"Yo, Naeema."

She turned just as Grip silently opened the door to the SUV.

Mone opened his mouth like he was ready to fire a dozen different questions at her but she recognized the exact moment he stepped back from his curiosity.

As she gave him another smile and slid onto the back-seat she didn't doubt he was remembering that curiosity was indeed the very thing that killed the cat.

"Are you sure about this, Naeema?"

She looked at the detailed sketch the tattoo artist

Shades had done, incorporating all nine of her son's school pictures interwoven with roses and scrolls and a cross to create what would be a full sleeve for her left arm. "Yup," she said, looking over at the tall, skinny white dude with blond dreads.

He was the same man that she—and Tank—had trusted to do the tattoo on her mound.

"I need at least two sessions—maybe three because of all the detail, and that swelling's gonna hurt like a bitch," he warned her.

"Two. I'm stronger than I look," she told him, tapping the top of the counter in the front of his one-room tattoo shop on Halsey Street in Newark.

"It's gonna cost you."

"It's already cost me more than you know, Shades," Naeema said, pausing for that familiar soul-searing pain she used to feel when she spoke of her son. It was there but not as strong. Not as piercing. Vengeance was healing her wounds. Time would erase them. *Thank God.*

She reached into her bag and pulled out the wad of cash to toss at him. "Are you tatting me up today or what, Shades?" she asked. Smiling although she felt the sadness in her eyes.

He caught it with one hand and removed the rubber band to count the stack of fifties. She knew it had to be three grand or better. "Shit, let's get it," he said, replacing the rubber band and tossing the stack into the register.

She dropped her purse on the floor and pulled up the sequined half-sweatshirt she wore, exposing her sports bra and the arm she wanted tatted, while he dropped down onto his stool and slid on a fresh pair of gloves. She lay back on the bench and extended her arm as she stared up at the colorful artwork covering the entire ceiling.

She finally felt free to spend the ill-gotten gwap. The inked memorial to her son—finally claiming him as she should have in the past—was perfect.

Epilogue

Eight months later

"*I* guess I should introduce myself," Naeema began, pushing her shades atop her closely shaven head as she looked down at the headstone of Brandon Dashawn Mack. "Then again I know you're in heaven and I believe you're looking down at everything . . . and so I guess you know I'm Naeema. I'm your mother."

She licked dryness from her lips and wished her eyes suffered in the same way. One lone tear raced down her cheek. She let it roll. "And I hope you can see now more than I ever showed while you were here on Earth that I loved you."

Naeema smoothed her hand up and down the length of her arm, stroking the many faces of her son depicted in her tattoo sleeve. "I don't do graveyards. The one and only time I fucked with one is when your great-grandfather Willie made me go for my parents'—your grandparents'—funeral. The whole time my little scaredy ass was thinking about all the dead bodies in the ground looking like zombies and shit."

She looked around at the many headstones and burial plots. "Just like I am now," she admitted softly with a half-smile that didn't reach her eyes.

Using her thumb she stroked the side of his ring that she wore constantly on the middle finger of her right hand. "I just . . . uh . . . . wanted to get as close to you as I could down here and let you know that I have so many fucking regrets when it comes to you. I shoulda did better by you. I coulda did better by you. So please forgive me."

Sniffing back more tears she lowered her shades over her eyes. She felt like there was much more she could or should say, but she released a heavy breath and pressed her lips together. The horse was dead and the milk was spilt.

"Happy birthday, Brandon," she whispered just as a cool spring breeze touched her face and swept away her words.

Naeema turned away with many more words left unsaid and made her way across the burial grounds, trying her best to maneuver between the plots to avoid stepping on the resting places of the dead. When she reached the concrete paved lane where she had parked her motorcycle she pulled on her pink helmet.

Soon she was driving through the streets of Newark with the sun warming her back and arms in the off-the-shoulder T-shirt she wore with capri jogging pants. She felt more relaxed and calm than she had in months.

The murders of Nelson, Red, and Bas were never very far from her thoughts. Justifiable? Yes, to her. Criminal? Yes, to the police.

She had moved through her life waiting for the police to bust her door open and drag her ass in. Every day for weeks she had stalked the news about them even being missing. She hadn't seen anything and didn't think it was smart to ask Tank to check with his contacts at the police department. Everything was copasetic and she could finally unclench her ass and get back to normal. For now.

And she wasn't the only one.

Two months after the murders her conscience had led her to hop on her bike and secretly check on some of the pawns in the chess game she won against her son's killer. Driving by Vivica's apartment and seeing Hammer press kisses to Viv's neck as they sat on the porch had almost made Naeema steer into oncoming traffic. The fuck? *Guess they're helping each other through their grief. Fuck 'em.*

Brianna, her son's first love, was still working at her grandmother's diner and Naeema was glad to see some of the sadness gone from her eyes as she passed the teenager waiting at a bus stop down the street from the diner. *God bless her.*

Rico hadn't let Naeema whipping his young ass in that hotel in front of his girl stop his fist flow. The black ribbon from the funeral home on the front door of his mother's home was a testament that his fight with Naeema wasn't the last one he'd lost. *Rest in more peace than you did while living . . .*

Mr. Warren had never returned to West Side High School but when Naeema discovered he was teaching at a private school near where he lived she had politely sent an anonymous email to the headmaster advising him of his newest teacher's sinful desires. Without any other real evidence it was the best she could do to at least put the school on alert. *Nasty-ass bastard.*

She was surprised when Chance, her sperm donor, showed up on her front step with his eyes more clear of his drug addiction. Thinking he had come to retaliate, she had squared up with her fists ready to fly until he asked her if she had a picture of Brandon. Long moments had passed as she stood there staring at the man who used to be the boy she loved. She was surprised by the pity she felt for him and even more surprised when she gave him not only an already framed photo but also Brandon's chain. With tears in his eyes as he promised to honor her request to never darken her step again, Chance had begun his long walk home with the chain clasped tightly in hand. *I can only pray he didn't sell it.*

They all had been changed. She knew she would never be the same. She shifted back and forth between being okay with that and not.

Releasing a breath less heavy with troubles, she turned her motorcycle around the corner of Eastern Parkway. Her eyes instantly fell on Coko's small brick home. The lights were on in the house like always but it was definitely empty. Naeema had no clue if the woman was dead or alive. High or sober. She hadn't seen Coko for more months than she could remember. She hoped she was in a long-term rehab facility. *Prayers up . . . blessings down.*

Naeema had just parked her motorcycle in the garage when her cell phone sounded off. After she removed her helmet she pulled it from inside her bra and checked the screen. With a smile she answered the call. "Hey, Ms. JuJu," she said.

"How'd it go?"

"It went good. Real good," Naeema assured her as she closed the garage door and locked it.

"And you like the headstone I chose?"

"Trust me, Ms. JuJu, when it comes to Brandon there is nothing I could have wanted you to do better," she said, still apologizing for a night when liquor, weed, and her guilt had sent her to the woman's house to accuse and blame.

The line stayed quiet for a few seconds and Naeema didn't fill the silence. Ms. JuJu had told her a long time ago to stop apologizing. Still Naeema knew the woman to whom she'd entrusted her child appreciated Naeema's thanks.

"I got banana nut bread," Ms. JuJu finally said.

Naeema smiled. "Then I got a trip to make to your house to get it," she said, crossing the backyard and stepping over the broken step to reach the back door to her house.

She paused.

The door was slightly ajar.

Her heart pounded.

"Ms. JuJu, let me call you back," Naeema said, ending the call.

There had been a dozen or more break-ins on the block in the last couple of weeks and Naeema knew Sarge would *never* leave the door open. Never. "Shit," she swore, wishing she had her registered gun in her hand and not hidden away in the living room.

She backed up to the door and used her elbow to slowly ease it open. The lights were off and she stood there trying to hear over the deafening pounding of her heart. It was quiet. Too quiet.

Naeema stealthily moved across the kitchen floor using what little light streamed beneath the kitchen's door to guide her steps. Leaning toward the door she listened. She tensed at the sound of a low moan. "Sarge," she whispered, pushing the door open.

Sarge's prone body lay by the open door. She raced over to him and stooped to gently turn him over. "Are you okay,

Sarge? What happened?" Naeema asked, her anger rising in a flash at the sight of blood oozing from his busted bottom lip.

"I snuck up on 'em," he said, sounding winded.

Naeema leaned his head against her lap as she looked around at her living room. Everything that didn't belong on the floor now lay there tossed aside like trash. The bins. Her dresser drawers. Her mattress. Her clothes. The pictures of Brandon she'd carefully placed in frames and hung proudly about the room. Her privacy. Her dignity.

All of it had been violated.

Naeema felt her breath coming in short puffs like she was trying to let off the steam rising off her white-hot anger. This was an intrusion she would not accept.

The front door had not been open when she first came home. All of this had to have gone down while she was parking her bike in the garage. They must have attacked Sarge and run out the front door just before she entered through the back.

Lucky motherfuckers.

She helped Sarge to his feet and led him to sit on the edge of the box spring. Naeema left his side just long enough to wet a washcloth in the bathroom and she brought it back to him to press to his swelling lip.

"I tried to stop 'em," Sarge said.

"Don't worry about it, Sarge. I know you did," Naeema said as she walked over to the fireplace and opened the empty ash pan. Relief flooded her that her gun had not been discovered. She picked it up.

"Call Tank," Sarge said, his voice stern.

Naeema shook her head. In the seesaw of their off-again,

on-again relationship they were definitely off again. And she was okay with that. "Trust me I'm gonna find out who is behind this and make them realize that they fucked with the wrong one," she said, checking that the gun was loaded before she cocked it.

Click.

Acknowledgments

$\mathscr{I}$ have to thank God for His continued blessings. I am so grateful for my career that continues to grow every day. I am finally walking this path with anticipation of everything He has in store for me.

The rest of this is to acknowledge the ladies in my life. I love my man, my brother, and all the men I am blessed to call family but this ain't 'bout them right now! Lol.

I am a woman who can say that I had the examples of extraordinary women to help raise me, guide me, nurture me, and protect me. My mother, Letha. My granny Bertha. My aunts, Rodger (aka Sister), Marsha, and Alberta. How blessed was I to have all of you? Strong, beautiful, independent women who left an imprint on my life that remains to this day. My mother, my guardian angel first on Earth and now from heaven above, I thank her for teaching me to listen to my gut. *I am finally getting it, Ma.* My grandmother Granny, I wonder almost every day if I am living up to the woman she helped mold me into. She always told me and the other young girls in the family that if we grew up keeping our panties up and our skirts down we would be alright. Lol. *That was just one of a million of your one-liners I need to write down one day, Granny.* My aunt Alberta taught me through example to never be afraid to laugh loudly and enjoy life. My aunt Marsha showed me how not to be afraid to strike out on my own. And last but not least, my aunt Sister has always pushed me to want and work for more. I thank her so much for everything she has ever done for me. I'll never forget how she purchased a box of my first book back in 2000. A box! Forty-eight books. *How awesome are you, Aunt Sister? You tried so very hard to fill the gap my father left behind. Please know you are appreciated and loved.*

Kim Louise, my sistah of the written word and my good friend, thank you for those three a.m. calls to check on me as I struggled to finish this book and the many times you answered when I called to run an idea by you. I put some serious teeth into a huge chunk of your life and you never shook me off. Not once. A true friend indeed.

Claudia, my agent. Eight years, huh? Please know I thank you for everything you have taught me about this business. I speak and deal with a confidence backed by a knowledge base you helped manufacture. I take comfort in knowing that above being an agent you are my friend and that friendship will last a lifetime.

Okay, enough with the mushy stuff. Lol.

To the team at Touchstone, thanks so much for the hard work and care you all have put into this book. I cannot say enough how much I enjoy working with you all. There are not enough words to express my gratitude to Melissa Vipperman Cohen, Martha Schwartz, Anne Cherry, Cherlynne Li, and Kyle Kabel. Phenomenal work. Great book inside and out. I appreciate you all.

To my online community, especially everyone who is so outgoing on my Facebook page, thanks so much for keeping me connected to the world. I appreciate all 8,600 of you talking books with me—mine and others!

Thank you to all the reviewers, literary publications,

bloggers, book vendors, bookstores, and anyone out there who supports the beauty of books and reading.

That's it for now. I have yet another deadline to meet. Forever grateful,

Meesha Mink

About the Author

MEESHA MINK is the bestselling and award-winning author of more than thirty books written under three names, including the explosive Hoodwives series (*Desperate Hoodwives, Shameless Hoodwives,* and *The Hood Life*), which she coauthored. Mink made her solo debut with the Real Wifeys trilogy (*Real Wifeys: On the Grind, Real Wifeys: Get Money,* and *Real Wifeys: Hustle Hard*). As Niobia Bryant she writes both romance fiction and commercial mainstream fiction. The Newark, New Jersey, native currently lives in South Carolina and writes full-time. For more information please visit www.meeshamink.com or www.niobiabryant.com.

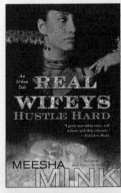
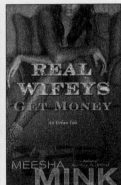
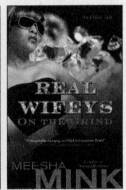

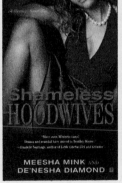